DEATH
THROUGH
DESTINY'S DOOR

A SPIRIT ROAD MYSTERY

Also by C. M. Wendelboe

BITTER WIND MYSTERIES
Hunting the Five Point Killer
Hunting the Saturday Night Strangler
Hunting the VA Slayer

SPIRIT ROAD MYSTERIES
Death Along the Spirit Road
Death Where the Bad Rocks Live
Death on the Greasy Grass
Death Etched in Stone

TUCKER ASHLEY WESTERN ADVENTURES
Backed to the Wall
Seeking Justice
When the Gold Dust Died in Deadwood

NELSON LANE FRONTIER MYSTERIES
The Marshal and the Moonshiner
The Marshal and the Sinister Still
The Marshal and the Mystical Mountain

DEATH
THROUGH
DESTINY'S DOOR

A SPIRIT ROAD MYSTERY

C. M. Wendelboe

Encircle Publications
Farmington, Maine, U.S.A.

Death through Destiny's Door Copyright © 2021 C. M. Wendelboe

Paperback ISBN 13: 978-1-64599-173-1
Hardcover ISBN 13: 978-1-64599-174-8
E-book ISBN 13: 978-1-64599-175-5
Kindle ISBN 13: 978-1-64599-176-2

Editor: Cynthia Brackett-Vincent
Cover design by Deirdre Wait
Cover photograph and author photograph by Heather M. Wendelboe

Published by:

Encircle Publications
PO Box 187
Farmington, ME 04938

info@encirclepub.com
http://encirclepub.com

Dedication

I would like to dedicate this novel to
Fred Steurer, friend and mentor.

Acknowledgments

I would like to thank Deb Michaels for her legal acumen and wisdom in steering me in the proper direction for portions of this book. To Ernie LaPointe for his advice concerning Lakota culture and history. To the Edward Clown Family of Pine Ridge, descendants of Crazy Horse. To Deirdre Wait for designing the book covers, and to Eddie Vincent for keeping the faith. And to my wife, Heather, who often steers me in the proper direction when writing, telling me exactly where I can go, and for taking so many of the photos used on my book covers.

Chapter 1

Red Cloud Agency Near Camp Robinson, Nebraska
May 5, 1877

Crazy Horse, the Sacred Man of the Oglala Lakota, rides ahead of his warriors. Their women. Their children. Many shuffling along behind in the trail of dust kicked up by nearly a thousand lathered, exhausted ponies, as more horses plod along behind. Not that the Sioux will get the chance to keep them after this day is done.

As they begin the final leg of their journey into Camp Robinson, loafers from the soldier camp join them along the way, once-proud warriors who had fought the *wasicu* as he had, only to surrender their honor for what scraps the white man tossed their way. Tagging along today in the hopes of being among those rewarded with food that the Indian agent deems fit for them to receive.

He pauses for a moment to look over his people, beaten down and war-weary from the constant attacks and pursuit by the horse soldiers. So this is how the mighty Oglala surrender to the *wasicu*, he thinks. But Crazy Horse's head is not hung in shame like the others, for he has no reason to feel dishonor. He has fought the white man with every fiber of his being in an effort to maintain their way of Lakota life, unhindered by

1

the white men's rules. Unhindered by boundaries. Yet, here they are, surrendering for the "privilege" of living within those boundaries set by others.

The Battle of the Greasy Grass had been a tremendous victory for the Lakota—yet, killing all of the horse soldiers commanded by yellow-hair Custer had also been the beginning of *this*. After their great triumph, the horse soldiers frothed at the mouth for blood, and hunted Crazy Horse and his followers even into their winter camps, killing indiscriminately the women and children. Sitting Bull had fled to Canada, but Crazy Horse believed it fruitless to expect sanctuary there, and had fought until... his warriors could fight no more. Could not protect their families. Could not hunt to provide for their loved ones.

And so, Crazy Horse had kept his people alive by the only way left to him—surrender to the soldiers, even though he expected no mercy. Expected no promises to be fulfilled by the white man who had broken so many promises in the past.

He had often thought of Chief American Horse—even Spotted Tail—headmen who had long ago gave into the whims and desires of the white man, and accepted reservation life— and for what? So that they could be the *Chiefs* that the soldiers recognized? Important men having the power of destiny over their own people? Crazy Horse long ago knew that a man's power came from what lived inside of him, not what this world could give him.

* * * * *

Crazy Horse and his people arrive at the outskirts of Camp Robinson for their formal surrender. Army Lieutenant William Philo and a company of horse soldiers meet Crazy Horse to escort them the rest of the way in. Warriors and women alike whisper among themselves, nervous being around an enemy who has sought them out for destruction at every turn.

The road into the soldier's camp is lined by several thousand Oglala and Miniconjou Sans Arc Lakota who have come out to glimpse the legendary fighting man. He pauses and strokes his sorrel's neck—the only other pony he owns, a war mount—calming him from the people crowding close to him. But why? For all his success as a headman and shirtwearer, all his prowess as a warrior, he remains humble as he has all his life. He has even heard some people say he is shy, and, perhaps he is. How many times has he thanked *Wakan Tanka Waste*, the Benevolent Gods, for every blessing in this life that he has received? Yet, when others would gladly devour the fruits of victorious battles, he has taken few things from his enemies besides their lives.

The moment he has dreaded is fast approaching, and he thinks that this will be his final journey. All he wants is to live in peace, and he has promised the *wasicu* he will fight no more, but there are agency politics he will need to battle against as fiercely as he fought the soldiers. Unlike Spotted Tail and Red Cloud, he wants nothing to do with war against the whites. Crazy Horse wishes to be what he is—an Oglala Lakota who has done as much for his people as he could. Unlike Spotted Tail and American Horse and Red Cloud, Crazy Horse will be like Sitting Bull—a warrior at heart to the end. *A conquered man*, the crowd hushes, but Crazy Horse will never let the soldiers conquer his spirit.

He halts a final time and the soldiers also stop as they nervously look back at the Indians. Crazy Horse wants to take a last look at freedom and bends his head to talk with friends Little Big Man and Little Hawk who flank him on this his final journey.

He turns in his saddle and watches as Big Road calms the people riding, walking, many covering their noses and mouths with trade cloth against the choking dust. Many he has talked with believe the white man's promises of abundant food for them and their families. Freedom to live their life as proud

Lakota after so many years of being hunted. But Crazy Horse knows better, for he went off by himself into the hills in the days leading up to his decision to surrender, asking *Wakan Tanka* for guidance. The Great Mysterious spoke back—*do not believe the promises of food. Of the ability to roam at will. Do what you can to protect your* tiospaye.

And yet, Crazy Horse's vision showed him he must lead what was left of his followers here and submit to the *wasicu*.

As he looks about at the thousands of people surrounding him, he hears the hush in the crowd. Crazy Horse is here.

Tashunke Witko has surrendered.

Chapter 2

Oglala Sioux Tribal police investigator Willie With Horn woke Manny Tanno from a restful, deep sleep. At least as restful as an FBI Agent working the reservation could get. "You need to get down here to the rez, ASAP," Willie said, out of breath at the other end of the line.

"What is it?" Clara Downing asked, rolling over in the bed to snap on the lamp beside the bedstead like she'd done dozens of times since Manny moved in with her. "Do I need to make a pot of coffee for you to take along?"

Manny covered the receiver and said, "Don't know yet."

He rubbed the sleep out of his eyes and asked Willie, "What do you have for me now?"

"You know Everett Black?"

Manny chuckled. "Who doesn't? What's he done this time, kicked the hell out another of his ranch hands? Stole his neighbor's bull again?"

"He wrecked his truck."

Manny covered the receiver once more and silently cursed Willie for waking him for a simple tribal case. "I won't be needing that coffee," he told Clara.

He checked the clock on the alarm: ten-thirty. Was he getting that old that he went to bed with the chickens, like his Uncle Marion used to say when he crawled into the sack early? "Last I heard, traffic accidents were tribal jurisdiction. Your bailiwick—"

5

"Not when the old man went speeding after a burglar he caught in his study tonight and took a Double Gainer off the high wall just west of his ranch. Hollow Thunder's there now. Says he can't even tell what pieces of the old man are still in the car, as bad mangled as it is. He's waitin' for the rollback to show up and winch the truck up."

"So, Everett's dead?"

"As dead as White Clay since they closed down the liquor stores," Willie said, thinking of the liquor stores across the Nebraska border that sold mostly to Indians and that the state had since closed down.

Manny hung up the phone and sighed deeply. Everett died chasing a burglar out of his house. A death connected to the commission of a felony. Murder. "Better make it a strong pot of coffee," Manny told Clara as he swung his legs over the bed to dress. He groped for his trousers, draped somewhere over the foot of the bed. "*Very* strong—I have to talk to the Black Family when I get down to Pine Ridge."

* * * * *

Willie held the screen door at the Black Ranch house for Manny and said, "Everett's kids are waiting in the den."

"Mourning their heads off, I'd wager."

Willie looked down the hallway as if he could look through the walls at Everett's heirs grieving the loss of their dear daddy. "The only thing they'd mourn is getting cut out of the will."

Manny reached inside his briefcase and grabbed his notebook. Stalling. As a tribal cop, Manny had dealt with Everett some years ago. The old man had reported his prize brood mare stolen by a neighbor, only to find out that Everett's fence had fallen into disrepair and the horse merely stepped over the downed wire. But that wasn't good enough for him—he later led his neighbor's bull into his pasture claiming it had "stepped over the same fence." Manny had called bullshit on that when he learned that one of Everett's ranch hands had repaired the fence weeks before. Manny shuddered as he prepared to conduct the initial interviews. If Everett's kids were anything like their father... "Let's get this over with."

Manny stepped through the entryway and draped his Stetson and coat over a hook on the mahogany hall tree that reached all the way to the ten-foot ceiling, carved decades ago with wildlife scenes—a six-by-six elk leading his ladies into a pasture to feed.

Manny avoided dry wall sheets propped against one wall while drywall knives and paper and buckets of mud waiting to be pasted on fresh board littered the room. Manny stepped over the mess and started to follow Willie down the hallway when Willie stopped and said, "Mary Comes Flying is consoling the *children* in their hour of need."

"Everett's woman?"

"Everett's live-in-housekeeper," Willie corrected.

"I'd say if she's lived with the old man more'n fifty years, that qualifies her as his *woman*."

Willie lowered his voice. "Just don't call her Everett's mistress or the old gal will thrash your backside."

"I'll remember that."

They resumed walking down the hallway, the sounds of laughter becoming louder until they reached the door going into Everett's den. Mary met them and shut it against the frivolity going on inside. "I am so glad you are here," she said, ringing her hands, looking up at Manny. Although he wasn't tall, Manny felt so next to the small woman in front of him. *Frail* came to mind, but—if her reputation around Pine Ridge was taken as gospel—Mary Comes Flying was anything but frail. For decades, she'd been Everett's housekeeper. His house manager. His house foreman who kept his spoiled twin children in line.

She had to be tough—probably ruthless—to deal with those two brats for so many years. "If I would have seen him run after… I would have stopped Ev…" her voice trailing off.

"Maybe we ought to go inside and visit," Manny said.

"Sure," Mary said. "Sure. But when you talk with the twins, please do not judge them by their reactions to their father's death."

Manny nodded knowingly. With every death notice he had ever given as a tribal officer and later as an FBI agent, he saw firsthand how differently people took the news of a love one's death. Some cried. Some fainted. Some went into a state resembling comatose. But—as Manny noted to himself as he followed Mary and Willie into the den—this was the first time that he'd ever seen a family *celebrate*. Or at least, that's what it appeared to him. Jimmy—the oldest twin by two minutes, Willie told him—sat behind Everett's enormous oak desk, the tinkling of ice in his tumbler greeting Manny as Jimmy Black held his glass high in a toast, his feet propped up on an open desk drawer. "The FBI has ridden in to save the Black family and avenge old Everett's death," he said, his voice slurring badly. A trickle of alcohol ran down his chin and onto his paisley pajamas but he made no effort to wipe it off. He looked through bleary eyes at Manny with that flushed florid face, one he'd recognized in other alcoholics. "Officer With Horn insists you have to talk with us."

Manny studied Jimmy. Although he was ten years younger than Manny, he looked that much older. The ravages of liquor had not been kind to Jimmy Black. *The bane of our people*, Manny thought.

"Please have a seat," Mary said as she indicated an overstuffed couch, tanned elk hides draped across the back, the legs of the couch made from the thick legs of buffalo.

"By all means, officers," Jimmy said, grabbing the side of the desk to stand, "have a seat and make yourselves at home. I am sure good ol' Dad would have wanted it that way." He walked on wobbly legs to a liquor cabinet and said over his shoulder, "Does the FBI allow you to take a little pick me up?" He poured five fingers of scotch and said to Willie, "I won't even ask you. *Holy men* take no alcohol, as you have told me many times. Well, mister agent man, do you want a nip?"

"I'll pass."

"It'll improve that grumpy expression of yours."

"Stoic."

Jimmy popped the top off the decanter and asked, "What's that you said?"

"Stoic," Many answered. "It's the stoic expression we agents get when we have to ride in to save the day."

Jimmy laughed, and his big belly jiggled under his robe. He staggered back to the huge desk, gouged in places, stained in others, with the character that told Manny it had probably been in the Black family for near a century. Manny imagined Everett sitting where Jimmy sat, conducting business related to his cattle ranch and horse breeding operation, making deals as he talked on the Bakelite telephone that looked like it had been here as long as the desk had.

Willie and Manny sat in captain's chairs in front of the desk. Manny took a notebook out of his briefcase that he hadn't written in in the six years since he had been back working Pine Ridge. Manny used the notebook as a prop—folks often expected investigators to write down their every word as if what they spoke was gospel. *Too damned many police shows on television with investigators showing the public the "real" way interrogations are conducted.*

Manny held his pen—with the ink that dried up about the time Bill Clinton got out of office—out of habit. Later, he would write what the witnesses had told him, and his FBI 302 notes would reflect that. But he wanted no distractions when he asked folks questions, distractions from his real desire—studying the witness to catch micro tics or eye movements or body shifting that told Manny whether they were being truthful or lying.

"Let's begin with you, Mary," Manny said, clicking the pen.

"Yes." Mary sat straight against a chair back. She maintained the upright posture Manny came to recognize in many older, traditional Lakota women.

"Officer With Horn said Everett surprised a burglar tonight."

Mary nodded and dropped her eyes. "Tantra was awake—working out in her gym upstairs at this ungodly hour, if you can believe that—when Everett yelled at her to call the law as he bolted out the door."

"That's all she said, 'call the law'?"

Mary nodded.

"Where's Tantra now?" Manny asked.

"My little sister wouldn't dare even think about entertaining visitors without getting all ladied-up," Jimmy said while he swirled bourbon around in his glass. "She's taking a shower."

"It wouldn't hurt you none to bathe now and again." Tantra Black walked into the den. No, Manny thought, she *glided* into the room. Tall and lithe, she wore a silvery pantsuit that accentuated her curves. Her damp hair had been hastily combed and pulled back, held together by a bone hair-tie. For being Jimmy's twin sister, she looked thirty years younger than her brother. And fitter. And right now, a whole lot more sober.

"Tell mister agent man, little sister," Jimmy slurred after he'd downed his drink, "just what dear old Dad yelled at you as he flew out the door on his final trip in this world."

Tantra glared at Jimmy before seeming to notice Manny for the first time. Her gaze lingered over him a little longer than Manny thought it should for a daughter grieving her father. She sat in a chair next to Manny and turned to face him. "Some bastard broke into the safe… he yelled at me—"

"How could you hear what your father said—my understanding is that your gym is upstairs?"

"Heater vents."

"How's that?"

"Heater vents," she repeated. "This old house has terrible acoustics except when father talked downstairs in the den or his reading room. Then it's like he was talking through an intercom, it comes through that clear."

"Please continue."

"After he yelled at me that his safe had been burglarized, I came off my treadmill and ran for the stairs just in time to see him run by." Tantra forced a grin. "For an old man, he could run pretty quick. Anyways, I got down the steps just in time to see him jump out of his new Ford pickup and hop in his old International and chase the other outfit."

"Did you get a look at the other truck?"

Tantra shook her head. "I barely saw their taillights before they disappeared down the drive." Her eyes welled up and she swiped a hand across them, smearing her mascara. She reached for a box of Kleenex on the desk and wiped her cheek. "That was the last time I saw him. I just wish he'd taken his new truck instead of that rat-trap-of-a-beater of his."

Manny appeared to be making notes when he said, "what was your father driving?"

"Like I said, he drove that old truck that he owned *forever*."

Willie flipped open his own notebook and thumbed pages, running his finger down until he said, "Robert Hollow Thunder investigated the accident. Everett was driving a '71 International three-quarter ton pickup, though by Robert's description of the truck at the bottom of that ravine, he couldn't actually tell what it was. If he didn't run the license plate, he wouldn't have known what make it was, all mangled and all…" Willie blushed and looked at Mary and Tantra. "Sorry for the graphic description—"

"No need to apologize, Tonto." Jimmy held up his glass and looked at Willie through it. "I can call you Tonto 'cause I'm Indian, too, though no one would ever know it, listening to Father." He stood and used the edge of the desk to make his way back to the liquor cabinet. "That old coot should have known better than to drive that beater of his." He filled his glass and eased himself back to the chair, somehow without spilling a drop. "About every male over the age of ten on this ranch has had to make repairs to that thing. That truck should have been in a museum." He reached into his robe pocket and grabbed a pack of Marlboros. He shook one out and stuck it between his lips.

"You know your father never allowed smoking in the house," Mary said.

"Well, dear ol' Dad's no longer here to tell me to snuff it out," Jimmy said and lit a kitchen match on the side of the desk. He held the match while he brought his shaking cigarette to it when…

Mary leaned over and blew the match out. "But I am here now. Do not light it."

Jimmy dropped the match in a round metal can beside the desk and said, "That's right—you *are* here. For now, old woman."

Manny quickly resumed his questioning. The last thing he needed was to get embroiled in another Black family fight. "Why didn't Everett take his new truck?"

"It wouldn't start," Tantra said. She stood and paced in front of the table, her hands gesturing wildly as she said, "He tried starting his new outfit. I heard the starter grind, and figured a computer module was bad—"

"Sounds as if you know something about vehicles," Willie said.

Tantra looked up at Willie. "I live on a ranch, big 'un. We all have to know something about the machines, even if we don't often work on them."

DEATH THROUGH DESTINY'S DOOR

"At what point did your father jump in his old truck?" Manny asked.

Tantra shrugged. "Must have been right away 'cause by the time I ran outside, he was already driving hell bent for leather after the burglar. I yelled at him. I did." She turned her head and grabbed another Kleenex to wipe her eyes. "But he didn't hear me. He just drove off."

Jimmy clapped and stood on unsteady legs. "My little sister can put on a show, though I didn't realize she took up acting in college."

"Damn you, Jimmy—"

"Sis, you didn't get along with the old fart any better than I did, so don't let on like you're a bit sorry he's dead. And now," he said as he made another assault on the liquor cabinet, "all that is left is to divvy up the spoils of the old man's will."

"Just for tonight," Mary scolded Jimmy, "keep quiet so these officers can do their job."

"Then tell the cops how much Daddy drank, and how he was usually drunk when he drove like a wild man." He lifted his filled glass and said, "here's to Daddy and his filthy lucre."

"Have *some* measure of decency. Just for tonight." Mary pleaded.

Manny quickly asked her, "did you talk with Everett before he ran out of the house?"

"For the briefest moment. He woke me when he was running down the hallway—"

"You mean the old man nudged you from your spot in the bed," Jimmy said and laughed once again.

She glared at Jimmy and said, "he banged on my door as he ran by." She rang her hands as she turned to Manny. "When I answered the door, Everett was half-hopping down the hall, trying to pull his boots on, yelling 'someone broke into my safe.'"

Many looked around the den but could see no safe. "What safe?"

"In his study down the hallway," Tantra volunteered. "It was Dad's only place where he could get away from…" she glared at Jimmy, "unpleasant people."

"Show me."

Manny and Willie followed Mary and Tantra down the long hallway with Jimmy staggering along behind them, ice in his glass tinkling every time he stumbled into the wall.

Everett's study—his quiet room, as Tantra explained—was little bigger than a walk-in closet. Willie and Manny crowded in. Tantra stood with her shoulder touching his, and Manny noted she *could* have given him more room, though with her fragrance wafting past his nose, her cologne was welcome in the musty room.

Mary squeezed into the room and stood to one side while Jimmy made it as far as the door jamb. He leaned against it as he craned his head around to look inside, drowning his grief in more Wild Turkey.

Manny looked about the tiny room to where a weathered occasional chair sat under an overhanging lamp. The shade depicted a branding scene, amber light filling the room, and Manny could imagine a man reading quietly here. A single five-high shelf barrister bookcase filled with classics adorned one wall beside the only window in the room. But it was the sheer *confusion* that amazed Manny the most. Where Everett's den where he conducted business was neat and orderly, this room was anything but. Newspapers and periodicals littered the floor, nearly every spare inch, with books occupying another pile in some convoluted system known only to the dead man.

And little else except an antique safe that spanned one wall, the door ajar. Black lacquered paint had long ago began flaking off, but the date could still be read in a fleur-de-lis pattern: 1889.

"That was the year granddad Henry was born," Tantra said. "His father—my Great Grandfather Black Heart—purchased it."

Willie whistled. "Take a good team of drays to move that."

"All the way from Omaha," Jimmy said. He had moved his operation from leaning against the door jamb to standing on shaky legs just inside the door. Whisky sloughed over the side of his glass onto the orange shag carpeting but he made no more effort to clean it up, any more than Everett had to clean the red scoria dust off all the *stuff* cluttering the room. "The house was literally built around that old safe. Great Granddad built this house the year he bought the ranch to expand his horse breeding bissness," he slurred.

Manny stood looking around, trying to understand what Everett had in mind by keeping all these newspapers and magazines and books cluttering the room when Mary seemed to read his mind. "Everett never allowed me to clean in here. He often said it was the only place that he felt truly comfortable in, and he was afraid if I cleaned it or straightened it up that somehow it would lose some of its character." She shook her head. "And what character this mess has."

Willie's cell phone rang, and he turned away to answer it. "My evidence technician is on the way," he said as he pocketed his phone. "Everyone step outside the room, please."

Mary walked past Tantra who bent over looking into the safe. When she didn't move, Willie took her by her arm.

She jerked away and glared at him. "If I want to see what's inside my father's safe, I will damn well do it."

Mary gently took Tantra by the arm and led her out of the room. "Let us just get out of the way of these officers. We can look inside when they are done."

Manny waited until Mary and Tantra stepped into the hallway to take a closer look at the burglary scene. Particularly the safe. With the open door revealing that there were things still inside, Manny wondered what the thief was after. He squatted and looked closer, careful not to disturb any latent

15

prints the burglar might have left. An entire corner of the safe was filled with collections of coins in blue books, and old paper money stored in archival plastic display sleeves. Next to the currency, an original Randall knife worth as much as Manny made in a month rested on a horn display stand. Bonds and stock certificates took up space in another corner along with books of stamps, all very valuable. All prime prey for a burglar. All left where they were as if Everett surprised the thief before he could steal anything. And all moved recently by the looks of the smudges on the dusty collections. Manny asked Tantra and Jimmy if they noticed anything missing.

"The old fart didn't open his safe for any of us," Jimmy volunteered.

Mary eased Jimmy aside and stood in the doorway looking in. "Jimmy's right—Everett never opened the safe when people were around. Including us. He wouldn't even leave it open when I was in the room."

"Well, it's open now," Manny said. "Who would have the combination besides Everett?"

Mary shrugged. "I do not know, Agent Tanno."

"He gave the combination to no one," Tantra said. "And as for what is missing, he showed me a cedar box several times. And each time he stashed it right back in his safe and closed it like I was going to steal it. I was looking for the box when your... *pardner* rushed me out of the room."

"I saw it once as well," Mary said. "Nothing special. Just a cedar box about a foot long."

"There must have been *something* special in that box," Willie said, squatting and peering inside the safe.

Willie was right—Lakota often kept things special, things sacred, inside boxes made from the cedar trees growing around the reservation.

Willie stood and brushed dust off his knees. "So, just what

was in the box, *Unci*?" he asked Mary, using the term of respect for her. *Grandmother*.

She looked away and Manny said, "Tell us. Please. It might be the only piece of evidence we have of Everett's burglar."

"A map," Mary whispered, barely audible. "Everett kept a map inside that box."

"Map of what?" Manny pressed.

Mary looked at the floor and nudged a piece of lint with her toe.

"Tell mister agent man what the map was," Jimmy taunted. "Or are you afraid the man himself might come back from his secret grave and haunt you."

"Everett kept a map of where... Crazy Horse was buried," Mary said at last, and she shuddered, looking about as if Jimmy's warning was imminent.

"Look at the old woman," Jimmy said. "She bullies us around damn near every day but she's afraid of some old curse." He waved at the air and more whisky spilled out of his glass. "But don't get too excited, *holy man*," he said to Willie. "If I bought every map people were selling showing just where Crazy Horse was buried, I'd have to cash in all of Dad's inheritance to pay for them."

"What inheritance?" Tantra said. "There is none."

The smirk left Jimmy's face and he said, "Of course there is— Dad was frugal as hell with his money. He had a bundle tied up in the ranch and securities. Who knows what business dealings he's had over the years. The man had a golden touch, you know that."

"He did," Tantra said, brushing close to Manny. "He and his attorney—that weaselly Mellis Considine—had several meetings in his office."

"How do you now that?" Willie asked.

"The acoustics," Tantra answered. "I heard them up in my

studio talking like they were in the next room. Father made out a new will and cut us out of it."

"Shit!" Jimmy said. "That's why Mellis had been coming by these last months. I figured it was just something to do with ranch business." He turned to Mary. "Did you know about this?"

"I suspected," Mary said. "But it was up to Everett what he intended to do with his money."

"What *did* he intend to do with it?" Jimmy asked Tantra.

"I overheard Father mention some charities he wanted to leave his money to."

"That enough talk about money," Mary said. "Your father died tonight and the least you could do is show some respect."

Jimmy laid his hand over his heart like he intended reciting some drunken Pledge of Allegiance. "There. That better?"

Mary cocked her hand like she was going to slap Jimmy when down the hall…

"Yo! Willie!"

Willie poked his head out of the room and yelled, "Down the hallway, Pee Pee."

The sounds of rollers wheeling heavy lab equipment grew louder until Pee Pee Pourier stopped in the doorway. "Give me a hand with these cases," he said, and Willie wheeled one case with Pee Pee's evidence equipment while he followed Willie inside the room wheeling another.

"Is this it?" Tantra asked, pointing to Pee Pee. "This… little man. Working alone? I would think the FBI would send more people to work this case. It is, after all, a murder, right?"

"Technically," Willie said, "Everett died as a result of chasing a felon—the burglar—out of his house. But the U. S. Attorney might not see it that way. Right now, what we have is an open safe that someone may or may not have opened without your father's permission. As for our evidence technician," he slapped Pee Pee on the back, "Precious Paul Pourier works a crime scene as good as anyone."

"This is bullshit!"

Mary took Tantra's arm but she jerked away. "Surely you don't think Father's death was an accident."

"Of course it was," Mary said, and looked up at Willie. "It *was* an accident. I mean, the burglar didn't run him off the road or anything?"

Willie sighed. He took out his pocket notebook and flipped pages. "According to Robert Hollow Thunder, Everett was traveling between sixty-two and sixty-six miles an hour when he drove off the rim of that ravine." He closed his notebook. "Doesn't look like anyone nudged him off."

"Tantra," Mary said, her voice revealing how exhausted the old woman was by the night's events, "let us leave these men to do their jobs. I made a pan of brownies with nuts, just like you like them. Let us sample a piece, shall we." She nudged Jimmy. "You, too. Something in your gullet to crowd out the whisky is not going to hurt any."

Jimmy didn't answer as he leaned against the wall, eyes drooping, drool seeping out of one side of his mouth, nearly falling asleep there in the hallway. Mary shook him and he tried focusing through bleary eyes as if seeing her for the first time.

"Let us go into the kitchen." Mary said, "or to bed, if you can make it that far." She eased Jimmy and Tantra down the hallway when she turned back and asked Manny, "You will keep us informed?"

"Of course," Manny answered as he took off his coat. "Tomorrow, perhaps the next day, we may have more questions. But tonight, why don't you and the Twins wind down."

"I'll try," Mary said. "But before you leave the house, could you knock on the kitchen door so we can visit?"

"I will," Manny said and watched as the three of them disappeared down the hallway.

Willie stood beside Manny and said, "You get an eyeful, watching her walk?"

Manny jerked his head back into the room. "Watching who walk?"

"Not Mary, that's for certain. I mean that woman who kept sidling up next to you—Tantra."

"Hard not to look."

"Make sure that's all you do," Willie said. "Clara would have your jewels skewered if you did anything else."

Manny lowered his voice and said, "Speaking of jewels, how's your... little problem coming along?"

Willie looked at Pee Pee dusting the safe with silver powder, paying them no mind. "The fertility clinic in Rapid City said my little swimmers just aren't swimming hard enough to get the job done."

"How'd they determine that?" Manny said as he pulled on a pair of latex gloves before answering his own question. "That's right—they make you go into a room by yourself with what... a copy of South Dakota farmer magazine?"

"Not hardly," Willie answered. "Do you know how embarrassing it is taking a *Hustler* into a room to help do the dirty deed?"

Manny shrugged as he stepped toward the safe and said over his shoulder, "Lot of guys read *Hustler*. What so embarrassing about that?"

"Nothing," Willie answered, "until you have to come out of the room and every other guy in the waiting room knows just why you had the copy of a girlie magazine in one hand and the plastic cup in the other."

Manny patted Willie on the back. "I wish I had an answer," Manny said, "but I'm too old to get your wife pregnant, even if you'd let me."

"Why not try artificial insemination?" Pee Pee asked. He stood and turned toward them, silver and black fingerprint powder smudging his face and forehead. "It worked for Molly."

Manny and Willie looked at each other. "I thought your girlfriend was that Joleen from Hill City?"

Pee Pee waved at the air and dusted fingerprint powder drifted off his hands. "Molly was that Blue Heeler I had." His tone turned serious and he told Willie, "But I think the vet messed up, as her puppies looked more like bulldogs. Be careful you don't get a kid that looks like a bulldog."

"You two aren't any help." Willie snatched his can of Copenhagen from his back pocket and stuffed his lower lip full before brushing the excess off onto his jeans. "It's just that I'm a bit squeamish with all that artificial insemination thing since I had to help with some cows up by Ft. Thompson when I was a kid—"

"Now you're thinking of Doreen as a *cow*?" Pee Pee asked, his voice sounding hollow from inside the safe where he resumed making a mess with the print powder.

"No I'm not," Willie said as he bent to the garbage can and fished out an empty can of Coke to spit in. "I just thought the process was a little… dehumanizing."

"Willie," Manny said, "cows can't be *dehumanized*. You're an educated man—surely you don't think the doctor would treat Doreen like some Charolais heifer getting sperm for the first time?"

Willie paused before saying, "You got a point. Still, I ought to be able to get the job done without all that artificial insemination stuff."

Chapter 3

Manny and Willie helped Pee Pee carry out boxes of evidence: books that Everett had recently read and were open on his desk. Newspaper articles that he had cut out and circled. A pair of slippers that may or may not have been the old man's. And much of the contents of the safe that showed where someone—Everett or the burglar—had moved the coin collection and stamps and stock certificates. "This will piss off those spoiled brats," Willie said, "taking some of their precious inheritance and locking it into evidence for God knows how long."

Manny chuckled. "As long as cases take to work, this *evidence* might be tied up for a very long time." He held the door for Pee Pee and said to Willie, "Help Pee Pee load his evidence van while I touch base with Mary again. There's a few things I'd like to ask her tonight."

"I won't be here when you leave," Willie said as he stepped over dry wall tools and nearly slipped in a pile of dust. "I need to get with Hollow Thunder. The wrecker hauled out Everett's truck with the old man still trapped inside it and they're headed for the impound lot now. I want to be there when they use the Jaws of Life to cut him out."

"And I need to take photos," Pee Pee said. "Be a first for me—taking snap shots of a corpse still inside their metal coffin."

"Don't sound so damned happy about it," Manny said.

Pee Pee shrugged. "It's something different from... you know, sloughing fingerprint powder around some poor guy's study."

"I'll stop by the Justice Building in the morning and we'll go over what we have," Manny said, and left Willie and Pee Pee to cart heavy bankers boxes of evidence to the van.

Manny turned and walked down the hallway to Mary's kitchen and rapped on the closed door. She told him to come in and the odor of strong, fresh coffee hung in the air along with something else... cake? Strudel? He couldn't place it, but he was hoping Mary could help him do so.

She set her beading project—a tiny turtle, maybe a lizard—in a small Tupperware box and said, "you deserve a cup of joe as long as you and young With Horn have been at it."

Manny hung his Stetson on a hat hook beside the door and said, "I could definitely use a cup."

Mary snatched a mug from a row of other mugs on hooks above the kitchen while Manny looked about. For as large as the house was, the kitchen was small. Efficient. A gas oven probably as old as the house itself—the white porcelain finish cracking but still usable—occupied one part of the room, contrasting with the new stainless steel-finished refrigerator beside it. A Formica table sat in the center of the room and the stems of wildflowers jutted out of an opaque flower vase in the center. "Comes from our greenhouse," Mary said as she set a cup of coffee in front of Manny. "I seen you lookin' at 'em."

"I figured that's where you picked them this time of the year." He wrapped his hand around the hot mug. "But where's Tantra and Jimmy, 'cause I don't feel like going another couple rounds with those two."

"Gone to bed," Mary said over her shoulder as she reloaded coffee in her dripolator. "At least Jimmy is—he's passed out in his room. I steered him toward his bed and he stumbled in, just like he always does." She poured hot water into the top of the dripolator before sitting down at the table and clutching her own mug. "But don't be too hard on them—they just lost their father."

"Not that you'd notice," Manny said and instantly regretted it. "Sorry. It's just that they seem more interested in Everett's inheritance that might come their way than their father's death."

"I am guessing there will be no inheritance," Mary said, then added, "you want a piece of rhubarb pie?"

"Do you need to ask?"

Mary smiled and turned to the counter. She peeled back tin foil covering a pie plate, and grabbed a spatula. "Those two can wear a person out," she said as she popped the pie in the microwave. "Whipped cream?"

"And spoil the natural taste?' Manny asked. "I'll take it straight."

"Just like Jimmy likes his booze."

"I saw that." Manny draped a napkin across his lap. Not that he feared anything would ruin his jeans—Pee Pee's fingerprint powder had already done that. It just… seemed like the right thing to do when one dined with a tribal elder.

Mary handed Manny the pie and sat across from him. He took that first bite, savoring the rhubarb as it slid slowly down his throat. "You mentioned there may be no inheritance. That's the second time tonight I heard that."

Mary stared at her cup like she was reading tea leaves. "Everett had pancreatic cancer," she began, "diagnosed five months ago. His kids never appreciated anything, even though he had given them the world. They never produced a thing of any real value. Never took an interest in the business. Never did anything except what they pleased, and Everett figured they would squander the money if he left it to them. He thought if he left them with diddley squat that it would force them into making a go on their own." She looked up at Manny, tears welling up at the corners of her eyes. "Right after his diagnosis, he began meeting with his attorney, Mellis Considine, figuring out where best to distribute his estate." She swiped her apron across her eyes. "The Twins will inherit little."

"How did the Twins take the news that their father was terminal?"

"They never knew," Mary answered. "Everett wanted it that way. He and Mellis were careful not to divulge why he came here or what Everett was doing at his law office in Rapid City. Tantra suspected, but she never really knew."

A sliver of hot, sticky rhubarb fell onto Manny's shirt front and he dabbed at it with his napkin. "Everett built up a considerable business. Largest horse breeding operation in five states, if I recall the article in *People* four years ago. It'd take some work to distribute all that wealth."

"Charities," Mary said. She walked to the sink and dampened a washcloth that she handed to Manny. "Best wash that off your shirt front 'fore it stains."

Manny rubbed until the pie filling was but a memory. "What kind of charities? I'd imagine he gave to many good causes."

"Oh, Everett had many charities in mind—not that he ever gave a cent to any of them when he was alive." She forced a laugh. "Not until he learned he was terminal, that is. Then it was 'Katie, bar the door,' shelling out money like it would buy his way safely along the *Wanagi Tacanku*."

"The Spirit Road," Manny said softly, as if repeating it loudly would offend the powerful spirits in the afterlife. "Willie said Everett didn't believe in the Lakota way."

"That is an understatement. Whenever I would invite Everett to a sweat or a powwow, he would get angry. 'My old man shoved that Indian crap down my throat when I was a kid.' Sad. Everett never believed in any aspect of our Lakota ways—especially since he was always bickering with his father,

Henry, when the old fellow was still on this side of the grass."
She shrugged. "I always thought that was why the Twins never
took to the traditional ways."

"Or maybe, Mary, they were too selfish. Walking the *Chunka
Duta*—the Red Road—takes sacrifice. It means helping others.
Putting them before self."

"In many ways, you are right," Mary said. "But it is too late to
change things now."

Manny finished his pie and downed his coffee before standing
to leave.

"If you are driving back to Rapid City in this dark," Mary
said, "be careful. There are many deer and livestock on the road.
One of the Jandreau boys hit a bull elk driving to Hermosa last
week."

Manny put his hat on and said, "All I have to do is make it
to Pine Ridge Village. The FBI maintains an apartment there
for agents to crash in when they are out in the field late." He
chuckled. "Especially me. I don't have the best track record
when it comes to driving in daylight, so a layover in the dark is
welcome."

"I will show you out," Mary said and fell in step beside Manny
as they walked down the hall.

As they neared the entryway, Mary stopped Manny before
the pile of construction tools and dry wall board and said, "I
hope you don't think this is the way I usually keep house." She
waved her hand around at the mess. "I told those two when
they started the job that I wanted them to clean up their mess
at the end of every day. Told them they needed to keep their
tools out of the way before someone stepped on them and hurt
themselves, and now look at this."

Manny squatted and read *BB* stenciled on the side of a
toolbox. "Double B—never heard of that except… " he stopped
and felt his face turn warm.

Mary giggled. "Do not feel ashamed thinking that's some woman's bra size." Her smile faded. "It stands for Buddy and Bobby Kramer. The father and son Everett hired to remodel this part of the house." She kicked a dry wall hammer. It slid across the worn oak floor and hit the far wall with a *clunk*.

"You sound none too happy with them," Manny said, looking around at the mess. "Don't blame you—I wouldn't be too happy, either. Unless they do exceptional work to make up for it."

Mary stood with her hands on her hips looking at everything that the Kramers had just left lying about. "They do all right when they actually *work*. They approached Everett with a deal he could not refuse. Everett saw a steal and he was always a little…"

"Cheap?"

"I prefer the term frugal, Agent Tanno. He always kept an eye out for the best deal. I suppose it was the businessman in him."

"It'll be nice when they finally finish it."

Mary threw up her hands. "Who knows when that will be. They worked for a couple hours this morning and then just… left. Probably went to Hot Springs for a drink, be my guess."

"If it were me," Manny said as he headed for the door, "I wouldn't pay them until the job was completed."

"And neither would Everett. He made that plain to the Kramers when he agreed on their price. That is why I cannot figure out why they did not want to finish the job—that is the only way they will get paid. I know I will not take money out of the house's operating budget to pay them."

Before Mary closed the door she said to Manny, "Just do what folks here on the reservation say you do best—find the man who broke into Everett's safe."

Manny waited on the porch for the tell-tale *click* of a lock after Mary closed the door, then remembered—rural folks rarely locked their door. Even ones like Mary who had no man-eating dog to alert them rarely thought about locking their doors. But, they had horses, and that reminded Manny of Crazy George He Crow's rabid-mean gelding. That junk yard horse would not only alert George if strangers approached the house, but the nasty old swayback would stomp a man to death if he got inside the horse's pasture. Manny kept that in mind as he walked to his car.

He had nearly gotten to his Crown Vic when someone *pssst* at him. He peered into the dark and strained to see who when Tantra ran, bent over, from the house towards him. When she got to his car, she squatted beside Manny and watched the house. "I wanted to catch you before you left."

"Mary said you'd turned in for the night."

"I stayed up watching for you. This is important—what did Mary tell you about my father?"

"She told me many things," Manny answered, finding himself squatting beside Tantra as if he also needed to hide. "Is there something you think Mary told me that concerns you?"

"No," Tantra said, lowering her voice and scooting closer to Manny, her cologne subtle yet sensuous. Like Tantra. "It's what she *didn't* tell you."

"How do you know what she said to me?"

A slight smile crossed Tantra's face that was lit up by the amber yard light twenty yards away. "Remember that acoustics thing in the house I mentioned? When I'm in my studio, I can hear conversations from pert'near every room."

Manny wanted to scoot back away from her, the thought of Clara popping into his mind. But Manny could not and he stayed close to the beauty squatted next to him. "I'm listening."

Tantra took a deep breath and said, "Mary didn't mention Hobart."

"She did not. Who is Hobart?"

"He is Mary's son."

"She might not have said anything about him because she thought he had nothing to do with your father's accident. Does Hobart live here?"

"He stays here now and again. But he had an apartment in Rapid City."

Manny saw a light in a house window blink out and he found himself lowering his voice. "You must think he has something to do with your father's death."

"Hobart knows the combination to the safe, the only person besides Father who did."

"Doesn't mean he was here tonight—"

"He and Father had a heated argument two days ago," Tantra blurted out. "In his reading room. They got to yelling at each other loud enough, I thought they'd go to blows." She looked back at the house. "Hobart stormed out. Or Father threw him out, I'm not sure."

"What was the argument about?" Manny stood and opened his car door to grab his Thermos of coffee when Tantra said, "Shut it, please. The dome light. Mary might see me talking with you."

"I take it you two don't get along."

"We have our moments," Tantra answered. A horse snorted in a corral behind the house and Manny jumped. "As for what Hobart and Father were arguing about, I couldn't tell."

"You couldn't hear what they were saying?"

Tantra shook her head. "You saw what his reading room was like—some kind of super-messy fallout shelter. Half the books and magazines cover the vents so I can't hear so great. But I think they were talking about that phony map father kept in his safe. At least I caught words to that effect."

"The Crazy Horse map?"

"The Crazy Horse map that was as phony as any of the other ones you see for sale. I think Hobart wanted Father to give him the map."

"Where can I find Hobart?"

"Like I said, he lives in Rapid. He's a teacher at Central High. He'll be easy to spot—he'll be the Indian with about ten pounds of traditional *crap* hung all over him."

"I'll remember that. Is there anything else you forgot to mention before?"

Tantra paused before saying, "Hanson Becker stopped by my studio this afternoon, but I wasn't there—I was out."

"How do you know this Becker stopped to see you?"

Tantra dug into her pocket and handed Manny Becker's business card. "Because he left this stuck in my door." *Native American Art Appraisals* was embossed in red lettering across the card.

"And his paying you a visit is germane to your father chasing after a burglar tonight?"

Tantra shrugged. "It might be nothing more than a coincidence."

"What did he want?"

"Probably wanted to low-ball me on buying some of my pieces. But," she chuckled as if at an inside joke, "Father would have put the boots to him if he knew he stopped to see me. They weren't exactly chums. I can text you his phone number if you want to talk with him."

"Thanks," Manny said, and told Tantra what his work phone number was.

"Do you have a personal phone?" she asked.

"Why?"

"I'd like the number."

"I don't know if that's a good idea—"

"You aren't married," Tantra said, brushing Manny's hand where a wedding ring should have been if he had gotten the courage to tie the knot with Clara. "You never know when some

single lady from Pine Ridge will call and invite you to lunch."
Tantra winked. "Or more."

Chapter 4

Evening; September 5, 1877
Camp Robinson, Nebraska

Crazy Horse watches behind him as he and Touch the Cloud ride side-by-side on the way to Camp Robinson while Standing Elk keeps an eye on those that have ridden out from the agency to glimpse Crazy Horse. Indian Agent Lee had promised he would arrange a meeting with Three Stars Bradley to discuss the terms they had agreed upon at Crazy Horse's surrender. "I do not trust Agent Lee," Crazy Horse tells his uncle.

The man—too big to sit most ponies—agreed. "Since when has the *wasicu* ever kept their word?"

"You are right. They did not keep their word to allow us a buffalo hunt this year. Why would they be honest with us now? I think that they are men without honor."

"I often thought about riding to the sacred *Sapa Paha* and hiding." Touch the Cloud cracked a grin. "But where would *I* be able to hide?" His smile faded. "Maybe you should, too."

"You know I must go and at least present our case. The soldiers agreed I could live at the Spotted Tail Agency with my *tiospaye*." He looks about at Red Cloud and Spotted Tail's warriors crowding him. Itching for a fight. "I do not wish for

32

our people to live subservient like Spotted Tail or Red Cloud's loafers."

"Perhaps this time the white man will keep his word..." Touch the Cloud says, but there is little conviction in his voice.

And there is little conviction in the heart of Crazy Horse. He first had his vision some time ago of this being his final place upon *Unci Makha*. Grandmother Earth. And several times since, he'd had visions of soon traveling the *Wanagi Tacanku*— the Spirit Road—to join those who had died in battle to preserve the Lakota way of life. As he nudges his pony toward the soldier camp, the feeling grows even stronger.

Will he breathe his last on this ground now owned by the soldier chief?

* * * * *

Crazy Horse—along with his warriors and Indian Agent Lee's escorts—crest the hill and get their first glimpse of Camp Robinson. People point to him and shout. It is not a greeting between friends, but angry, menacing cries.

A lone rider approaches. He Dog, Crazy Horse's friend, rides a lathered pony toward them and skids to a stop beside Touch the Cloud and Crazy Horse. "My friend," He Dog says, pointing to the soldier camp, "there is danger there. You must not go."

Crazy Horse nods and looks past He Dog. "I can see that there are people there that want to hurt me. But I have to go. I have to argue my wishes."

"But once you get into the soldier camp, you cannot escape— American Horse and Red Cloud have positioned their warriors all around the camp to prevent you from leaving."

Crazy Horse's spirit is saddened, for he knows he *will* escape this day. But not an escape such as He Dog thinks. "It will be all right, my friend," Crazy Horse says and rides toward the camp.

They ride past warriors shouting that Crazy Horse must die, but those people are afraid to challenge the sacred man until they dismount at the camp and Little Big Man pushes his way through the crowd and grabs him by the arm. He shoves Crazy Horse towards the camp adjutant's office where he will speak with Three Stars about moving to Spotted Tail Agency. And about the promise that Crazy Horse and his followers will get their own agency in the sacred Black Hills.

Little Big Man shoves Crazy Horse into the adjutant's office, watching over his shoulder at the giant, Touch the Cloud, and several other followers of Crazy Horse. "Wait inside," Little Big Man orders, and Crazy Horse—wanting only peace now that he has surrendered to the *wasicu*—walks calmly into the office.

He stands with the others along one wall for much time before Indian Agent Lee enters the office. Through an interpreter, Agent Lee says that he has not spoken with Three Stars Bradley. Nor is the general going to arrive at the camp this day and speak with Crazy Horse.

"This soldier is Lieutenant Kennington. He will be your escort here in camp," Lee says through the interpreter before turning to Touch the Cloud and the other warriors accompanying Crazy Horse inside the office. "I would speak with you men alone."

When Crazy Horse's uncle and his followers leave the office, Little Big Man and soldier Kennington, along with the Indian Police the Lieutenant has summoned, flank Crazy Horse and lead him outside.

Crazy Horse's followers push toward the sacred man. Cries arise. Knives are unsheathed. Pistols cocked. Warning him of his peril. The danger he is in should he follow the soldiers and Indian Police.

Followers of American Horse and Red Cloud smother Crazy Horse's warriors' mournful cries, rising and falling with the stench of impending death that hangs in the air.

For they know, as surely as they know *Wakan Tanka* will watch over the sacred man in death.

They know Crazy Horse will not see the next sun rise.

Chapter 5

"Where the hell's that rookie of yours?" Police Chief Lumpy Looks Twice said to Manny. Lumpy glared at Pee Pee picking at his dentures with the tip of a pencil. "Will you put those damned teeth back in your head!"

Precious Paul Pourier flicked a piece of donut from between the fake teeth before slipping them back into his mouth and checking the fit.

"That's damn disgusting," Lumpy said.

"They don't fit so good," Pee Pee said, now fidgeting with the braid hanging onto his chest. "Stuff gets under them."

"If you wouldn't use them to open beer bottles they *would* stay in your mouth."

"Chief," Pee Pee said, lowering his voice, soothingly, "calm down. It's not our fault this meeting is going to start late."

"Well, I'm not going to calm down." Lumpy bit off a corner of his own donut and said to Manny, "I have business to attend to. The annual budget meeting with the tribal council—"

"Is that where you go in and fight for raises for us *we* folk?" Willie said from his seat at the end of the conference table. "Like you fought for your *own* raise this summer?"

Lumpy's face turned red. "The raise I got was automatic when the tribal council appointed me permanent Police Chief."

"That's enough bickering for one morning," Manny said. "He'll be here," though he had little conviction in his voice that he

36

would. Since Shannon "The Animal" Henderson was assigned to Manny for training last month, the man had been on time once. Once. And Manny was convinced that the one time was purely by accident when Shannon's alarm actually went off on time.

Willie stood and walked to the coffee pot, bringing the carafe to his nose. He sniffed the thick, black liquid the consistency of Penzoil and scrunched up his nose before pouring himself a cup. *Willie's a whole lot braver than I am,* Manny thought.

"Chief," Willie said, "that The Animal's charm—being late? That what they expected of him when he played pro ball?"

"If he had been late when he played for the Brows," Lumpy laughed, "maybe Cleveland would have actually celebrated a win that year instead of going O-for-sixteen. And the team wouldn't have had to shell out mega-bucks for their star draft pick."

Heavy *thudding* sent ripples in Manny's cup of tea like the ripples in a Jurassic Park mud puddle as the T-Rex approaches, a sure sign that The Animal was in the building and tramping this way. "I wouldn't say anything about his... injuries. He's kinda sensitive about it, and you wouldn't want *him* going off on you."

Lumpy started to speak when he wisely clothed his mouth as Special-Agent-in-Training Shannon Henderson opened the door, smacking his head on the top of the door jamb. His eyes rolled back into his head, and he put his hand on the side, swaying. Manny looked frantically about—he was the closest to the big man. If he fell, Manny would have to try to catch him. *That's all I need,* he thought, *a triple hernia catching Shannon.*

But the man recovered and regained his balance, looking around the conference room. "What, you've never seen a black man before?"

"Just have a seat, Agent Henderson," Manny said and watched with trepidation as Shannon staggered to the far side of the table and dropped into a flimsy office chair. The chrome legs flared out and Manny expected the chair to give way, but it held. For being such an intimidating man, Shannon had proven to be somewhat of a delicate feller. Sidelined four times in his rookie season for injuries on the field—anything from twisting his ankle before the game even started to falling off the bench and spraining his wrist—he had been cut from the team at the end of that first season. It had only been through the grace of some benevolent FBI football fanatic that Shannon had been recruited by the Bureau. And even then, it had taken Shannon two academy sessions to graduate because of injuries received in custody and control class.

Manny tossed the rest of his tea into the trash and walked to the soda machine. He dug into his pocket and asked Shannon, "Want a Coke?"

"I am mighty thirsty," he answered.

Manny punched in a Diet Coke and was about to punch in a regular Coke when Shannon said, "I am strictly a Pepsi man, Agent Tanno."

Manny turned and popped the top off his can. "But the machine only has Coke products."

Shannon shook his head. "Call it luck."

"How's that?"

"Luck," Shannon repeated. "Drinking Pepsi has always been lucky for me."

"I'll bet you weren't drinking Pepsi those times you were injured on the field," Lumpy said.

Shannon glared at the chief who stood. Manny noted his head was about even with Shannon's. *Sitting down.* "All right," Lumpy said, "where are we exactly on this Everett Black Heart case."

"You mean Everett *Black*," Manny corrected.

Lumpy laid his pudgy hands on his hips as he rocked back and forth on his heels like a drunken penguin while he smiled at Manny. "Did I hear you right—the mighty secret agent man is in the dark about the Black Hearts?' He motioned to Willie. "Fill Mister Know-It-All in about that bunch while I hunt up some fresh coffee."

Manny watched Lumpy leave the room when he asked, "What's Lumpy talking about?"

"What he's referring to is that 'Black' was not Everett's legal name. And it's not the Twins' name either," Shannon said and turned to Willie. "Didn't mean to steal your thunder."

"Steal away," Willie said with a wave of his hand.

Shannon opened his briefcase and took out a legal pad smeared with what appeared to be jelly, perhaps from a donut. "That was why I was late this morning, Agent Tanno. I went to the Tribal Office as soon as they opened to do some research."

"On Everett?"

"On the Black Heart family." The big man stood and, with pad in hand to refer to, began pacing in front of the table as if educating a jury. "Everett Black was born Everett Black Heart. But he dropped the 'Heart' when he was in is twenties." He looked at his notes and squinted. "About the same time that his own father—Henry Black Heart—grew old and wanted nothing more to do with the family business." He flipped a page. "Right about that time, he turned the business over to Everett."

"What's that got to do with Everett changing his name?" Pee Pee asked, his dentures out once more now that Lumpy was out of the room.

Shannon stopped pacing and set his notebook down. "Anecdotal evidence from the ladies at the Tribal Office is that Everett figured if folks knew they were dealing with an Indian horse breeder that they might take advantage of him. So, he changed his name so folks wouldn't know."

Manny laughed. "I met Everett a time or two and he was as Indian-looking as anyone on the reservation. Hell, he looked like Iron Eyes Cody on steroids."

"Iron Eyes Cody was some Italian dude," Pee Pee said.

Manny waved the air. "You know what I mean. He could never pass for a white man."

"He could if Everett conducted most of his business over the phone. The mails," Willie said and turned to Shannon. "No to steal *your* thunder."

"What my little friend means," Shannon emphasized *little*, something few people could do when referring to Willie, "is that Everett sold and shipped horses all over the world. His quarter horses were known for their stamina. They're bred for performance and, as such, don't quite look as pretty as your ordinary quarter horse or thoroughbred.

"Many Black Ranch horses were shipped without anyone ever meeting Everett. They've been shipped all over the world without anyone ever meeting the old man or coming to his ranch to inspect the horses they're buying."

"I've heard the Black Ranch's reputation is strong," Manny said, "but I didn't think they were that trusted."

"Many of Everett's horses went to Long Riders Guild members," Lumpy said. He entered the room holding an oversized coffee mug in the shape of the character Goofy. *Appropriate*, Manny thought as he threw up his hands. "Does everyone know all about Everett Black… Heart's business but me?"

"*Kola*," Lumpy said, "if you lived here like us *rez* Indians, you'd know such things."

Chapter 6

Manny breathed a sigh of relief when Shannon tramped out of the room after Pee Pee to retrieve the brake lines to be sent to the lab, and Lumpy left the room for his budget meeting. "Finally, I might just get some straight answers," Manny said. "Like what do you know about the Black family that might remotely help, 'cause that bit of gibberish I just heard helps very little."

Willie stretched his long legs out under the conference table and popped the top on his can of soda. "One thing I can tell you is that, over the years, we've gotten more than a few calls to the Black Ranch—even before I was on the force. Anything from the time Everett took his neighbor's bred heifer for spite to the old man putting the run on a couple Mormon boys doing their mission to kicking the shit out of that portentous Hanson Becker."

"The art critic?"

"The same. I almost got his autograph, but he was gone by the time I got to the station the next morning."

"What's the connection between him and Everett?"

Willie shrugged. "Who knew with Everett? The old man had dealings with all sorts of folks, though I doubt Becker was there to buy a horse. Fat as he is, I doubt he can even sit a horse." Soda went up Willie's nose and he snatched his bandana, wiping it before tossing the can in the trash. "Point is, the old man was always putting the run on somebody—he just seems to have bulled his way through life."

A light rap came then on the conference room door. A young secretary from Records poked her head inside and said, "Here's the printout of the calls you wanted."

Willie stood and took the manilla folder from her, her eyes meeting his and a slight smile crossing her face before she shut the door.

"That's one you want to be careful around," Manny said.

"How's that?"

"That girl from records? Did you not see the way she looked at you? Doreen gets wind another woman is interested in her *married* man and she'll go off her rocker."

"Sylvia's just a nice kid, is all."

"It's always the prey that doesn't notice the hunter that gets pounced on the hardest."

"Voltaire?"

"Homer Simpson," Manny answered.

Willie laid the manilla folder on the table in front of Manny. "Then you best watch out for Tantra Black—she definitely has her eye on you."

Manny scoffed as he opened the file. "Tantra's a spoiled rich kid—"

"Who most likely *always* gets her way," Willie said. "I saw the way she looked at you last night and I'm saying Clara will have *your* jewels roasting on an open fire if she even suspects another woman's staked her claim on you."

Manny ignored Willie as he took out the two pages which documented the calls the police had responded to from the Black Ranch in the past ten years. He ran his finger down the dates and said, "Last year Everett put a hurt on a Jake Comes Flying when he came around the ranch. Is that Mary's ex-husband?"

"Truth be known," Willie said, "they were never actually

divorced. The rumor I heard was that Jake snakes around Mary now and again trying to rekindle the old romance."

"Apparently, Everett would have none of it," Manny said. He flipped the page. "But there's no mention that either Hanson Becker or Jake Comes Flying ever pressed charges for the assaults."

Willie broke off a corner of his Bismarck and dunked it into his coffee. Unlike Pee Pee, he didn't have the luxury of grabbing another pair of teeth if any broke. "My guess is that the old man paid them off not to prosecute. That was another of his loveable traits—throwing his money around. Bullying folks into his way of thinking. And," he lobbed the hard pastry into the trash, "thinking his money would buy him out of anything." He stood and eyed the Wheel of Death as he fished coins from his pocket. "Hungry?"

"Not for something that's been in that machine for God knows how long."

"Suit yourself," Willie said over his shoulder. He stood in front of the vending machine and selected a ham and cheese. "It still brings us back to the burglary," Willie said. "How Everett scared the thief off, and how—I'm just guessing here—the thief got absolutely nothing for his trouble." He sat at the table and opened a mustard pack to spread on his sandwich. "He must have left empty-handed—all the valuables were still in the safe when Everett surprised him."

"I disagree," Manny said, wiping mustard off Willie's cheek. "I think the thief came away with something considerably more valuable than those coin sets and stamp sets he left behind."

"What was that?"

Many leaned closer and lowered his voice as if *wanagi*—ghosts—lurked somewhere in the room with them. "That map of where Crazy Horse is buried. That's what's missing."

Willie must have felt as Manny did as he shuddered and said

barely in a whisper, "You know Crazy Horse's final burial spot has never been found because there *is* no map. If Everett had a map, it was surely fake, just like the others that crop up claiming to know where the sacred man was buried. All offered at more money than I spent on my last truck. And all bogus."

"And there is absolutely *no* possibility that Everett's map is authentic?"

Willie looked at his boots and nudged a piece of paper with his toe, avoiding Manny's gaze.

"Then there is a chance that it's genuine—"

"Quiet," Willie said, looking at the door as if expecting someone to enter and catch them talking about something *wakan.* Sacred. "All right, I'll tell you about a local legend, but it's just a legend, mind you."

"I'm all ears," Manny said, standing and walking to the coffee pot, his courage finally up enough to grab a cup.

"The legend says that Black Heart, Everett's grandfather, was one of those chosen to accompany Crazy Horse's parents when they drove the body in a wagon away from Camp Robinson for burial. Later, his son Henry Black Heart—Everett's dad—asked Black Heart to draw a map of where the sacred man was buried, and he did. From memory."

"And you think the map in Everett's safe was that map?"

Willie said nothing.

"Is it possible—"

"I don't know," Willie said, tossing the rest of his sandwich into the garbage and standing, pacing. "Old *Chante Sapa* was fifteen years old when he accompanied Crazy's Horse's body. And fifty years later he draws a map. From memory. From what the terrain *used to be.*" He faced Manny. "You know how things change over the years. Even over a few years. So, even if it is authentic, the chance that it will lead anyone to the burial spot is chancy, at best. Look." Willie dragged a laptop over and signed into the internet. His fingers glided over the keys before hitting *search* and he turned the screen so that Manny could see it. "Look at all the maps for sale that claim to know where the sacred man is buried. Enough to paper your wall. And most, be my guess, offered for sale by *wasicu* just looking to cash in on the mystique of Crazy Horse."

Manny put on his readers and said, "There are plenty offered for sale by native folks, too."

"That may be, but the fact remains that the map taken from Everett's safe is a fake. Just like all the others."

"Just maybe," Manny softened his voice, "you don't want *any* map to be genuine. You don't want to know where Crazy Horse is buried."

Willie nodded. "You might be right. *Tashunke Witko* was buried in secrecy so that no one—Indian or white alike—would find his remains. Can you think how the grave would be desecrated if anyone actually found the burial spot?"

Manny knew. When he instructed at the FBI Academy in Quantico before being reassigned to the Rapid City Field Office, rarely a week went by that the newspaper didn't mention some Civil War hero or battlefield being desecrated by overzealous souvenir seekers. And the same for Sitting Bull's grave in North Dakota before a group of brave men and women got together in the middle of the night and moved his remains to South Dakota where they were interred below concrete to prevent such sacrilege. "I think the most important thing about the map," Manny said, "is that someone *believes* it's the real map that points the way to the grave site."

Willie agreed. "But maybe the map was just a distraction."

"How's that?"

"Perhaps it was taken, like Tantra thought, knowing that she or Mary would spot it missing right off. They both surely know the legend of the map. Mary might even think it's genuine."

Manny had thought of that last night at the FBI apartment here on the reservation while he was being kept awake by The Animal's snoring in the next room. He thought how the theft of the map—subtle, not like taking the coins or stamps or securities—might look like the thief targeted Everett for something specific. But the thought crossed his mind last night that perhaps, just perhaps, the thief's only reason for taking it was to lure Everett into his truck. The one with the brake lines cut.

Last night he had also thought long about Mary's son. "Tantra claimed that Hobart knew the combination and that he and Everett had a heated argument a few nights before the old man did a *Thelma and Louise* impression, sans *Louise*, off that high wall."

"Why would Everett give Hobart the combination to his safe if they despised one another?" Willie asked. "In my way of thinking, that causes him to float to the top of my suspect heap."

"We'll know when we talk with him." Manny stuffed Pee Pee's official crumpled-up note into his briefcase and snapped the clasp. "And let's not forget the Twins. If they thought their cushy lifestyle was in danger with Everett willing everything to charity, one—or both—of them might figure that dear old Dad needed to have that accident before the new will was officially recorded. I'll let you know what Hobart says as soon as we interview him."

Manny grabbed his briefcase and walked out of the justice building, thinking back to the other person who might be harmed by a change of the will—Mary Comes Flying. Having not seen a copy of the will, Manny didn't know for certain if Everett had left his trusted housekeeper—and woman—anything. Mary would be out in the cold just like the Twins if the new will had actually been executed and recorded.

Chapter 7

M anny stood in the shadow of The Animal outside the body shop waiting for the Enterprise Rental service to drop off a vehicle. "Sorry, Agent Tanno." Shannon stood wringing his hands as if he were attending a funeral and waiting to shake hands with the family of the dear departed. Except this "dearly departed" had nothing to do with a death. "I just don't know what happened."

Manny took deep, calming breaths before answering Shannon. It had been two months since Manny had a wreck, and he was looking good for his yearly eval. Until today, when he had to drop off the government's Crown Vic for repair. And the Senior Agent had been angry at Manny and refused to issue another government car. "I'll tell you what happened... you've been using the door of my car to haul your big butt off the seat. *That's* what broke the hinges on the door. I've told you before that cars aren't designed for someone like... you."

"I'll do better with your next car."

"There's not going to be a next *car*," Manny said. "The Bureau specified a truck when they called Enterprise. One that even you'll fit in."

A Toyota pickup rounded the corner and drove toward the body shop, stopping beside Manny and Shannon. A man—more like a boy—climbed out. With his pimply face and tousled red hair, he dangled keys from his hand, his nails painted black. He exaggerated a look up and down Shannon before asking, "I'm supposed to drop this off with some old dude here. That be you?"

"I'm the old dude," Manny said and walked around the pickup with Shannon following, appraising the truck with a destructive look in his eye. "I thought you said the Bureau rented a full-sized truck? How am I going to fit in *that*?"

Manny wondered, too, as he opened the door, imagining the wriggling Shannon would have to do to climb inside the compact pickup. When Manny spoke with his secretary before she called for the rental, she said most of the trucks were usually spoken for, with more folks renting four-wheel-drives in the wintertime than in other seasons. "I'll do the best I can," she assured Manny.

"I was under the impression we were renting a *big* truck—an F-150. Maybe a Ram."

The kid stood staring up at Shannon until Manny snapped his fingers in front of the kid's eyes. "The truck! Where's the full-sized truck we ordered?"

Pimply Face snapped out of it and turned his attention to Manny. "I don't know, dude. We had a run on trucks since this last big snow fall and we're plumb out." He rubbed at what appeared to be spaghetti sauce splotched on his white shirt. "This is the last truck we have on the lot."

The kid hopped into another car with *Enterprise* splashed across the door, driven by another kid as young as the first. They pointed to the truck and giggled as they sped away from the body shop.

Manny turned to the "truck" and said, "might as well figure out how to get in."

As he watched Shannon, Manny was certain that the Bureau would have to rent horses for them next after Shannon was through trashing this vehicle.

*   *   *   *   *

Manny maneuvered the tiny pickup between cars in the teachers' parking lot of Rapid City's Central High, and all the while, Shannon fidgeted to get comfortable. Manny steered well away from the other cars, thinking the last thing he needed was for Shannon to snap his door open and catch another car door.

Shannon pointed to three Fords parked in a row and said, "I think it's one of those. They're just like the one you turned in for repair."

When Manny talked with Hobart Comes Flying—going by "Black" now—he told Manny to meet him out back at the end of the school day and that he would be driving a Crown Vic. As Manny parked several spaces down from the three Crown Vics in the lot, he noted all had Pennington County plates. Local.

"One of them's gotta be his," Shannon said as he rolled the window down and half-leaned out the door.

"We'll know soon enough when the kids bail out that door."

The school bell rang loud like a ship's claxon on a foggy night—cutting through the din of kids screaming and laughing as they burst out of the doors toward their own cars. Manny sat with his arm smashed against the side glass, Shannon taking up the rest of the room in the single-cab truck.

"You sure he's meeting us here?" Shannon asked.

Manny checked his watch. "He told me to meet him at the Crown Vic right when school got out for the day. He said he wouldn't wait long, as he'll be as anxious as all the kids are to get out of the school building at quitting time."

Teachers rushed to their cars parked in the teachers' lot, the kids into their jalopies in the student parking area. Manny watched as teachers drove away in the three Crown Vics with no sight of Hobart.

"He's evading us," Shannon said as he stared at the now-empty parking lot. "He's hiding something, that's why he doesn't want to meet us. The academy instructors went over how suspects

49

elude and evade police."

"He's not a suspect." Manny was on the verge of agreeing with Shannon when a muffled horn tooted beside the pickup. Shannon pointed his fat finger and said, "What's *that* driving toward us?"

Manny turned in his seat as best he could and watched a car drive slowly towards them. "That, Agent-in-Training Shannon Henderson, *is* a Crown Vic."

A man hunched over the wheel of the vintage Ford Crown Victoria, the stainless steel trim wrapping over the top of the car, reflecting the afternoon light dulled only by the snow cloud that hung over the Black Hills.

Manny got out of the truck and turned his collar up against the skiff of snow that had begun in the last hour. By the time the Ford had stopped in front of the Toyota, Shannon had extricated himself and stood staring at the car the same way the rental kid had stared at Shannon earlier.

A man Willie's size—but not nearly as large as Shannon—climbed out from behind the wheel of his vintage car. A tiny beaded lizard dangled from one ear lobe while his *wophiwe*—his medicine bundle in the shape of a lizard—hung from his neck by a rawhide thong. "You Agent Tanno?"

"I am. And you must be Hobart Black."

"I am," he answered. "Where the hell you been? I've been waiting over there for damn near a half-hour," he pointed to an overhanging car port at the rear of the school building.

"We thought you were driving a Crown Vic," Shannon said, still eyeing the car.

"And I thought you said you'd be in some kind of full-sized truck," he smirked at the Toyota. "Not a clown car."

Shannon circled the Ford and Manny hoped he didn't get close enough to damage it. "And we weren't expecting... *this*."

"What Agent Henderson means," Manny said as he slipped

on his gloves against the cold, "is that we were looking for a *new* Crown Vic, not…" he looked over the car again. "What year is this anyway?"

"'55," Hobart answered.

Shannon whistled. "This must have set you back a mint."

"It did, but it's not the only collector car I have. Being single, I can collect whatever the hell I want. Cars. Guns. Antiques. It's the only vice I have. But you didn't come hunting me up to talk about my collections…" He stopped and approached Shannon as if realizing for the first time who Manny's trainee was. "You're The Animal. Played for the Cleveland Browns, didn't you?"

Shannon straightened up to his full six-foot-eight height and smiled wide. "I suppose you want an autograph."

"No," Hobart said. "I want my money back."

"How's that?"

"Money. You owe me a goodly amount."

"I've never even seen you before."

"But I've seen you," Hobart said, "running across the field that night of your rookie game. Running and tripping and spraining your damn fool ankle. Limping off the field with three poor schmucks helping you. You were hyped as the meanest defensive end to come out of the draft in years."

"What's that got to do with me owing you money—"

"Because I drove all the way to Cleveland for that home game just to watch you play. Cost me a fortune in gas and motels, and you never even took the field long enough for one God-blessed play."

Manny stepped between them, instantly regretting it. If Hobart decided to take out his wasted trip on Shannon, Manny would be the little guy in the middle getting crushed between two bruisers. "Perhaps there's someplace where we can talk besides the school parking lot. The offer's still good to meet at the FBI Office."

"Like I told you over the phone, I don't trust the Feds," Hobart said and held up his hand. "Nothing personal against you... you seem like a nice enough feller. I meant I don't trust the FBI in general."

"All right then," Manny said, "pick a spot."

"Stone Cold Creamery on West Main Street," Hobart said, exaggeratedly looking over the rental truck. "That's if that little thing can make it that far."

"It'll make it," Shannon said, patting the fender affectionately like he'd patted the bench many times in his brief pro football career, "but you'll have to ride in the bed."

"How's that?"

"After we follow you to your house and drop your car off."

"I still don't understand—"

"Your classic car," Shannon said. "I can't imagine you wanting to drive a vintage pink car in this snow."

"Rose," Hobart said. "The color is tropical rose."

"Whatever," Shannon said. "The point is that all three of us can't fit in the cab."

Hobart turned to Manny. "What's this goofy bastard talking about?"

"About parking your Ford out in this weather," Manny explained. "Unless you want to drive your classic car in the snow."

Hobart chuckled. "I drive all my cars anytime, even in the winter. Now keep up with me if you think this little truck can."

Hobart climbed back behind the wheel and didn't wait for Shannon to squeeze into the pickup before he sped off. Manny did his best to stay with the Crown Vic as Hobart wove through traffic the two miles to the ice cream parlor. As quick as they drove to the ice cream shop, by the time they pulled to a stop in front of Cold Stone, the tables inside were already filled with high schoolers fresh out of class.

Manny bailed out of the truck and ran around to the passenger side. He took Shannon's arm before he grabbed the door and helped him wiggle out of the pickup before he broke yet another vehicle. Once he was extricated, Shannon followed Manny and Hobart into the ice cream shop. Manny motioned to the kids filling all the seats, slurping shakes, chocolate dripping over their banana splits and waffle bowls of ice cream. "Looks like we'll have to find some other place to talk."

Hobart grinned at him. "What's the matter, you're not *Lakota* enough to take a little cold. There's tables outside. That's if you and The Animal can handle it."

"But it's twenty degrees outside..." Shannon started to say, but added, "I played college ball in colder temperatures than this."

"Then let's order something that'll make us *really* cold," Hobart said and ordered what Cold Stone billed as a Mud Pie Mojo.

Manny looked at the menu tacked on the wall and calculated Hobart's order—with the Oreos smothered by almond fudge and peanut butter—would use up all the calories Clara the Calorie Nazi allowed him. "I don't see a *Weight Watchers* special on the menu."

"When Granddad Henry took me anywhere like this, he always ordered a fruit sorbet. Even into his eighties, he ate right."

Manny ordered pineapple sorbet for him and Shannon and followed Hobart outside to the metal tables positioned around the courtyard. Manny gritted his teeth as he sat on an icy chair across a small round table from Hobart, praying that his butt wouldn't stick to it when he stood to leave after the interview.

Manny's hand trembled with the cold as he grabbed his notebook and pen with the dried-up ink and said, "I need to ask you some questions concerning Everett Black."

Hobart wiped chocolate off his chin before setting his Mud Pie Mojo on the table and leaning back. "I figured you'd eventually get around to asking me about Everett. To be up front about it, I had little use for the old bastard. He wasn't at all like Granddad

Henry." Hobart motioned around the ice cream parlor. "Old Everett wouldn't be caught dead here. With common folks. Like Grandpa Henry and me used to do now and again." He looked away at something Manny could only guess at. He sat quiet, knowing people often took moments to get past memories— either good or bad—before they continued.

After several moments, Hobart turned back around. A tear had frozen to his cheek and he flicked it off. "I suppose I need to get this out of the way so's you don't think that I'm scamming you... I go by Black Heart, though you know me by my given name of Comes Flying if you talked with my mother."

Once again, Manny remained quiet, knowing silence often loosened people's tongues as much as questions. Cars passed along Main Street, oblivious to the murder of crows hunting overhead. Shannon slurped at his sorbet, clueless to Manny's technique of silence, hoping it would induce Hobart to continue.

"Mother and I moved from Crow Creek to live with Everett and my *Tunkasilai* when I was eight."

Between shivering lips and clicking teeth, Shannon asked, "your what?"

"Agent," Hobart said, "you're going to have to learn my language if you intend on working the rez."

"He's new," Manny said and turned to Shannon. "Hobart means he came to live with Everett and Henry Black Heart."

Shannon set the rest of his sorbet down and shoved his hands into his coat pockets. "Now I am confused. Did Everett adopt you or something?"

"Bite your tongue," Hobart said. "Everett never was my dad. The man was as cold as these chairs we're sitting on. When my mother answered an ad for a live-in housekeeper, she'd just split from my alcoholic father in Ft. Thompson. We moved into Everett's ranch house, but by then he wanted few people outside the rez to know he was Lakota, and that's when he started going by Black. See, Henry Black Heart had given over the ranch by then and he took me under his wing. Treated me like his *takoja*. His grandson. We did many things together. He taught me to walk the *Chunka Duta*—the Red Road of honor and integrity... the essence of what it means to be Lakota." Hobart once again flicked a frozen tear off of his cheek. "And we did so until the day he died. I was ten then, and devastated. I had lost my best friend." He leaned closer to Shannon and said, "You're turning a little pale."

Shannon's teeth clicked like a telegraph terminal. "That's funny—a black man turning pale."

"Probably from the cold. Perhaps we ought to go inside before you turn into a big icicle. You don't have the stamina for this weather like we Indians," Hobart said, but Manny noticed Hobart had buttoned his own coat and turned his collar up against the wind. Just like Manny had done twenty minutes ago when the wind picked up. "School kids are cleared out. We can go inside if you want."

Shannon abruptly stood and tossed the rest of his sorbet into the trash as he shuffled inside the ice cream parlor. Hobart looked after him and smiled. "Your trainee isn't too tough, is he?"

"He's just not used to this cold this early. If you like, we can stay out here and talk where it's cool," Manny said, but Hobart had already headed in through the Cold Stone doors.

Chapter 8

Manny felt the welcome, warm air rush over him as he stepped into the ice cream shop, empty of the school kids now. Empty of other customers, too. Something about one not wanting ice cream in twenty-degree weather, Manny reasoned.

Manny walked to the corner table where Hobart and Shannon sat and once more opened his notebook, his useless pen at the ready. He had gotten into the habit of not taking notes early in his law enforcement career, opting instead to concentrate on what the other person was saying. Catching any untruths, inconsistencies. Voice inflections and facial tics that revealed how a witness really felt at the time. He would write his 302 report later from memory, but now he wanted to ask Hobart more questions. "I understand you and Everett had a heated argument a few days before his death."

"Who told you that—"

"And it almost went to fisticuffs. And Everett went chasing after someone which resulted in his fatal wreck. The brake lines were probably cut."

Hobart's face turned red and he said, "Sure, we had an argument. And it got heated. If he were a younger man, I'd have put the boots to him, but I damn sure never messed with his truck."

"By the sounds of it," Shannon said, balancing precariously on the small chair beside the flimsy table, "old Everett was a handful

DEATH THROUGH DESTINY'S DOOR

for everyone until the day he died. You might not have been able to put the boots to him, as you put it."

Hobart's jaw clenched and Manny quickly said, "What did you two argue about?"

"His will," Hobart said without hesitation. "Mother said Everett intended to change his will—"

"And you were angry because he was cutting you out of it," Shannon interrupted.

Manny leaned over and whispered to Shannon, "Keep quiet and you just might learn how to interview someone without pissing them off." He turned back to Hobart. "Tell me something about this... discussion you had concerning Everett's will."

"For starters, I didn't want a dime of the old man's money for myself," Hobart glared at Shannon. "Mother said Everett intended cutting the Twins out of his will and donating his estate to charities. I was there trying to talk the old bastard into giving some of his money to my heritage center."

"What heritage center?" Manny asked.

Hobart looked away and took a deep breath. "The one I've been campaigning for over the last four years. Spending every weekend traveling around the area, trying to drum up funds for it." He leaned across the table, his anger gone, replaced by enthusiasm. "I want a heritage center that teaches Indian kids what it truly means to be *Indian*, and I don't care if it's Lakota or Arapaho or Shoshone or even Crow. I just want someplace where they can go and study. Someplace where they walk that Red Road that Grandpa Henry led me down."

"You must have been upset that Everett wasn't donating much to it?"

"Not much!" Hobart said, his anger resurfacing as his hand slapped the table. "He said he would donate *nothing*. Nada. The old coot would rather have thrown his money at the 'Save the Eucalyptus Tree' or 'Save the Sand Flea' charities than give a dime to promoting Indian culture. Agent Tanno, I just wanted Everett to donate *something* to help out, but he was so set against his Indian roots that he refused. And laughed about it when he told me to hit the bricks."

"I don't understand," Shannon broke his silence. "If Everett was Sioux—like you and your grandfather—what did he have against Indians?"

"It all came down to money," Hobart said. "It always came down to money with Everett. To people not connecting him to the tribe." He stood. "You two want more ice cream?"

When Manny and Shannon declined, Hobart stood and walked to the ordering counter. Manny thought this was a good time to educate his trainee and said in a low voice, "Many folks deny their Indian heritage as if there's something shameful about it. It's common for folks living off the reservation to dress like white folks. Act and talk white. It sounds like Everett denied his roots all those years, and I suspect it had more to do with just money."

"I knew people back in the day from the projects. People who crawled up out of the ghetto and made their fortunes. Most acted uppity. Aloof. Like they were something special. I can see Everett not telling anyone who didn't know him that he was Indian. It would affect his bottom line."

Hobart returned to the table with a double sundae. He threw his braids over his back out of the way of the sticky chocolate and licked some that had dripped onto his hand. "You must think I had a jaundiced opinion of the old man?"

Manny shrugged. "It does sound a little harsh, but then I didn't know him."

"Do you understand *skopa*, Agent Tanno?"

Manny nodded. "It refers to a man that is crooked. Bad in his dealings with others."

"That fit good old Everett to a *T*. When I was growing up

in the house, I saw firsthand what he was like—lying about a mare's lineage. Claiming a horse had pure mustang blood when it wasn't true. And presenting paperwork to prove his lies." He wiped whipped cream off his lips. "That's why I wanted nothing to do with his money."

"Until you came begging for money for your heritage center."

Hobart jabbed the air with his spoon. "You're damned right I wanted his money. Wanted it to go to a good cause. If I couldn't convince him to will a sizeable donation to the center, it would go to any charity but Indian." He set the empty bowl on the table. "Except Everett's original will now stands and my heritage center gets nothing. So you can stop accusing me of cutting the old man's brake lines."

Manny flipped a page in his notebook as if he were actually going to write down what Hobart told him. "I'm not accusing you of anything. I'm just in the information-gathering phase. Such as... it's a little odd that you had so little use for Everett, yet you adored his father. Even calling him *Grandfather*."

A slight smile crept over Hobart's otherwise angry expression as he told Manny, "Old Henry was my *Tunkasila*. I called him Grandfather not just because I used that term of respect. He was my grandfather in the Lakota way of thinking, and I was his *takoja*."

Hobart stood and walked to the trash can to toss his empty bowl. "When mother took the job of housekeeper after his wife died, I was only six when we moved into the ranch house. By then, Henry Black Heart—my *Tunkasila*—had long since signed over the ranch to Everett, who wanted little to do with his father. And nothing to do with the Lakota traditions."

He sat back down at the table, his smile widening. "But old Henry was still set in the Indian ways. He lived it and taught me about walking the honorable Red Road. We did everything together—hiking the reservation. Hunting game. Teaching me about the old ways, and how people survived back in the day. He was a loving man and my mentor except when…"

Manny waited for Hobart to continue, but he sat staring at the tiled floor like he was reading tea leaves.

"Except when?" Manny asked.

Hobart stared at the floor so long Manny thought he had not heard him when he looked up, the smile gone, the dour expression on his face returning. "Except when Grandfather caught me straying from him and going through Destiny's Door one summer afternoon."

"What's Destiny's Door?"

"Not what," Hobart answered. "Where. It's on the reservation. Granddad Henry said it was a sacred place and gave me what-for when he caught me."

Manny thought back to the many times as a boy that he and Unk had hiked the hills throughout Pine Ridge Reservation, but he could not recall any place called Destiny's Door. "Where is that, just out of curiosity?"

"If I told you, you might be inclined to visit that place, which I would not recommend," Hobart said.

He stood and swiped a hand across his eyes. "When Grandad Henry died, I was only ten and had no one in the household to continue leading me down the *Chunka Duta*. Over time, I forgot much of Henry's teachings and strayed, I have to admit. When I graduated high school, good old kindly Everett gave me the bum's rush. 'Get your ass out into the world,' he said. 'You've been sucking this family's teat for way too long.'"

"Seems a bit harsh, even for him," Manny said.

Hobart snickered. "Didn't help my cause any that Everett caught me and Tantra smooching in the barn one afternoon. The last thing he wanted was for her little girl to hook up with another Indian."

"So you two had a fling?" Shannon said, stretching his long

legs out as he perched precariously on the small chair. "Got into doing the wild thing?"

Hobart pulled his braids back down onto his chest and twirled the end of one. "Not hardly. She just played me like she plays other guys. Taunting me. Teasing me. Bringing me right up to the edge where I thought there was going to be something more. You can understand a young man's hormones, right?"

Manny could, at least what he remembered of a young man's hormones. When he went to his senior prom with Ivy Dupree, they had become intimate afterwards in the back seat of her old Buick. When it came time that she wanted more, Manny got control of his emotions and backed off. Somehow. He understood what Hobart felt as a young guy right out of high school.

"By the way, that was the first and last time I ever touched Tantra," Hobart said. "But I always wondered if she had tipped Everett off that we were in the barn so he would catch us. Always wondered if she wanted me out of the house."

"Getting kicked out must have had a positive effect on you," Manny said. "Getting your college degree. Working your way up to football coach."

Hobart laughed. "Yeah, after about fifteen years on the sauce. You know those rummies that hang around Prairie Market and stop whoever is unlucky enough to pass by for a handout?"

"Many times," Manny answered. "Sometimes they get a little aggressive if you don't give them money for booze. Why?"

"That was me," Hobart said. "I'd hang out there, harass people walking by until my... sponsor helped me to get clean. Got me into rehab and I haven't missed an AA meeting since. Even when I was working my way through college, I attended a meeting at least once a week. More if I could, just to keep me honest."

Hobart breathed deeply, his medicine bundle on the thong around his chest rising and falling less the calmer he became. "But you didn't ask me here to talk about my checkered past. No offense, I just don't trust the FBI, so ask me whatever else you think you need to. I have a football team to coach."

Manny clicked his pen and held it over his notebook as he asked, "Everett's safe wasn't opened by any explosive, and it wasn't peeled. It was someone who knew the combination."

"Or the old fart left it open. That day I went there asking for a donation, it was open for a moment before he slammed it shut. Like he thought I was going to steal something."

"According to Jimmy and your mother, Everett kept it closed. Always, unless he was in the room."

Hobart fidgeted in his seat, his temper flaring once again as he asked, "What the hell's your point?"

"My point," Manny said, "is that only you and Everett knew the combination. Which seems another oddity, giving your... tenuous relationship with the old man."

"I knew the combination at one time, Agent Tanno, because Grandfather Henry gave it to me when I was a little pot licker. *He* trusted me with the combination to the safe. Said I should have it if anything ever happened to him, I could get to necessary documents that were stored in there." He leaned forward, his hand gripping the table, his knuckles white. "As to why it was opened the night Everett died, you'll have to look elsewhere. I haven't turned the dial on that safe since I was younger. I don't even know if I remember the combination."

"Fair enough," Manny said, clicking his pen again before asking, "who do *you* think opened the safe, then?"

Hobart shrugged. "How should I know? Probably someone at the ranch."

"Like a ranch hand?"

"Could be, though the old bastard never trusted his employees any more than he trusted the rest of us living in the house, so I don't know how they could have known the combination."

Shannon scooted his chair close and rested his massive forearms on the table as he jabbed a finger at Hobart. "How about that map of where Crazy Horse was buried…" the leg of his chair buckling. Shannon tilted sideways like the leaning Tower of Pisa and seemed to hover in the air for a moment as if he was in some gravity chamber before toppling over. He thrust out his hand to break his fall and went sprawling onto the tile floor.

Manny sprang from his chair to help him up, but Shannon waved him off while he looked about the ice cream parlor. "It's embarrassing enough falling without having some… old dude help me up."

Shannon grabbed onto the edge of the table to stand, but lost his grip and fell back to the floor. He held his wrist and said, "I think I hyper-extended it. It's the same one that I sprained against the Ravens that time."

"Give me a hand," Manny said to Hobart, and together they managed to help Shannon to his feet without developing triple hernias. "Go to the counter and ask for a Ziploc bag of ice," Manny said. "Then sit in that corner booth where you can't fall off and keep the ice bag on your wrist."

Hobart looked after Shannon shambling toward the counter. "Now I see why he never made it through a game."

"He does have his moments though."

"How's that?"

"By bringing up a good point," Manny said. "When he asked you about the map of where Crazy Horse is buried."

"What about it?"

"It's missing from Everett's safe."

Hobart shrugged again. "Got nothing to do with me."

Manny tapped his notebook with his pen. "For argument's sake, in some alternate universe, let us presume that you knew the map was in the safe. If I understood you correctly, you didn't care about Everett's money for yourself—"

"I did not—"

63

"...and so you wouldn't want the map for the purpose of selling it to anyone."

Hobart face flushed. "Of course I wouldn't sell it, even if it were authentic."

"And how can you be so certain that the map isn't genuine?"

Hobart leaned across the table again and met Manny's gaze. "I know that it's fake because *Everett* claimed it was genuine. And I know how many times that scoundrel lied over the years."

Manny sat back and closed his notebook. "Why would Everett lie about the map?"

Hobart rubbed his thumb and finger together. "Moolah. Greenbacks. The old fart had been touting that that map was real for as long as I can remember. I always figured he came up with that story—and passed the rumor around—in case he needed money one day in an emergency. Would've offered it to the highest bidder, of which there would have been many. *If* it were authentic."

"I think if it were, he would have let me look at it." Hobart sat back in his chair. "More than a few times when I was growing up, I asked Everett to look at it. But every time he'd put the run on me. Way I figure it, the old bastard didn't want anyone to see that it *was* a fake."

"And you never laid your hands on it?" Manny asked. "Never saw it up close?"

A *tic*. Just a faint micro tic at the corner of Hobart's eye told Manny he had seen it.

"When did you look at it?"

"I told you I never—"

"Hobart," Manny said, "I have been doing this job for a long time and I am very good at it. Just now—when I asked if you'd seen it—your face gave you away. You saw it. Now when?"

"Well, it sure as hell wasn't recently—"

"When?"

Hobart sat up in his chair and said, "when I was a youngster. I must not have been more'n ten or eleven. At least that old, as it was right after Grandfather passed away. I made the mistake of sneaking into Everett's study and taking a look at the map. I had only gotten a moment's glimpse before the old man came in and caught me. Tanned my backside. And that was the *only* time I saw it."

"So then, how are you sure that it isn't *the* map to Crazy Horse's burial place?"

"I don't know," Hobart said. "I just don't know. When I was a kid looking at it, I thought it had to be genuine. But that was only a kid's thinking, is all."

Manny looked over at Shannon sitting in the booth holding the bag of ice on his wrist before turning back and saying, "But in this alternate universe we're talking about… if it *were* a real map, I'd imagine you wouldn't want the Twins getting their hands on it."

"I wouldn't!" Hobart blurted. "They'd just sell it to the highest bidder."

"Why would you care about the map at all if you know it's a fake?"

"I *think* it's phony. But if it isn't… believe me… I have tossed Everett's claim around in my head ever since I can remember," Hobart said.

"And what if it *is* genuine?" Manny asked.

"I'll tell you what," Hobart answered. "The location of Crazy Horse's burial site would come out. And you know that location—wherever it is—is sacred. It would be desecrated."

Manny put the notebook and pen in his briefcase and said, "If you thought it were authentic, you would go to great lengths to ensure it did not fall into the wrong hands."

"I would have done most anything… short of setting Everett up to die in a truck crash."

"Then, there is one way to settle the speculation that you took the cedar box containing the map. Let me look in your apartment—"

"The hell I will!"

"We could get a search warrant," Shannon said. He had come up behind them, holding the Ziploc bag of ice to his wrist while he towered over them. "We could toss your place looking for the map. Be a real mess when we finished. Better to just give us your consent—"

Hobart stood abruptly, knocking his chair over. He stepped close to Shannon and stood looking defiantly up at him. "Go ahead and get your search warrant, if you think you can get a judge to issue one. Do that and my attorney will have your ass by the time he's done."

Shannon began to say something when Hobart turned and stomped out of the ice cream shop.

Manny looked at Shannon and shook his head. "That went really well, Trainee Henderson."

"What? We could get a search warrant."

"Did they not teach you anything in the academy? We don't even have reasonable suspicion, let alone probable cause to apply for a search warrant."

"But... but you were convinced Hobart had something to do with the missing map. If we could find the map at his place we could tie him to the burglary."

"I was just tossing words out," Manny said, "to gauge his reaction. We have nothing on him for certain. And now," Manny motioned to the classic Ford fishtailing away in the snow, "Hobart may never talk to us again."

Shannon held the ice bag and looked down at his size fifteens. "Sorry, agent Tanno."

Many waved it away. "Forget it. Let's just get you in the car and to the ER so they can look at your wrist before you fall again. Be a real rodeo if you went down with just me trying to help you up."

Chapter 9

Willie insisted that Manny park his rental truck at the Justice Building and hop in with him. Almost like he suspected Manny was more than a little dangerous behind the wheel. "Where's Man Mountain Mike?"

"The Senior Agent in charge gave him the day off to mend his sprained wrist," Manny answered as he closed the door against the biting wind.

"And you didn't object? The man's in the training program, for God's sake. He ought to man-up even when he's in a little pain."

Manny smiled. "Would you like him to try squeezing in here with us?"

"Good point," Willie said as he pulled out of Pine Ridge Village on the way to the Black Ranch. "By the way, I did manage to call Hanson Becker. He was covering paintings at the Prairie Edge in Rapid City. Not a lot for art critics to do here in the Wild West, and he agreed to meet me at the Justice Building this week. Want to sit in?"

"Does a fat baby drool? Of course. I want to find out what he knows about the Black family."

Willie slammed on his brakes when a porcupine waddled up from the ditch and shuffled across the road. He snatched a military wool blanket from the back seat and bailed out of the door, running after the porcupine. He approached the critter with the blanket up as a shield as it stopped and eyed Willie a moment before he tossed the blanket on top of the hapless creature. It wiggled and squealed and—when it managed to squirm out from under the blanket—its back was bare of quills.

Willie let it scurry away before recovering the blanket, folding it carefully so the quills that had stuck in the blanket didn't jab him. He returned to the SUV and placed the blanket carefully on the back floorboard. "I'll pick out the quills later," he said.

"Didn't know you were into quilling," Manny said.

"I'm not. Mary Catches said to keep an eye out for a porcupine for some projects she wants to tackle."

"Your sacred woman?"

Willie nodded. "My *winyan wakan*. She's been mentoring me," he said, and no more was needed, for Manny knew the bond between the sacred woman and her student of many years, studying the *wakan* ways—the sacred ways—on Willie's journey to evolving into a sacred man himself.

"She still live in Porcupine?"

"She does."

Manny chuckled. "She lives in Porcupine but can't get enough porcupine quills."

Willie climbed back behind the wheel and resumed the drive toward the Black Ranch when Manny asked, "Have you ever heard of a place called Destiny's Door here on Pine Ridge?"

Willie took his can of Copenhagen from his pocket and stuffed his lip. "Can't say that I have, but then I didn't grow up on this reservation. Why?"

Manny eyed the can of Copenhagen. He'd never dipped, but he had smoked for many years and the sight of any tobacco triggered a yearning for a cigarette. He quickly grabbed a piece of Dubble Bubble from his own shirt pocket and said, "It's just something Hobart mentioned. He told me to forget finding the place, but I noticed he shuddered when he said it, like it's sacred. But I can't imagine much frightening a man that size—your

69

size—especially the way he stood up to Shannon in Cold Stone. His temper got away from him and I thought he was going to punch my trainee."

Willie turned onto State Road 32 towards the grasslands, pronghorn grazing beside the road and into the meandering hills, paying the Expedition no mind. But Manny knew that, come hunting season in this part of the reservation, those same animals would be as elusive as Everett's reason for changing his will. "Why do you think the old man wanted to cut his children entirely out of his estate?"

Willie slowed when they arrived at the quarter-mile long drive that led to the Black Ranch house. "If the other night is any indication, I'd say the old man figured his kids were a couple sniveling asses and thought they didn't deserve squat."

"Kids! They're older than you," Manny pointed out.

"You know what I mean," Willie said. "If I were Everett, I'd consider it a gift cutting them out of the estate. Make them get off their tails and work just to make ends meet like the rest of us."

"You might have a point," Manny said, thin tendrils of wood smoke from the ranch house filtering above the short rise right before the house came into view. "But now with Everett's death before he could execute the new will, they're sure to inherit a bundle."

"How much, do you suppose?" Willie asked, passing corrals on either side of the road, one holding horses, the other two, Angus bulls.

"We'll know soon enough when the will is read," Manny answered. "Park next to that fancy Tesla."

"Jesa!" Willie said. "Somebody must have some lucky bucks."

"Mellis Considine," Manny answered.

"Since when does he handle high dollar cases? I thought he only handled divorce and drunk driving cases. Drug cases."

"Since he fleeced some old lady out of her estate and got a taste of the big money," Manny said. "So, now he has enough to blow. Like on a Tesla."

Manny had met the attorney only once when he represented a client whom Lumpy and Manny had arrested on a traffic stop when they were both tribal cops. A K-9 search of the suspect's car yielded a trunk full of marijuana, all in Ziploc bags for distribution. Mellis had argued that the car should have been returned to his client. The tribal judge thought otherwise and allowed the police department to keep the car under forfeiture laws—a year-old Jaguar. For the next year, policemen took turns touring the reservation in style, until Lumpy plowed into a buffalo crossing the road over by Kyle and totaled it.

Willie parked between the Tesla and the Ford F250—the one that wouldn't start the night Everett ran out of his house. They climbed out and started for the house when Mary Comes Flying met them on the porch. "Don't expect a warm welcome from the Twins… they think you're going to accuse them of setting up Everett's accident—"

Manny held up his hand to stop her. "Right now, we still don't know for certain if those brake lines were cut." *But I will know once I talk with Reuben,* Manny thought. "So, reassure the Twins that all we're doing here is sitting in on the reading of the will. We'll talk about the burglary and the accident another time."

"Thank you," Mary said. "Follow me to the Great Room."

Manny and Willie fell in behind her as she led them through the construction project that hadn't been touched since the night of the initial call. Manny stepped over dry wall knives and skirted a bucket of dry wall mud as he followed Mary down the hallway into Everett's Great Room. Animal heads adorned two walls, deer and antelope beside a full mountain lion mount. As they entered the room, Willie had to duck to avoid running into a bull buffalo head larger than any Manny had ever seen on the reservation, and he stepped around a bear rug in the center of the room.

Jimmy Black sat teetering on the arm of a leather couch draped with elk hides. Ice tinkled in his tumbler as he raised it high in a mock toast. "The FBI has arrived." He downed the drink. "And his trusted Tonto-like *pardner* Officer With Horn." His smile faded and he glared at Mary. "Though it wasn't my idea to invite the local law to this private event."

"No, it was Mary's decision to have law enforcement sit in," Mellis said. He set his glasses down on Everett's enormous mahogany desk and stood. He walked around it and faced Manny but did not offer his hand. "Were it up me, I would not allow police to be present when the will is read. But Mary insisted, and so I have no choice."

"And if it were up to me," Manny said, "I wouldn't be here with a… small-time lawyer."

Mellis snickered. "See that Tesla out front… you think I'm still a ham-and-egger attorney?"

"You'll always be small time," Manny said, "no matter what kind of car you drive. Even a fancy Tesla."

Mellis snapped his fingers. "That's where I remember you… you railroaded my client out of his new Jag when I was a criminal defense attorney."

"Isn't that a little redundant?" Willie asked. "Saying 'criminal' and 'attorney' in the same sentence?"

Mellis' face flushed as red as his crimson-colored tie. He turned on his heels and tramped back behind the desk. "Can we begin sometime today?" he asked Mary.

"We're waiting on Tantra. She's resting. Her headaches, you know—"

"You mean she's passed out," Jimmy said and tilted his head back and laughed heartily. Scotch spilled over the side of his glass onto his hand and he licked it off. "My little sister was a *baaaaad* girl last night. I'm afraid she drove into Rapid. Did some clubbing and barely made it home before the sun came up. She's a little… 'stoned' is how we old duffers put it—"

"I'm quite all right," Tantra said as she entered the room. "And I am not *stoned*, as you put it. I was just out late trying to get my mind off Father's death."

"Like hell," Jimmy said. "You were out celebrating raking in the dough, just like I would have if I didn't have my drug of choice right here." He stood on wobbly legs and managed to make it to the liquor cart without falling down. Somehow.

Tantra turned to Mary and said, "I did not fall off the wagon last night. I was out late because I ran into… an old friend."

"Must have been a good friend if you stayed out until sunup," Mary said.

A slight smile tugged at the corners of Tantra's mouth. "He used to be a *very* good friend."

"That's all well and good," Mellis interrupted. "And I can stay here waiting for you and Jimmy to stop arguing and for you making excuses to Mary. Really, I can stay here *all day*. I'd actually prefer it—I will bill the estate for however long I am here."

"Mellis is right," Mary said. "Let us just sit down and give Mr. Considine some respect to read your father's will. Jimmy."

He put the stopper back on the scotch decanter and started to stagger back to the couch when Mellis motioned for him to sit beside Tantra in a captain's chair in front of the desk.

Manny and Willie sat on the couch in back of them as Mellis cleared his throat. "Now that everyone is present—"

"My son, Hobart, is not here," Mary said.

Mellis waved the air with his reading glasses as if dismissing it. "Doesn't really matter. Hobart will receive very little of the estate. He can come into my office next week and I will give him a copy of Everett's will and a check. Now, can we begin?"

Mellis donned his reading glasses and opened a red paisley folder. He took out the documents and looked through his readers as he said, "To my dear loving children—"

"The old bastard must have written that about thirty years ago," Jimmy said, "when he thought we were actually salvageable."

"Written twenty-four years ago, to be precise," Mellis said. "Before you... *grateful* children had a falling out with your father."

"No," Tantra said, "Father had a falling out with *us*. About the time he made his first million. When he figured there was more for the taking and began ignoring us except to berate us for some perceived flaw."

Jimmy guffawed. "*Perceived* flaw? Dear sister, we are rife with flaws, you and me, and Father was perceptive enough to notice them. I'll give him that."

"That's the only thing you ever gave him!" she blurted out.

"Mellis," Manny said, quickly. The last thing he wanted to do this morning was hear two brats fight, "that will was written years ago when you were still doing criminal defense work. How is it that you're handling the estate?"

"Though I owe you no explanation, I will explain for the sake of the heirs." He stood and walked around the desk. "The man who represented Everett—Saul Hormey—brought me into his firm a few years ago before he died."

"Then you never talked with Everett about his will?" Manny asked.

"I did. Twice. Once when I came here, and the other time when he dropped by my office in Rapid City. He wanted to amend his will, but he died before it could be executed. Now can we please continue?"

When he got no objection, he walked back around and sat at the desk. He resumed reading Everett's wishes of twenty-four years ago. "To my dear loving children, Tantra and James, I leave the ranch, the horse and cattle operations, as well as the holdings in the aforelisted banks." He listed five banks in the region, all with varying amounts.

"Ha!" Jimmy yelled and tossed his whisky glass against a wall. It shattered and he nudged Tantra. "We are *very* wealthy, little sister." He turned in his seat and nodded to Mary sitting on an occasional chair beside the couch. "That means, out-of-a-home-Mary Comes Flying, that I can break my glass here whenever I want. Or break anything else I feel like and you can't do a damned thing about it."

"Except evict you," Mellis said, and for the first time he smiled.

"How's that?"

"Mary—my obnoxious friend—is left with the ranch house and control of everything within these walls. She can give you the bum's rush herself if she so wishes."

Jimmy shrugged. "What the hell do I care? With the old man's money, we can go live wherever we want."

"Not quite." Mellis handed Mary and the Twins each a document. "As you can see, for you to reap the yearly income, Everett demanded each of you remain in this house. Working the business."

"That's bullshit!" Jimmy said and flung the papers across the floor.

"It may be," Mellis said, "but I chalk it up to the old man's morbid sense of humor. I can just imagine all of you living here and working closely together. It'll be a marvel if one or all of you don't get charged with assault on the others."

"Jimmy's right. This is horseshit." Tantra stood and dropped her papers in front of Mellis. "I always thought when Father died, we'd be free of this… this dump. *And* of each other."

Jimmy staggered to the liquor cart and managed to get the stopper off the decanter of whiskey. "We're not in defeat yet, little sister." He turned around and held his full glass high. "We control the purse strings. Perhaps we'll cut the old bat's wages and she'll be forced to move out."

Manny leaned over and whispered to Willie, "I guess Everett was devious even in his younger days when he wrote that will. I'd love to be a mouse in the corner and watch the fireworks."

"And there'll be fireworks in spades," Willie said, shielding his mouth with his hand. "The only thing that kept these spoiled misfits from each other's throats was Everett's strong hand."

Mellis cleared his throat and said, "You may want to sit for this, James." He waited until Jimmy had staggered back and dropped into his chair. "You can cut Mary's wages. That is your prerogative with the will. But I doubt that she'll care much, as Everett left her a... sizeable amount sitting in an Omaha bank. If these figures are correct, she may never need a paycheck again. Between that and the other properties—"

"What properties?" Tantra asked. "Father never mentioned any other land."

"Not land," Mellis said. "Rental properties. A four-plex in Pine Ridge Village and a duplex in Hot Springs that haven't been rented out in years. All could be sold or fixed up to make Mary money."

Mary slumped in her chair. "Everett... left me money?" she breathed.

"More than you could make in a lifetime as a housekeeper," Mellis answered. Tantra glared at Mary as if she were suddenly an enemy and Jimmy's jaw muscles tightened. "So we're stuck here?" he asked.

Mellis closed his briefcase and checked his watch. "I'm afraid so. You're all one big dysfunctional family now. Just like when Everett was alive."

"You never said exactly what my son will inherit," Mary said.

"The son-of-a-bitch better not get much!" Jimmy blurted out. He stood on wobbly legs and looked down at Mary, his fists clenching and unclenching, when Willie said, "You want some time in the pokey? Go ahead, swing on Mary and see what shape you're in when you get to jail."

After a long pause, it registered in Jimmy's foggy mind that an ass-whooping was a heartbeat away and he backed off from Mary. "I just don't think Hobart deserves any."

Mellis slid an envelope across the desk and Mary opened it.

"Everett only left Hobart a thousand dollars."

"Read the note he scratched on the other side."

Mary turned it over and read, "Here's a stipend for keeping old Henry out of my hair the last years of his life."

Jimmy chuckled. "That's appropriate—Hobart never was a Black, even though he insists on using our name."

After Mellis left the room, Mary stood and said, "It's been some morning, for sure. If anyone is interested, I have fresh German chocolate cake in the kitchen."

"All I want to do is go back to bed," Tantra said.

"And I want to figure out the best way to get out from under Dad's bullshit will," Jimmy added, "and out from under you two."

Mary shook her head as she watched the Twins stomp out of the room. She faced Manny and said, "The offer stands for you, too."

"Mary," he said, "I, for one, would happily take a slice of cake from the world's wealthiest housekeeper."

Willie stood and stretched. "I better come along and assist. Manny's been known to eat more cake than two grown men."

Chapter 10

Manny stopped at the pile of dry wall equipment and loose boards and buckets of screws and nails cluttering the floor just before the entryway and shook his head. "I'd have thought the Kramers smart enough to come get their equipment if they're not going to finish the job."

"All the tools and crap you see here are probably stolen anyway," Willie said while he buttoned his coat.

Manny squatted and picked up a dry wall hammer. He had used one many times working his way through college but had no desire to do so again. He had worked far too long to soften his hands and he'd be damned if hard work would change that. "That's the second time you mentioned that the Kramers are a little bit shady."

"I'd just be happy if they came back and cleaned their mess up," Mary said. "This is my house now and I aim to find someone who can finish the job."

"Did you ever call them and demand they come get their equipment?" Willie asked.

"I did. Eventually," Mary said. "That moron kid of Buddy's said they landed a roofing job and could not get back here to finish this. Then Buddy came on the line and assured me they would come and get their stuff. That was two days ago."

Manny stood and brushed white dry wall dust off his trousers, something tugging at the corners of his mind that he couldn't get a grip on. "Mind if Officer With Horn and I wander around here for a few moments?"

"Wander away," Mary said. "But with the Twins skulking about, I do not know if I would go upstairs."

"I don't need to go up there into the spoiled lions' den."

"Then take your time," Mary said and walked back down the hallway.

Willie waited until Mary had disappeared into the kitchen before saying, "You must see something, 'cause I recognize that look."

"What look?"

"That look where there ought to be a light bulb sparking over your head. What is it?"

Manny slapped his hands together and dry wall lingered in the air a moment before falling onto the floor. "I knelt where I shouldn't have."

Willie threw up his hands. "That's your great epiphany—you just got sloppy and kneeled into some dry wall dust?"

"It is," Manny said. "Follow me."

He led Willie down the hallway past the kitchen and the Great Room into the last room along the hallway, Everett's tiny reading room. After they walked into the room Manny asked Willie, "What do you see here?"

Willie stood with his hand on the butt of his gun. "I see chaos. Papers and magazines and books taking most of the floor space. I see the safe is still open." He clicked on his cell phone's flashlight and shined it inside the ancient safe. "I see everything that we left is still there. The baseball card collection and the comics haven't been taken." He stood and turned off the light. "What do *you* see?"

"How big are the Kramers?"

"Buddy, the old man, is about five-nine. Goes about two-twenty. Bobby is an honest six-footer but slimmer. Why?"

"Because either may have a hard time fitting inside this small space to steal anything. They'd have to get right down on the floor. If they did, they'd leave *that*," Manny said as he pointed to gray-colored dust just outside the safe and on the bottom of the opening. "Just like I did just now out in the entryway."

Willie bent over and ran his hand over the dust. "Jesa! I'd say that is dry wall dust. I musta missed it the first time."

"You and me both," Manny said. "I thought it was from Pee Pee flinging fingerprint powder around just to piss the homeowner off like he usually does, but I was wrong." Manny clapped his hands together and more dust flew into the air. "Even though Everett was active, I doubt he'd have knelt and transferred dry wall dust from that construction area by the entryway. And I doubt Mary could get down there, as stoved-in as she is."

"Then it almost has to be the Kramers," Willie said.

"We need to get them in for an interview anyways, and this might loosen their tongues if they figure we know they've been in here."

"That might be easier said than done."

"Thought they lived on the reservation?"

"They do," Willie said. He shifted some magazines cluttering the desk and sat on one corner. "But they are as shy of law enforcement as they are of bath water. If they even suspect we're looking for them, they'll figure we have them for *something* and they'll rabbit."

Manny bent over and looked another time inside the safe. "They moved those coin and stamp collections looking for the cedar box containing the map, I am convinced."

"The map that everyone swears is a fake?"

"Except Hobart," Manny said. He stood and put his hands on the small of his back, stretching. "Hobart thinks the map is genuine. He denied it, but when I asked him, it showed—he is convinced the map Everett's father drew fifty years ago is for real. A map that Hobart would die to prevent it landing into the hands of the money-hungry Twins."

Willie nodded. "I thought about him, too, and put him right up there on my suspect list."

Light from the lamp cast an odd color atop the bookshelf amidst the dust. Manny squinted. Faint specks of red dust mixed with the dust that had surely accumulated over years had caught Manny's attention. He tore off a piece of paper from his notebook and folded it into a bindle, using the side of his pen to scrape the red dust off into the tiny envelope. "Where's this dust come from here on the reservation?"

Willie chuckled. "A ton of places. That red scoria dust gets into everything. Why?"

Manny pocketed the envelope of dust to pass on to Pee Pee later. "It doesn't belong. Doesn't mean it's important. Just that it doesn't belong here in Everett's study."

Manny looked about the room imagining what Everett saw every time he hid out in here from the chaos of the Twins and relaxing from his business dealings. As he often did, Manny wanted to know what the victim saw in his last hours, his last moments alive. He sat in Everett's tattered occasional chair situated under the dim, overhanging reading lamp, and crossed one leg over the other as he thought Everett might have done here in his sanctuary.

Manny closed his eyes, breathing deeply. These times were the few moments when he wished for one of his haunting visions that would help him solve the problem before him. But no vision came to him and he opened his eyes. He looked from Everett's vantage point, staring at the clutter that hadn't been cleaned in years, at dust that had settled on everything in the room.

Except for one spot a few feet in front of the chair that contained no dust at all.

Sticking out from a pile of decades-old magazines was a

faded folder devoid of any dirt and grime. Manny bent over and carefully slid it out from between old *Look* magazines. "DD" had been scribbled on one corner of the folder. He thought back to the Kramers, recalling that the "BB" inscribed on the tools wasn't a bra size but stood for "Buddy" and "Bobbie." Just like this "DD" wasn't a bra size, but something entirely different.

"Whatcha looking at?" Willie said, squatting beside the chair.

"This… folder. The corner was sticking out, and there's no dust caked on it like the rest of the clutter. This folder's been taken out and replaced more than a few times."

"You gonna open it or stare at it?"

Manny untied the string holding the flap over the folder and looked inside before cautiously sliding a piece of canvas about ten inches square out. The canvas was brittle, the coloring faded. As it should have been if it were drawn decades ago. "My God!"

"What is it?"

Manny tapped the folder. "This is why 'DD' is scribbled on the front."

Willie turned the light and squatted beside Manny. "Jesa! This is *the* map. The 'DD' on the outside has to mean Destiny's Door."

Manny reverently slid it back inside the folder and tied the string. He'd examine it later.

"I don't understand why this wasn't in the safe," Willie said. "Why would Everett leave it out here in the open where anyone could take it?"

"For one thing, I am betting Everett knew this was *the* map." Manny laid the envelope carefully on the floor. "I'd wager he took it out often when he was sitting in this chair with no one in the room to see it except him. Like the art thief who looks at his stolen masterpiece every day—a masterpiece reserved for only his eyes. As for why not keep it in that old safe that a pound of C4 couldn't open? Everett must have been worried that someone might one day get into that safe. Perhaps the day he caught

Hobart, he realized the kid had the combination. I don't know. But I bet Everett figured no one would ever think about looking for it in this… mess."

"Let's say he figured out old Black Heart had given Hobart the combination to the safe when he was a youngster," Willie said, still looking in awe at the envelope containing the map. "Everett might have been hiding it from Hobart, fearing he'd one day get into the safe."

"That is a possibility."

Willie snapped his fingers. "Then there must be another map. One that Everett kept in the cedar box. So, the thief took the wrong one. The one in the safe was a phony, and… who besides Everett would know the map in the safe is a fake?"

"Tantra knew, she said it was a fake. And Hobart said it was a fake, too. But something told him that the map he saw when he was a youngster was genuine, though he wouldn't admit that when I talked with him." Manny stood and looked about the room.

"Unless," Willie said, "both of them said that to throw suspicion off of themselves."

Manny ran his hand over the folder and said, "Unless the real one was the one in the safe and this one is the phony." He rubbed his temple against a rising headache. "We have several possibilities—one, that this is the only map and Everett took it out of the cedar box at some point. Or, two, that there actually is another map that Tantra was certain was fake. We won't know for sure unless we find the other one and have it tested—if there *is* another one. This one we need to get into evidence—"

"You will do no such thing!" Tantra stormed into the room and stood in front of Manny, holding out her hand. "Give me the map. It's mine."

"We can't do that," Manny said. "This is evidence that we need processed."

"And just where the hell did you find that?" she said and pointed at the folder. "I thought the map was stolen from Father's safe."

Manny motioned to the pile of magazines that looked like every other pile in the room. "Perhaps the only thing the thief made off with was a cedar box that he—or she—*thought* contained the map."

"Then there is just the one map?"

Manny shrugged.

"Don't matter," she said. "Give it to me."

"Like I said, it's evidence—"

"Of what?" Tantra said. "The map is a fake."

"Oh?" Manny said, feeling his anger rising. "Are you an antiquities expert?"

"Of course not. I have no time for that."

"Then how do you know this is not genuine, especially without even looking at it? You don't. But if it is a fake, then me seizing it for evidence will deprive you and Jimmy of nothing."

"What is the commotion down here?" Mary walked into the room. She dried her hands on her apron and said to Tantra, "What are you yelling about like a crazy person?"

"Agent Tanno insists on taking the map that he knows is a fake."

"What map?"

"The map of where Crazy Horse is buried."

"I don't understand," Mary said. "I thought the map was stolen from Everett's safe the night he had his accident."

"I'm not sure what is going on exactly." Manny motioned Mary closer while keeping the folder away from Tantra as he carefully opened it once again. "Either the burglar made off with a cedar box and nothing more, or there are two maps. This one Everett kept hidden in plain sight between that stack of magazines. Have you ever seen this map?"

"On two occasions."

"And you would know if it's genuine?"

"I am pretty certain," Mary said, "though it's been years."

Manny nodded to Willie who moved between Manny and Tantra, in case she lunged for it and tried to slide the canvas out.

"May I?"

Manny handed Mary the map and she put on reading glasses dangling from a chain around her neck. After she looked at it, she handed it back to Manny. "I am certain—this is not the map Everett claimed was genuine. This is a reproduction. Many people sell Crazy Horse maps that have been made to look authentic by using some sort of aging method. Someone probably did the same thing to this one."

"Then maybe you can answer this," Manny said as he slid the map back into the folder, "why would Everett take it out often and look at it if is a fake?"

"Because the old man was nutso," Jimmy said, crowding into the reading room with the others. He tapped his temple and said, "The brain cancer affected him, though he was always off in a mean kind of way even before he developed that. He was losing it this last year and forgot shit all the time." He chuckled. "I can see the old fart forgetting which was the real map, whether it was this one or the one in the safe that was authentic."

"Then it's settled," Willie said. He took the folder from Manny and held it away from Tantra. "This might be a fake. A reproduction. Something like you'd see for sale on the internet or at roadside stands." He looked at the Twins. "You two should have no objection to us seizing a *fake* map."

"But I haven't even seen it to verity that it is a reproduction," Tantra said.

"Mary's opinion is good enough for the moment," Manny said.

He motioned to Willie and they squeezed past the Twins and into the hallway when Mary said, "Supper is on, and it's getting a little late to drive back into Rapid City."

"Thanks for the offer," Manny answered, "but I think I'll stay here at the government apartment for the night."

Or stay at a sacred man's house.

One who might be able to decipher the map.

Brother Reuben.

Chapter 11

Manny paused as he often did when approaching his brother's trailer house, especially at night. Reuben had spent twenty-five years in the South Dakota State Penitentiary for a '70s homicide and he detested law enforcement. About the only one he tolerated was Manny, but even that was often sketchy. And that's if he recognized what vehicle Manny drove down Reuben's long driveway. Tonight, Reuben would have no way of knowing who pulled up in the Toyota truck, and so Manny laid on the horn to alert him.

He honked twice, then waited for a second before tooting again—their signal that he was not there to arrest Reuben, even though they both knew it would take more than Manny to arrest the big man.

Manny slowly stepped from the truck and stood beside the open door with his hands on top of the cab. He held the folder containing the map as he looked around the shadows for his brother when Reuben said from somewhere behind him, "you don't need to be so sneaky. Just step away from that little pickup and walk up to the door and knock like every Jehovah's Witness or Mormon does. They're not afraid to."

"They don't know you," Manny said.

Reuben emerged from the shadow cast by a thick cottonwood tree to one side of his driveway. He clutched a short-barreled shotgun beside his leg and noticed Manny eyeing it. "This gun's not stolen, if that's what you're thinking."

"How would you know, with the serial number ground off?"

Reuben kept the gun tight against his leg. "What makes you think that?"

Manny smiled. "Because I know you. Besides, felons aren't allowed to have guns."

"You just stopped by to see if you can build some cockamamie case of a felon in possession of a firearm, or what?"

Manny motioned to the walk leading to the back of Reuben's house and said, "I have other things I have to do today. Maybe tomorrow I'll build a case. Let's talk."

Manny led Reuben around back on his icy, treacherous walkway—perhaps the only man Manny would trust behind him with a loaded gun—and stopped abruptly when he reached the back yard. He stared at the enclosure that was new since the last time he'd visited and said, "You said you were going to build a screened porch back here but this is… different."

"Different good or different bad?"

Manny looked over Reuben's new enclosure spanning the length of the trailer house, large enough to sleep several people. Enough for people to gather and visit. In good weather. "Right now, it's a different bad. No offense, but a screened porch in twenty-degree weather is of no use."

"I know. I know." Reuben leaned the shotgun against a lawn chair. "I intended installing those removable storm windows but ran out of money."

"Perhaps if you mechanicked full time you would have enough to put storm windows in."

"As in a full-time job? Bite your tongue, little brother, and grab a chair. I'll go fetch us some tea."

While Manny stepped through the screen door into the enclosed porch, Reuben disappeared into his house. He had ditched the old lawn chairs for new, thick canvas reclining ones that looked impervious to the wind and snow spitting through the screens. A rag rug lay in the middle of the floor and a coffee table fabricated from a slab of oak sat atop it. Reuben had installed overhead lighting, and heat from a wood burner somehow kept the cold at bay. *Honey despite the cold*, Manny thought as he settled back into a recliner. He checked his watch. He'd called Clara telling her that he wouldn't be making it back to Rapid City tonight. "I'll just grab some sleep at the FBI apartment here on the rez."

"Again!" she said, and Manny caught the despair in her voice. Perhaps frustration, but then he'd been frustrated with himself as of late, wondering just where his relationship with Clara Downing was headed. Since Willie's wedding, she had pressed Manny to set their own date. But did he actually want to take on such a commitment at this stage of his life? And was she ready for it?

Reuben entered the porch carrying a silver tray with a teapot and two cups. "Here goes, *misun*."

Manny ran his hand over the silver platter, slightly tarnished like real silver gets when not polished. "Getting pretty sophisticated. Not to pry—"

"Then don't—"

"...this must have set you back a pretty penny, especially on a part-time mechanic, part-time holy man's wages."

Reuben took of the top of the sugar bowl and heaped spoonfuls into his tea. "I didn't steal it, if that's what you're implying—"

"It's not," Manny said, knowing his brother would not steal from anyone. Reuben might kill the same man who stole from *him*, but he'd never lay hands on another's property. "I just wondered if the mechanic business was picking up any."

"I don't want it to pick up," Reuben said. "I have all the business I want for a disabled vet."

Manny blew on his tea before deciding it was still too hot

to drink and set it back on the table. "I didn't know you were disabled."

"Me, either," Reuben said, "until that VA rep who came through the rez this summer got to checking. He figured my four purple hearts ought to be worth something and he got me fifty-percent. Just enough to qualify for medication and monthly checks that I can splurge on this," he tapped the silver setting. "But you'd know that if you ever stopped by more than once every couple months just when you need something from me." He leaned across the coffee table and said, "You *do* want something from me, no?"

Manny remained silent as if afraid to admit Reuben was right.

"Come on, *misun*... what brings you here?"

Manny handed the folder across the table. "I want you to look at this."

Reuben turned the folder over in his hand before untying the clasp and said, "What is it?"

"A map of where Crazy Horse is buried."

Reuben dropped the folder on the table and backed away. "You're saying this is *the* map I've been hearing about all my life?"

Manny shrugged. "Like your disability, I am fifty-percent sure."

"Where did you get it?"

"Everett Black's house. It may be the one that his father, Black Heart, drew many years ago."

Reuben stood. "Then I am not going to look at it until I get clean." He smiled at Manny. "When was the last time you got cleansed so you're worthy enough to look at such a map of where the sacred man is buried."

Manny groaned. "I have the feeling that we are going to get clean together."

"You are so perceptive," Reuben said. "I'll grab a pair of shorts and a towel for you and meet you down at the sweat lodge."

Chapter 12

In back of Reuben's porch and down a shallow ravine sat his sweat lodge—made out of bent tree saplings with canvas stretched over the frame. In the old days, Lakota draped buffalo hides over the framework to hold the heat in. In the old days. Back when buffalo were plentiful.

Manny made his way down the slippery ravine to the lodge at the bottom. Except for still having to slide down the dirt embankment to get to it as he'd done so many times before, Reuben had built steps since the last time. With a handrail. *Has it been so long since I entered the womb of Mother Earth for purification?* Manny vowed, as he always did, to be more diligent in connecting with his Lakota roots.

"You look surprised by my improvements," Reuben said as he looked up at Manny gingerly coming down the steps. Reuben threw off the towel, snow pelting his cheeks and bare chest and legs. As many times as Manny had seen them, he had to look again at the scars across Reuben's thick chest, compliments of a North Vietnamese mortar attack at Hue during TET in 1968. He focused on Manny with his one good eye, the other one clouded where it had caught shrapnel somewhere north of Con Thien during his final tour of 'Nam. "I hate to admit it," Reuben said, "but I'm getting a little long in the tooth to keep sliding my butt down here every time I want to sweat."

"About time. What changed?"

"A sliver from a cottonwood branch sticking in my keister. Got infected, too. I would have called you to dig it out and put some medication on it—"

"And it would still be there," Manny said. "Us FBI folks don't treat old butts."

Manny took off his towel and draped it on the branch beside the log. *Waziyata*—the surly and chilling north wind said to kill anything it contacts—instantly chilled Manny to the core, and he flapped his arm to get some circulation back. "It'd help if I got inside the lodge to warm up."

"Soon enough, *misun*." Reuben stoked the fire in the small pit in front of the lodge. He laid rocks atop the embers and knelt, blowing on the fire. It flared up and, for a moment, Manny felt *some* heat on his near-naked body.

After the fire had heated the rocks sufficiently, Reuben scoped up some with a small pitchfork and disappeared through the flap over the lodge opening. He returned moments later with an empty pitchfork and scooped more rocks. "Good thing you didn't bring your trainee along," Reuben said as he turned back to the lodge. "As big as he is, he'd have a hard time fitting inside. Would have had to build an ever bigger *initipi* for that man."

"You met Shannon?" Manny asked, flapping his arms so fast he feared he'd start to hover.

"Never."

"Then how do you know how big he is?"

"Moccasin telegraph," Reuben answered. "Folks say he can barely fit into your car or that little truck you're driving now." He disappeared a last time inside the lodge. When he came out, he handed Manny a tin of *Prince Albert* tobacco.

"I don't smoke."

"It has been a while since you entered the lodge," Reuben said. "The tobacco is for the offering afterward. Now face east—I'll call when I'm ready."

For purification, and as Reuben had told him to, Manny faced east before entering the lodge. The heat inside warmed Manny's back and bare legs, the chills leaving him. Or was that the result of *Wakan Tanka*—the Great Mysterious—answering his internal lamentations about the freezing cold.

"*Yahpayo!*" Reuben cried from inside and Manny ducked through the flap. He closed it, plunging the lodge into total darkness except for the glowing rocks in the center.

Manny remained silent as he watched his brother across the rock pit, squatted back on his heels. He held a deer hide bladder and scooped water from a bucket beside him. When he dribbled water over the hot rocks, angry steam *hsssed,* rising, obscuring Reuben's form as he rocked back and forth, a faint chant from deep inside his gut rising and falling.

The steam drove the cold from Manny, replaced by an overwhelming damp heat that caused his vision to blur the longer he sat in the lodge.

When the steam died down, he began telling Reuben more water over the rocks was needed, but he found he could not speak, the humidity seeming to constrict his throat. He leaned over and took the ladle from the bucket himself and poured sacred *mni* over the rocks. The steam filled the lodged once again and Manny struggled to make out Reuben in the fog.

But he was gone.

Replaced by a scene as vivid as any drive-in theater: A man approaches a light-haired Oglala and hands him a revolver; a woman hands him a blanket that he drapes over his shoulder to conceal a pistol… Manny squints and brushes steam out of his eyes.

Tashunke Witko, Manny uttered through a parched throat. *Crazy Horse.*

From his uncle's tales as a boy, Manny struggled to recall the last days of the sacred man, Crazy Horse. *He was betrayed…*

stands out in his memory. As Crazy Horse is escorted to the post adjutant's office... "Do not go, *Tashunke Witko!*" Manny cried. Or had he just imagined shouting a warning, remembering that, once out the adjutant's office, Crazy Horse would be seized and made a prisoner.

Manny forced his lips to part as if held by some unearthly glue. To cry out again. To warn Crazy Horse that he would be set upon...

"Do not go, *Tashunke Witko*. Do not go with them. Do not—"

"*Misun!*" Reuben shouted. Manny's eyes opened and he looked frantically about, his arm thrashing about in the snow. He lay on his back in front of the sweat lodge. Reuben kneeled over him, shaking his shoulders, rubbing snow across Manny's cheeks to revive him. "Come out of it, little brother."

Manny tried sitting. Fell back down, his head, his eyes blurry, his vision slowly recovering as he focused on Reuben.

"Let's get you into the porch where you can rest," Reuben said as he stood Manny up. Reuben draped his arm around Manny's shoulder and carefully ascended the steps up to the porch. He eased Manny into a recliner before grabbing a blanket and wrapping it around him. "Don't move. I'm going to fetch us more tea."

After what felt like an hour, Reuben returned with the silver set and placed it on the rustic oak table. "Here," Reuben said and dropped a tea bag into a cup of hot water.

Manny leaned closer to the cup, pushing the tea bag under the water with a spoon like he wanted to push the memory of the vision he'd just had under his mind. But he couldn't. The memory vivid—like all his visions—would stay with him like a vengeful, waking daymare. Manny's only saving grace was that he had a sacred man to help him interpret what his visions meant—his brother Reuben, who sat quietly across from him, knowing Manny would ask his help when he was ready.

After two cups of tea, that moment came. "I saw *Tashunke Witko* being led to the trap that would result in his murder. I… I felt as if I could have stopped it somehow."

Reuben sipped his tea daintily before refilling his cup. He added a heaping spoonful of sugar and sat looking into his tea. He finally broke his silence and asked, "How do you feel being right there at the time Crazy Horse was being set up to be murdered and unable to help him?"

"Guilty," Manny said without hesitation. "I felt guilt. I… me, being an Oglala Lakota just like Crazy Horse, I should have done *something* to help him." He set his cup onto the table before his trembling hand spilled tea onto the rug. "But I was weak. Helpless."

"Like so many others that day that were frozen with fear… wanting to do something to help him but could not."

Manny nodded and stirred his tea.

"What do you think you would have done?" Reuben asked.

"I just don't know. Run to his side. Muster his allies—"

"Tell me," Reuben said, standing and drying himself with a towel, "were there others around *Tashunke Witko* crowding him? Wanting to lay their hands on him?"

Manny thought back to his vision that was slowly fading, as they always did. But like all his visions, it would reappear at the most frightening time. When he wasn't prepared for it. "There were American Horse warriors. Red Cloud's followers that I *sensed* wanted to kill him…" he stopped. "How did I know that?"

"You know that forces were aligned against the sacred man that day—jealous forces who did not wish him to survive—because you were *there*. *Waken Tanka* spoke to you, as he often does inside the *initipi*, and showed you what Crazy Horse was up against that day."

Manny rubbed at his now-growing headache. It throbbed with

each passing moment, as if this was his penance for experiencing his vision.

"Look at me," Reuben said. "If you were with Crazy Horse at Ft. Robinson in 1877, what could you have done that others could not?"

Manny's mind had cleared sufficiently so that he was once again in control of the analytical part of his brain when he concluded, "I could have done nothing to help him."

Reuben leaned over and laid his hand on Manny's shoulder. "From what I have been told—passed down in the oral tradition of our people—*Tashunke Witko* himself knew there was nothing anyone could do to alter the events of that day. He *sensed*—as you did—that he walked his final walk that day as he was escorted to the adjutant's office."

"Then why the hell do I feel so guilty?"

Reuben crow-hopped as he slipped on dry jeans before sitting across from Manny again. "Your guilt is the guilt of the entire Oglala nation. Our people's guilt that they did nothing to help Crazy Horse is now upon you to do something to make amends."

"Do what?" Manny asked. "It's been... nearly 150 years since Crazy Horse was murdered."

Reuben gestured to the envelope containing the map still resting safely on the undershelf of the coffee table. "Perhaps it is your duty to ensure that no one—*no one*—ever finds where the holy man is buried." He set his empty teacup on the table. "I think it's time we take a look at that map, little brother."

Chapter 13

Camp Robinson, Nebraska
Evening, September 5, 1877

Crazy Horse walks calmly toward a large building, Agent Lee to one side, soldier Kennington to the other, Indian police crowding close to the sacred man as they skirt the parade ground. When they reach the building, Crazy Horse stops. He stiffens as he sees the bars on the building. A low soldier opens the door, revealing white prisoners behind bars, some shackled, all looking unkempt in their filth.

This was the camp guardhouse.

Crazy Horse would not enter, even if it meant his life. "I will not walk into that *wasicu* jail," he said, his voice clear, loud over the din of the hundreds of Indians that crowded Crazy Horse, some his followers, others followers of Red Cloud and American Horse, jealous of his celebrity status.

Little Big Man grabs onto him a moment before soldier Kennington does. They force him into the jail.

Crazy Horse breaks away. His blanket falls from his shoulders, his pistol exposed.

An Indian policeman snatches his revolver before Crazy Horse can grab it just as Little Big Man pulls his knife.

Crazy Horse lunges through the Indian police, running

outside, Little Big Man running after him. He throws himself onto Crazy Horse, wrestling with him, when Crazy Horse jerks an arm free. Grabs Little Big Man's knife. Cuts him. He howls in pain, his grip on the sacred man gone.

"Kill Crazy Horse!" cries go up from American Horse's followers. From Red Cloud's warriors.

"Kill the bastard!" screams soldier Kennington.

The crowd has worked into a frenzy, pushing, lunging for the sacred man, hate in their voices. Death fills the air.

Little Big Man rushes at Crazy Horse and grabs him. Crazy horse jerks free. Stumbles back.

Into the outstretched rifle of a soldier. His bayonet pierces the sacred man's side. The soldier reacts. Stabs Crazy Horse again. He collapses, mortally wounded as a hush falls over the hate-filled Lakota.

Touch The Cloud rallies Crazy Horse's followers and they form a protective circle around him as his uncle kneels and examines Crazy Horse's wounds. He knows his nephew must be carried to a place of quietude to await his eventual death, confirmed by the camp surgeon McGillycuddy.

The soldiers refuse. But the Lakota—even those who had screamed for his death—angrily demand that the holy man be taken to the adjutant's office, not the guardhouse.

Touch The Cloud motions to Spotted Eagle and Hump Two and they carefully carry Crazy Horse's body into the post adjutant's office and lay him on the floor.

Dr. McGillycuddy digs into his bag and grabs a vial of morphine, injecting the holy man to relieve his intense pain. It is all the doctor can do.

Crazy Horse lingers between this life and the *Wanagi Takanku*, the Spirit Road, awaiting those who would escort him to the other side when his father enters the room. Waglula cradles his son's head and speaks soothingly. Crazy Horse tries to speak, but cannot.

In the late hours of this night a cry goes up from the Lakota outside and from those inside the adjutant's office. *Tasunka witko ktepi.*

Crazy Horse is killed.

Chapter 14

M anny never saw his brother tremble before. He had served three tours in Viet Nam in the 1960s, and had been an enforcer for the American Indian Movement in the 1970s after he was discharged from the Marines. He was later sentenced to twenty-five years in the state penitentiary for a homicide and had refused parole, wanting to be beholden to no one once he had served his time. And he had never been afraid of the Devil himself.

Until now.

His hands shook as he smudged the envelope containing the map with *peji hota*, the sweet odor of sage wafting over him and Manny, dispersed by the wind whipping through the screens of the porch.

After long, reverent moments, Reuben snubbed the sage out in an ashtray and took hold of the envelope. He sighed deeply, his lips muttering softly as he prayed, and he untied the string holding the flap over the envelope. He paused, setting it aside as if steeling himself to look at it.

He put on his reading glasses and slid the map out of the folder.

"Well?" Manny asked. "Is it authentic?"

Reuben held up his hand for silence while he turned the map to look at it from different angles. After taking his time studying the map, he sat back in his chair and wiped sweat off his forehead despite the cold wind whipping through the porch. "This is, little brother, *the* map of where *Tashunke Witko* is buried."

Manny leaned forward and looked at the map. "How can you be so certain? There have been so many maps purported to show the secret burial place of Crazy Horse."

Reuben set the map away from the tea pot and poured another cup of hot water. He dunked a tea bag in the water and sat silent.

Like Reuben had done—sitting quiet until Manny felt he could tell his vision—Manny remained quiet waiting for Reuben to gather his thoughts. "Destiny's Door." Manny breathed deeply and stirred sugar into his drink.

"That's the second time I've heard about that in the last couple days," Manny said as he pulled a blanket tighter around his shoulders. "Like it's some place here on the reservation that we should know about. But in all those times that Unk took me hiking, we never ran across anywhere called Destiny's Door."

"Me either." Reuben continued staring at the map before he broke and slipped a hoodie on. "It isn't on any map," he said, breathing deeply. Calming himself. "I thought it was a myth all along. A legend."

Manny wrapped his hand around his cup of hot tea and said, "I've never even heard it as a legend. Where did you hear that?"

Reuben leaned over and opened the door of his wood burner, tossing two large cottonwood logs inside before settling back in his chair, his gaze returning to the map. "I heard about the place when I was a youngster. Me and Bobbie the Gimp—a kid no one wanted to hang with 'cause he limped from a club foot so he couldn't keep up with anyone—heard about it when we were no more'n twelve." He sipped lightly and set his cup on the table. "It was summertime and school was out. Me and The Gimp were walking back from Oglala Lake with a nice string of crappies and come onto an old man—at least he was old to us at the time." Reuben paused as if telling of something painful deep in his memory. "He was walking about as fast as The Gimp, as the old feller had a prosthetic leg courtesy of the Germans in World War I. 'You boys got any money?' he asked us.

"Well, we butterflied our pockets and had all of a dollar-eighty between us. 'You walk me into town, boys,' he said, 'and make a trip down to White Clay to buy me a bottle, and I will give you both a treasure map. Worth all the money you can imagine.' I'm telling you, *misun*, that me and The Gimp got real excited and practically ran into White Clay—me running with Bobbie limping behind as fast as he could go with that bum foot of his. The old man plodding behind us. We pooled our money and bought the old man a forty of Budweiser."

"Even I know that a forty-ounce bottle of beer costs more than that."

Reuben shrugged. "OK, so I made off with the bottle while The Gimp did his best to distract the store clerk by hobbling around the store. In the end, the old feller was good to his word and traded us a map for the beer when we got back to the rez."

Manny reached for the pot of hot water, but it was empty. *Guess we have been here mulling over the map longer than I realized.* "Still doesn't tell me how you know about Destiny's Door."

"I'm getting enough… *itka* built up to tell you."

"Enough what?"

"*Itka. Cajones*," Reuben said. He stood and paced in front of the table, holding his empty teacup, his eyes locked onto the map. "Being the biggest of the two, I tucked the old man's treasure map into my shirt to look at it after supper. But that night when I spread it out on the kitchen table, Dad asked where I got it. When I told him some old rummy needing a drink, he looked at it for the briefest time before backing away. 'That there map shows Destiny's Door,' he said. 'Get it out of my house. Throw it away.'"

"Why was he so scared of it?" Manny asked.

"My *ate* just stood there shaking like I'm shaking now," Reuben answered as he looked at his trembling hands before setting his cup on the table. "This is one of those times I wish I still drank." He sat back down and leaned closer to Manny, his voice low as if afraid to alert spirits close to the map. "I hustled over to Bobby's house right off and gave him the map. The next morning, I went to Bobby's house with a fresh can of nightcrawlers and figured him and me would drown some worms. But he was gone. Lit out early with that map, his Ma said."

"What did he find when he finally made it back home?"

"He never did," Reuben said. "That's my point. The Gimp never made it home that day. Or any day. Bobby's dad called the cops and they searched everywhere. Asked me about the map, and the only thing I remembered about it was some terrain features and a notation of Destiny's Door."

"You're telling me Bobby was never found?"

"Neither him nor that place called Destiny's Door, though I tried dozens of times to find it even though Dad forbade it. Said Bobby's *wanagi*, his spirit, roamed over that area now."

Manny felt a new chill, though he was mere feet from the wood stove. "Then that map was authentic, you think?"

"I just don't know." Reuben nodded to the map spread out on the coffee table. "There were some terrain features that I recall as the same, but a lot is different from this one."

"You said this is *the* map," Manny said. "How do you know this?"

"After listening to you just now describing your vision, *Wankan Tanka* surely would never have given you a vision concerning a phony map. Besides," he shuddered, "I *feel* it is the genuine map as well."

"Where's this Destiny's Door?"

"Someplace south of Slim Butte, if this map is correct."

"Reuben," Manny said, "I know you are a sacred man after

much study and introspection. But do you really believe this *Destiny's Door* is a… haunted place?"

"I do," Reuben said immediately. He tossed another log into the wood stove and said, "Firehawker—my *wicasa wakan* mentor while I was in prison—asked me one day if there was anything I wished to ask him, as I was a little down in the tooth thinking back to Bobby The Gimp. Firehawker was a Stone Dreamer and had conducted the *yowipi* ceremony to find lost people before he went into prison. Lost objects. I told him I wanted to find Bobby's remains when I was released. I figured Bobby lost his balance as he often did and fell off a cliff. 'Where did this happen?' Firehawker asked. When I told him someplace called Destiny's Door, he shut me down just like Dad did years before. 'That place is sacred. If your friend died there with no guardian *sicun* to escort him along the Spirit Road, his *wanagi* still roams. Along with… a holy man, it is said.' Years later, I heard rumors that Crazy Horse was buried there, and I felt that I should leave well enough alone."

"Yet there was that map the old man gave you," Manny said and then nodded to the map in front of them. "Like the one that Everett had hidden in his room?"

Reuben looked down at the map and shook his head. "Not the same. There are some similarities that I recall, and many more terrain features that are different. But I do know this— both maps had Destiny's Door noted on it."

"Do you think the map of your youth was a map to where Crazy Horse is buried?"

"I think," Reuben said, "someone heard rumors of where the sacred man was buried and fabricated that map like so many fake maps nowadays. With some of the same features the faker heard about. That is all. *This*," he motioned to Everett's map, "is the map that Black Heart drew for his son Henry. I am certain of it. Which brings us back to your vision."

Manny squirmed in his chair. He didn't want to think about it if he didn't have to. But he had to, he knew, for it all had to be connected. "What do *you* think my vision was telling me?" he asked Reuben.

"I think that you saw Crazy Horse killed. No one else can say that. I think you were given that vision because you need to see that Crazy Horse's burial place has never been revealed."

"But I'm here on the reservation to investigate Everett's murder... that has nothing to do with Crazy Horse."

"I think it does," Reuben said. "*Tashunke Witko* was known as one who sought justice. Everett's grandfather, Black Heart, accompanied Crazy Horse's parents. Everett's murder going unsolved would disrespect that deed."

"I'm still not convinced it was murder."

"*Misun*, I examined the brake lines on that old International truck myself. I'm telling you, the line was sawed ever so finely right after it left the master cylinder."

"Everett surely would have noticed that," Manny said.

"Not at first," Reuben explained. "At the first pumps of the pedal, the brakes would work. Until down the road when he needed it and mashed all the way down on the pedal. By then, the fluid would have bled out and he'd have nothing."

"I just don't know what this has to do with my vision."

"No?" Reuben said. "Then why dream of the death of the sacred man now? You know *Wakan Tanka* gives you visions that usually connect to the deaths you are investigating. And I do believe the answer to Everett's murder may be found at Destiny's Door. In that area where Crazy Horse is buried."

Manny thought of that. As usual in these matters of his frightening visions, Reuben was right. "Then, best guess, where is Destiny's Door?"

Reuben scooted his chair close to Manny and turned the map to orient them. "The map has no legend, so there is no way of knowing how far it is. But by these terrain features, it looks like it is somewhere between Slim Butte and Oglala." He put on his glasses once more and bent close to the map. "What's this notation?"

Manny looked to where Reuben pointed and took his reading glasses from him as he squinted. "*NOTCH.* Scribbled on the canvas."

"Word or name?"

Manny shrugged and handed Reuben his glasses back "But it is on the other side of what's said to be *DD*, two high hills on either side of a trail."

Reuben sat back and tented his fingers on his belly. "That would put it somewhere in the grasslands, but I don't recall any high hills surrounding a path. But then, this was written decades ago and the lay of the land changes over time. These high hills drawn on the map might not even be there anymore."

"Then the sooner we get started, the sooner we'll find the place—"

"Whoa, little brother," Reuben said. "I want nothing to do with that place."

"Aren't you even a little curious what happened to Bobby The Gimp when he trekked to Destiny's Door?"

"Do you know what the odds are of finding his body after all these years?"

"Pretty slim—" Manny's cell phone rang and he dug it out of his jeans. He spoke with the Pine Ridge Police dispatcher for a moment before hanging up. "Seems like I'll have to go to that area sooner than I figured. Want to come along?"

"Not on your life… what do you have?"

"What I have is a dead body—a victim—waiting for me so it can tell me what happened."

"You're not going to let up on me, are you?"

"No," Manny said. "Eventually we'll have to look for Destiny's

Door. Besides, it'll piss Lumpy off to know I have a felon riding with me to a crime scene."

"That alone will be worth the trip," Reuben said as he grabbed socks and insulated boots. "Where is this body?"

Manny lightly tapped the map. "By the dispatcher's description, it is right where 'NOTCH' is scribbled on the map."

Chapter 15

"I don't know if I'm more frightened of where we're going or of your crappy driving," Reuben said as Manny narrowly missed an antelope that bolted across the road.

"I haven't had a real accident in... months. All right, I just nicked the corner of the Federal Building in Rapid going to testify in a case, but I didn't report it to the Senior Agent." He chuckled. "Like speeding—it never happened if the cops don't catch you."

Reuben sat scrunched up in the cab of the little truck, his knees rubbing against the dash, fingers digging into the dash pad. "Just the same, you could slow down a little."

"Willie and Shannon are already at the scene, and I want to make sure I get there before my trainee screws something up."

"Thought your rookie was sitting the day out?"

"He said he felt as badly taking off work as he did sitting out a game for injuries. Seems like he stumbled into the Justice Building just as Willie was headed out to this call and guilt tripped him into riding along."

They drove Highway 18 past Oglala, and Reuben pointed to two old men huddled on the bank. Fishing poles were stuck in the sandy shore and they stared at Manny's truck as it went by. "Another month and the lake will be frozen over," Manny said, then asked, "do you recall any other rumors or legends about this Destiny's Door?"

Reuben turned to look at the passing grasslands, and Manny wasn't sure he'd even heard the question, as his hearing wasn't what it was, the result of him being around artillery in 'Nam. He finally said, "When I was a kid, I tried asking the elders about the legends and rumors. All they would say was that bad *wanagi* roam that part of the reservation. And not just Bobby The Gimp's spirit, either. 'You find that place,' one old woman told me, 'you get out double quick, or you may never be seen on this side of the grass again.'"

"Little dramatic, don't you think?"

"As a boy, such a warning did have a dramatic effect. But I still kept searching for it."

"Surely you don't believe in ghosts," Manny caught himself. *Of course, Reuben believes in* wanagi, *spirits, bad ones that can lure a man to do terrible things, awful things.* And, in a way, Manny knew he did, too, on some level—his visions told him so.

"*Misun*," Reuben said softly, using the term for 'little brother,' "I have sought to teach you the ways of our people and still you fight it."

"Perhaps the old ways are just a little too frightening," Manny said as he slowed to allow a black-white-face cow to cross the road. He turned in the seat to face Reuben, the floor shift lever nudging his leg, and he cursed the rental company. "Besides, I am a law officer. I deal with tangible things. Those things that can be proved and disproved. I have to. I can't allow the ethereal to influence my thinking. If it looks like I'll have to go to a place that is sacred—one with bad *wanagi*—I just have to pray I'll make it out in one piece. Or without losing my mind."

Manny called Willie right before he lost cell service, and Willie said he was in the area. He would leave a piece of yellow plastic evidence tape tied to a clump of sage brush where he had turned off the road.

"Hope the four-wheel drive in this little truck of yours works,"

Reuben said, "'cause this is a little rougher country than I remember here... there!" Reuben pointed to Willie's evidence tape stuck in the sage brush beside a two-track path. With just one eye working and fifteen years older, he still had better eyesight than Manny.

Even without the tape, Manny could see where vehicles had driven off the road, breaking up four inches of snow. Manny kicked the Toyota into four-low and followed the tracks that led gradually down a grade. "Think this is where the elders thought Destiny's Door was?"

Reuben looked around. "By Slim Butte. I thought at the time they circulated rumors of ghosts figuring they would scare off someone—like a snot-nosed kid—from finding their whiskey still or something. Maybe someplace they went to party. As a kid, it made me all the more determined to find it. Back then, I was not... attuned to the old ways. I could not *sense* when I neared a sacred place." He rubbed his forehead. "Like I *sense* we are nearing now."

Manny sensed it, too, though he told himself it was just Reuben's superstitions rubbing off on him when he spotted Shannon. His big, goofy head poked up from the other side of a shallow hill, and Manny headed for him, keeping the truck in the ruts made by Willie's big Expedition.

When they had gone another hundred yards, they topped the short rise that looked down on Willie and Shannon standing beside another Indian Manny didn't recognize. He wore an orange hunter's vest with a scoped rifle slung over one shoulder. He stood beside Willie as he looked through binoculars at something farther down the hill to the west.

Manny parked beside the Expedition and climbed out. Reuben winched himself out of the truck in the same manner as Shannon did—by grabbing onto the doorjamb and grunting.

Manny waited until Reuben was free before walking to where

the others stood. Shannon shivered in the cold, wearing only the blue FBI windbreaker. "What 'cha looking at?" Manny asked.

Willie brought the binos down from his eyes and handed them to Manny. "Dead body. Been there a few days, by the looks of him, but not so fresh that the coyotes found him and snacked on him yet."

Manny held the binoculars to his eyes and adjusted the focus. He followed where Willie pointed and saw a corpse in the snow two hundred yards down the steep slope, through two sandstone spires that rose twenty feet into the air. Just like a door jamb with the trail leading between them.

"I think he's been there a long time," Shannon blurted out. "See how he's bloated-up?"

"He could just be a fat man," Reuben said.

Manny handed the glasses back to Willie and said to Shannon, "Reuben's right—he could just be fat. Bloating is rare in these freezing temperatures."

He turned to the man in the vest and said, "You the hunter who found him?"

"I did," the man said and offered his hand. "Joey Woman Hide." He nervously glanced at the corpse as he spoke. "But I ain't touched him, I swear," he held up his hands. "If he's missing anything, it weren't me."

"Just tell Agent Tanno how you came to find the body." Willie put the binos to his eyes again and went back to glassing the corpse and the surrounding hills.

"Okay. Okay." He ran a gloved hand across the snot that was dripping off his nose onto his scraggly mustache. "Up that hill," he pointed to a slope looking down on the spires, "I injuned-up on a nice five-by-five buck." He laughed nervously. "You know us *injuns* do the best *injuning* up on game."

Manny kept quiet while he waited for Joey's nervousness to leave him. When his shaking subsided, he got up the courage to say, "I spotted a nice mulie buck when I was on the other side of that ridge up there only 'bout three hundred yards off. It should have been an easy shot except the wind or something caused me to pull the shot. Mr. Buck bounded over that hill, and I ran as fast as I could to try to get another shot when I seen that," he pointed to the corpse.

"Did you go down there to look—"

"Not on your life," Joey said and started shaking again. "I steer clear of dead people. Bad news getting close to them. They might just get you."

Manny looked at Willie who stifled a grin. "Joey here's a fan of *The Walking Dead*."

"The Walking Dead?" Manny asked.

"Sure," Shannon said. "Zombies. No telling who they'll start munching on next."

Manny shook his head. "Zombies?"

"Sure. I learned in the academy that the Bureau has a plan to stop them if they get a zombie outbreak."

Manny finally understood what his trainee was doing when he was sidelined in the locker room at football games—watching zombie movies. The scary thing was that Shannon actually seemed to believe in the myth.

"What did you do when you saw the body?" Manny asked.

"I ran back up the road until I could get cell service," Joey said, "and called the police right away." He chanced a look at the corpse again. "Can I go now, 'cause I sure don't trust them… bodies?"

"As soon as you give Agent Henderson here a written statement," Manny said and motioned to Shannon. "Take Joey and sit in my truck. Statement forms are in my briefcase behind the seat. Wouldn't want you two brave fellas exposed to a potential zombie."

Shannon started for the truck when Manny stopped him. "And

Shannon, don't break anything getting in or out of the truck."

After they had walked out of earshot, Manny said to Reuben and Willie, "I hate to admit it but I do kinda feel a little odd here, too, but it can't be that dead body."

"It's that." Reuben pointed to the sandstone formations on either side of the trail leading to the victim. "If he died suddenly with no one close, his *nagi*—his spirit—will still linger. I have been sensing something that is not natural the closer we walked down the hill. Something that makes me... a little jittery, and it's not just because it's getting dark in another hour or so. Don't you sense it, too?"

"Of course not," Manny answered, but he had begun feeling that something was not right. Feeling as if something was warning him not to approach any closer. An evil *wanagi?* Manny started to dismiss the notion, because he knew better than to believe in superstitions. Still, there was a man dead in the snow, and he and Willie had to set their feelings aside and function as lawmen investigating a death. "We're not going to find out anything about that man standing around here," he said to Willie. "You ready?"

"Don't have much choice," Willie said and zipped up his parka.

Manny pulled his gloves on and said to Reuben, "You want to come on down and have a look?"

"Not on your life."

"That's what I thought, But you can still help... keep your eye open for Pee Pee and his evidence van. When he comes, show him where we are."

Willie led the way down the steep slope, crumbling red rock underfoot causing them to slip and pick their way carefully down, trying to avoid cactus and sharp spines of sage brush. He stopped suddenly a hundred yards from the body just before the trail led between the two sandstone spires. "There's no reason to go any farther."

"What's that?" Manny asked.

Willie turned his back and jerked his thumb toward the corpse as if afraid to look at it. "We've seen enough. Let's go."

"What do you mean, we've seen enough?" Manny said, stepping around and looking up at Willie. "We have to go down there and look at the scene."

He started walking back up the hill when Manny grabbed his arm. He jerked away and faced Manny, a look of *something* crossing his face. Willie shook his head to clear it. "I guess I don't know what I mean. Let's get down there."

Willie started back down the trail. As they neared the passage between the *door*, a feeling overcame Manny that told him Willie was right—there wasn't a reason to continue down to the corpse—when Willie stopped. He bent over, holding his gut and puked up that morning's breakfast. He stood and brushed his hand across his mouth before saying, "Let's get out of here." He started up the hill again when Manny grabbed his arm once more.

Willie's hand dropped to the butt of his gun as he spun out of Manny grip. Anger, bitter and violent, glared back at Manny who suddenly became aware that his own hand rested on the butt of his gun. And he had unsnapped the retention strap. As had Willie.

Manny jerked his hand away. "What the hell is happening?"

Willie looked down at his own hand on his gun and let go. He trembled when he said, "I don't know why I did that." He nodded to the doorway flanking the trail. "Something *there* clouded my mind for a brief moment."

"That could have been our last moment," Manny said. He slowly took his Glock out of the holster by his thumb and forefinger and laid it in the snow. "Whatever it is down there, it's affecting us. Doing what it can to keep us from going farther."

Willie slid his own pistol out and laid it beside Manny's. "Whatever it is, we were at each other's throats a minute ago.

We need to get down there, but we need to be safe."

"You still keep a stalk of sage with you?" Manny asked, feeling himself taking up the old ways. For some reason. "Maybe we ought to smudge before we go farther. Ask *Waken Tanka* for protection."

"I always keep sage," Willie said and reached inside his coat pocket, coming away with a stalk. He lit it with a Bic lighter, sweet smoke filtering upwards, and he waved it over Manny first, then himself. He offered prayers to the four directions, to the sky, Mother Earth. When he had finished, he hesitated as if he needed to offer prayers once again, or stalling the inevitable, before snubbing the sage out in the snow. "Let's get this done while we're freshly blessed."

They started back down the trail, Manny sensing a presence as they neared the doorway. He looked back at Willie and said, "You doing OK?"

"I'm maintaining."

Manny breathed deeply, calming himself, and walked through the natural 'doorway.'

When Manny was in the Army, his unit had to periodically go through what was termed the *Gas Chamber*, a rolling semi-trailer that traveled from fort to fort with the express purpose of periodically certifying soldiers in the use of tear gas. Every time Manny went into that trailer with the other soldiers and the gas master closed the door, his apprehension heightened all the more, even before the first release of CS and CN gas. Then it was a stifling, choking, constricting feeling that began in his throat all the way down into his chest, as if a six-by truck had rolled over him. Manny began feeling that constriction now. As if evil *wanagi* wanted him gone.

But he also felt something else, too, something he had experienced in his last vision. Something that told him—though he had known Crazy Horse would soon die just outside the guard house—the sacred man would be at Manny's side. Protecting him even as he walked farther into *Destiny's Door* as he neared the victim frozen in the snow.

When they had walked the last fifty yards and were within ten yards of the victim, Manny said, "Take a look around the body."

Willie began walking a lose circle around the corpse, studying the ground, stooping now and again to feel a broken sage twig, a rock overturned. Looking for any evidence left at the crime scene. If, in fact, this *was* a crime scene, and not just someone who had wandered off into the cold and gotten hypothermia. For as capable a tracker as Manny used to be, he had lived in the white man's cities for too long to keep up his skills. Not so Willie, who had lived his entire life on Indian reservations and had honed his ability to read signs while working as a lawman.

At the far side from where they had just walked down the hill, Willie knelt next to the body and said, "We couldn't see it from where we were, but there's a small amount of blood on the side of his head."

"As a result of a fall?"

"No," Willie said at last, as he stood and brushed snow off his trousers. "As a result of an exit wound. It appears this man leaned into a bullet going by. He is now officially a homicide victim." He looked up at the surrounding hills. "Proves my point that death is the number one killer of people."

Head wounds, particularly those from a projectile, often bled little, the heart ceasing to pump the instant the bullet shut the brain down. This man was no exception. "See anything around the body?"

Willie stood with his hands on his hips and looked around. "We might broom this snow off, but I doubt we'd find any tracks, as hard as this ground is. And all I can say for sure is this man has been here for at least a day, given the absence of tracks in the snow, what with this wind and all."

"All right then," Manny said, squatting beside the victim. "Let's see what he has to tell us."

Manny made a mental note: the man appeared to have died right where he lay, the bullet doing its job efficiently on the white man with the big belly. Manny brushed aside the man's flowing, white hair where the blood had matted and later frozen where the bullet had exited his head. "Know him?"

"Never seen him on the rez," Willie answered. He knelt again beside the victim, this time close enough to gently pull the man's stiff, frozen jacket aside. He felt inside the trouser and coat pockets and said, "Hello!" Willie held up a fancy-stitched wallet and carefully opened it up. He handed Manny a driver's license. "I think we've finally met the renowned art critic Hanson Becker."

Manny took the driver's license from Willie and quickly gave it back. Manny had other things he was interesting in looking at as he pried Becker's frozen fingers open. A torn piece of what looked to be an ancient, brown parchment fell onto the snow.

"What is that?"

"Can't say for sure," Manny said.

He felt inside Becker's coat. Nothing.

Until he ran his hand toward the back of the victim's coat. "Help me ease him off the ground."

Willie bent over and grunted, as much from the man's weight as from the body stuck to the ground, when it finally gave way and Manny was able to retrieve what he'd felt. He carefully unfolded the parchment paper and held it to the dying light of day. "This looks like a map of sorts. Let's see that piece we found in his hand."

Willie handed him the torn piece of paper and it matched.

"What 'cha make of it?" Willie asked.

Manny closed his eyes, thinking, reconstructing the death scene over in his mind, trying to see what the victim saw in his last moments. "Becker was chased here—"

"As fat as he was," Willie said, "he must not have been chased very far."

Manny agreed with Willie: Becker was morbidly obese and would have run out of steam in a short time. He looked up the hill and said, "He had to have parked a vehicle up about where we're parked." He pulled his stocking cap lower over his ears. "Like you said, he wasn't chased far. Probably sucking air for all he was worth by the time he got to this spot."

"Until somebody capped him."

"Until somebody capped him," Manny repeated. "My best guess is that, whoever shot Becker was after this," he motioned to the map." Manny closed his eyes again, imagining... "Becker quickly stuffed the map inside his coat as he ran. This small piece of paper stuck to his hand as he was stuffing it inside his coat to hide it."

"Then why didn't the killer search Becker for the map?" Willie asked.

Manny shrugged and stood, stretching his back, looking up the hill to where Shannon now stood beside Reuben looking down. "Maybe the shooter did search Becker but didn't find it. Maybe the shooter was scared off."

"By what?"

Manny shuddered and nodded to the *doorway*. "By the same sense of dread that nearly scared us off—Destiny's Door."

Chapter 16

Once he had cell service, Manny stopped the Toyota on a hill. He called the Fall River County Sheriff's Office in Hot Springs and asked for Sergeant Fick. When he came on the line, Manny said, "I need you to secure Hanson Becker's house. If his driver's license is correct, his house is right outside of town—"

"We've already done that. Secured the crime scene and my evidence tech is on the way."

"I don't understand," Manny said. "What I need is the house secured until I can get a search warrant."

"For what?" Fick asked.

"Murder. Hanson Becker's been murdered." He explained that Becker had been found shot on Pine Ridge by a small caliber gun by the looks of the entry hole. "What are you there for?"

"Someone burglarized Becker's house."

"When? How'd you find out?"

"A neighbor called it in," Fick said. "Last night. Becker's neighbor to the north said he heard the crashing of glass inside Becker's house. They didn't think much of it at the time as the man liked... liked wild-ass parties with younger ladies, to quote the neighbor. We've had several noise complaints at the house in the last few years.

"Then this morning, that same neighbor noticed the screen door swinging against the house and saw the front glass broken, so he called our office. Deputies made entry thinking something

119

happened to Becker." He chuckled. "And apparently, it did, though way over on the reservation."

"When will you have it processed?"

"By tomorrow morning. But I'm telling you, there's nothing to see except a house that's been tossed... nearly every drawer to every dresser and cabinet yanked out and emptied onto the floor. Photos on the walls knocked down and the backs ripped off. Carpeting ripped up. But you're welcome to come on over. With any luck, by the time you get here, we'll be finished processing it and you can help clean up."

"I think I'll settle for looking at the crime scene photos and your report when you're finished," Manny said. He started to disconnect when he asked, "Was Becker's car or truck at his house?"

"There was no vehicle in the garage or parked outside," Fick said. "I take it his outfit wasn't at the murder scene?"

Manny said that no vehicle Becker might have driven was found.

"We just figured Becker had gone off someplace and wasn't even looking for his car. I'll run a 10-28, find out what he drives, and BOLO it."

Reuben squirmed in the seat and tried moving his knee off the dash as Manny hung up. "Bad news?"

"Somebody broke into Becker's house in Hot Springs and ransacked it. From what Sergeant Fick described, someone was sure the hell after something." He took the parchment map he'd taken from Becker's body, and handed it to Reuben. "They might have been after this. A map of sorts. Can't tell much about it as it looks like some has been torn away."

Reuben flicked on the dome light and held the paper up. "This looks familiar," he said while he ran his finger over a trail marked on the map, "though I can't recall now. Maybe it'll come to me at about three in the morning a month from now."

Manny put the truck in gear and crawled along the snow-crusted road. "I am of the assumption that Becker drove his car or truck or whatever he drives down close to where his body was found. I can't see a man as obese as he was walking very far."

"I can hear those FBI instincts seeping through," Reuben said.

"Here's what I think happened," Manny said. "Unbeknownst to Becker, his killer followed him there. Becker got out, following the map along the trail when his murderer chased after him expecting to get the map. But Becker was just lucid enough after running until his heart burst to stash it where it might not be found."

"I hear a 'but' somewhere."

Manny nodded. "But what if he were killed somewhere else and the body transported to where he was found?"

"What do you think Becker weighed? 'Cause from where I saw you and Willie and Shannon helping Pee Pee with the body bag, he looked like a handful."

"Close to three hundred," Manny guessed. "I know what you're getting at—if Becker was killed somewhere else, it'd take an awfully strong person to tote the body down to where he was found."

"Or *two* strong people," Reuben added, his head rubbing against the roof of the truck as he tried scooting down in the seat.

"I thought of that," Manny said. "And the Kramers came to mind immediately."

"And if there were just one killer?" Reuben said.

"Hobart Black... Comes Flying." The brief time that Manny had talked with Hobart the day at the ice cream shop, he appeared nearly as heavy as Willie. Coaching football probably kept Hobart in good shape. He had the size, but would he be able to carry Becker down that steep hill and through Destiny's Door?

121

Manny stopped the truck when it crested the state road and grabbed a Thermos of coffee from behind the seat. He poured each of them a cup when Reuben asked, "Did Becker have spittle frozen around his mouth or lips? You got sugar?"

"I do not," Manny said before adding, "as a matter of fact he did. Why?"

"A terrified victim would work up a sweat, even if he wasn't running from a pursuer. If he was shot just where you found him, well… you see how the spit would be frozen to his lips. Perhaps his chin."

"How do you know…" Manny stopped mid-sentence. Reuben had been an AIM enforcer prior to the homicide that sent him to the state penitentiary. Manny doubted his brother had ever actually murdered anyone, but he could see Reuben chasing a man down in the wintertime to give him a beating. Manny just didn't want to know. "So you think he *was* killed there. Not killed some other place and hauled to Destiny's Door?"

"All I'm saying is there are so many possibilities, you ought not paint yourself into a corner."

Manny smiled. "You always keep me honest." *But when I find Hanson Becker's car or truck, I will know a hell of a lot more than I do now.*

Chapter 17

"They're in the big interview room," Willie said. "You can thank your trainee for the Kramers being here."

"Thank him how?" Manny asked, walking beside Willie down the hallway towards the room.

"After you told me to pick up The Animal from the FBI apartment, we stopped at Big Bat's for a cup of coffee and donuts. And who should be there with the same idea—the Kramers in all their smelly glory. They took one look at me and headed for the exit but Shannon blocked their way. By the time I caught up with the pair, they both had stiff necks from looking up at him." Willie chuckled. "Shannon intimidated the hell out of them just standing there. Little do they know that all they had to do was throw anything in his path, and the big man would trip and fall and they'd easily make their getaway."

"Did you tell them what we wanted to talk with them about?"

"I figured I'd give you that little piece of pleasure," Willie said and opened the interview room for Manny.

Shannon stood in one corner of the room, his arms crossed, glaring at the Kramers. Buddy Kramer sat with one arm draped over the chair and one leg resting on the table. His tattered Carhartt coat showed nearly as much dirt as his scraggly, graying beard that carried what he'd had for breakfast that morning. The top two buttons on his shirt were missing, a single gray hair sticking out of his grimy T-shirt. He looked the part of the down-and-out bum crisscrossing the country looking for handouts, just some middle-aged man wanting to hurt nobody. Harmless.

Except his eyes. They followed Willie and Manny when they entered, and a coldness overcame Manny. *Cunning*, he thought immediately. Behind the man's stare was a barely controlled viciousness.

In contrast, his son Bobby sat with his feet flat on the floor. A lanky, gaunt kid in his early twenties, he bowed his head as he stared at his boots. He looked up for a brief moment before dropping his eyes back to the floor once again.

"Agent Tanno," Buddy said as he stood. He wiped his hand on trousers only slightly greasier than his hand and extended it. Manny ignored the handshake and walked to the opposite side of the table. He kept silent as he took out the Kramers' file folder that the Pine Ridge PD had supplied him.

"What's this all about? Me and my kid was minding our own business in Big Bat's when this... this big bastard stopped us. I have half a notion to make a formal complaint."

"Make sure it's just half a notion."

"What's that?" Buddy said.

Manny nodded to Shannon who towered over everyone else in the room. "Did Agent Henderson threaten you?"

"Well... Bobbie," he slapped his son on the shoulder, "you felt like you were fixin' to get a mud hole stomped in your ass by this big guy, didn't you?"

Bobby looked up at his father through red-rimmed eyes and picked at an open sore on his cheek that matched several on his neck. *Meth head.* "Sure, Daddy. I felt... scared."

Buddy threw up his hands and sat back down. "There you have it. We was both scared, and we intend filing a formal complaint."

"That would entail you actually writing," Willie said, looking down at the old man. "And I doubt you can. And your *learned* kid here dropped out in the eighth grade, so he can't either."

"Ninth," Bobbie corrected.

"Ninth," Willie said. "What's one grade in school. Just one more in which little Bobbie here could knife more classmates." Willie leaned down, his face inches away from Bobbie's, "And one more incident like *that*, he gets sent away to juvenile detention."

Buddy stood abruptly from his chair when he saw Shannon over his shoulder still looking on, and he sat back down. "This what you're harassing us about—Bobbie having a learning disorder?"

"His learning disorder is called *drugs*," Willie said. "But that's not the reason why you're here. We want to know about your relationship with Everett Black."

Buddy sat back and started putting his foot back on the table when he saw Shannon motioning him to drop it on the floor. "What relationship? The old fart hired us to do some remodeling on that house of his. He kicked the bucket in that truck wreck, so now we're not getting paid. That's the end of our relationship."

"When was the last time you two were in Everett's house?"

"We was there—"

"Shut up," Buddy said. "We don't have to tell these fools anything."

Manny leaned across the table and said, "Is there a reason you don't want your boy to answer my question?"

Buddy scooted his chair back and laid his hand on Bobbie's shoulder. "Naw, it's just that the kid gets things wrong now and again."

"Then answer the question," Willie pressed.

"All right. We was there the day that kind old Everett took a dive off that cliff." Buddy scratched his groin and nudged Bobbie. "Wouldn't you say it was that afternoon?"

"Yeah," Bobbie said, still looking down at the floor. "Sure. That was the last time."

"Ever snoop around Everett's safe in his study?"

"Course not," Buddy answered. "No reason to. We was hanging dry wall in the entryway and down that first hallway, not his study."

Manny flipped to a blank page in the report as if reading something significant, but held it away from Buddy when he asked, "What if I told you your fingerprints were all over that safe?"

Buddy sat in his chair and kept quiet. He crossed his arms and glared at Manny. "I got nothin' to say." He crossed his legs and a slight discoloration showed on the instep of one boot.

Manny leaned closer and Buddy saw him staring at his boots. "What?"

"Take off your boots."

"Why should I? Don't you need a search warrant to look at them? Besides, what you need them for anyway?"

"We do not need a search warrant—plain view," Shannon said and stepped closer. "Now take your shoes off."

"Okay. Okay," Buddy said, and slipped his boots off.

Manny took both of Buddy's worn lace-up boots and donned his reading glasses. He reached over to a stack of photocopy paper and snatched a blank piece that he set on the table. "Looks like you traipsed through something brown. No, more red, I'd say." Manny knew he'd seen that tint of dust before. *Everett's study.* He took the boots by the tops and smacked each sole onto the piece of paper. Dirt and rocks and pieces of sage dropped onto the paper. Along with the odd colored flakes of something else.

He bent and looked closer at the flecks and motioned to Willie. "Jesa!" he said. "We've seen that before."

Buddy leaned forward and looked at the paper. "So, I got dirt on my boots. You can't charge a man for that," he laughed nervously.

"No," Manny said, using the tip of his pen to separate the

flecks. "We saw this same color of dust right in front of Everett's open safe."

"That's it?" Buddy laughed heartily. Bobbie, sitting beside him, took the cue and began laughing, too. "You think that's significant? We do a lot of jobs around the rez that take us to places where we step on red rock. Hello, Mr. Agent Man, have you never seen scoria dust before?"

"We'll know if it's scoria dust or not as soon as the lab studies it." Manny handed Buddy his shoes back. "Put these on before the odor makes me pass out."

"That would be a blessing," Buddy said, slipping on his boots and standing. "Now if there's nothing else—"

"Sit down," Willie said. "Agent Tanno's not finished."

Buddy paused as if weighing the chances of taking on Willie *and* Shannon, but he chose to sit back down in his chair and glare at Manny. "Okay, ask away so we can get back to work."

Manny sifted through other papers and came away with Buddy's bio. "Funny you should mention your work. Says here you two run a handyman business."

"That's us," Buddy said. "B&B Builders."

"You do remodeling?" Manny asked.

"We do."

"New construction?"

"That, too."

"Are you going to a job today?"

"We are."

"Remodeling job like Everett's?" Manny asked.

"Sure," Buddy said. "My boy Bobbie here is hell with a drywall knife. You ought to see him sling mud over the tape and—"

"What are you doing for tools?"

"What?"

"Tools," Manny repeated. "Are you so wealthy you have several sets of tools?"

Buddy crossed himself like he had seen others do it, Manny thought, and said, "We's just poor fellers eking out a living doing odd jobs—"

"With no tools? You left your drywall equipment at Everett's house, along with a skill saw and sander." Manny leaned in. "What are you using for tools? Or are you two figuring to do something besides work today? Perhaps returning to Everett's under the guise of grabbing your tools only to try and look in Everett's safe? Or did you already look inside his safe that last time you were there?"

Buddy looked at Manny, then to Willie and Shannon before saying, "We was never close to Everett's safe. Sure, we went back to the old house intending on picking up our tools, but that Hobart character came driving up and we… what do you say we did, Bobbie, protect our hides?"

Bobbie looked up and answered, "That's just what happened, Agent Tanno. We needed our tools in a bad way, but we didn't need for that Hobart to catch us and open a can of whoop-ass on us. He might figure we was there to steal things and he's a big boy." He held up his hands as if surrender. "Besides, we never steal. Now, can we go?"

"You have anything else Agent Shannon?" Manny asked.

"Nothing right this moment," Shannon answered. "But I'm sure I'll think of something later."

"Willie?"

Willie chuckled. "Just that odd statement Bobbie made that they never steal. He should have said the cops just haven't been able to make a case. But I have nothing else to ask of them just now."

"Then you two are free to leave," Manny said.

Bobbie and Buddy scooted their chairs back and zipped their jackets up against the cold. They started out the door when Manny said, "You guys ever do any mechanic work?"

Buddy turned slowly and faced Manny. "Of course. We have to. All we can afford is beater trucks we buy down in Gordon, and Bobbie here keeps them running. He's a pretty good little mechanic. Why?"

"No reason in particular," Manny said. "Just wondered if you ever did any brake work."

Bobbie began to answer when his father cut him short. "We got nothin' else to say," and they disappeared through the door and headed towards the parking lot.

"You thinking they'd be good for cutting Everett's brake lines?" Willie asked.

Manny shrugged. "If they didn't do it, it'll still make them nervous wondering why I asked about it."

*   *   *   *   *

After he dropped the flecks of dust off with Pee Pee for analysis, Manny began driving the reservation looking for Becker's truck. Sergeant Fick had called with the license number and description, and Manny hoped the killer was still driving it. "Any luck?" he asked Willie when he picked up the phone. "I've traveled all over the South Unit of the Badlands with no luck."

"Been more than a few outfits dumped there," Willie said. "But I haven't had any luck finding that truck and neither has any of the other units."

Manny hung up and pulled to the side of the road. He once more put his binoculars to his eyes, but it was getting late and it was hard to see. He hated driving these roads at night with all the animals crossing the road, and decided it was too dark to drive home. But was it *really* too late to drive back to Rapid City like Manny had told Clara a moment before calling Willie? Or was this just another night where Manny needed space? Needed to shake off that feeling of his chest tightening every time he walked through the door at home to parry questions from Clara. She peppered him with questions nearly every night over dinner, questions that ultimately came back to them setting their wedding date. "I can't live here unmarried like we've been doing much longer," she told Manny two nights ago.

"I wish I had an answer for you," he told her, "but I'm still not sure the Bureau is going to keep me here. My next station could be Fairbanks, for all I know."

Clara put her hands on her hips and looked at Manny like his mother used to do. At least what he remembered of his mother, dead when Manny was but a boy. "You are the *only* one who works the reservations. No other agent wants anything to do with the rez. I cannot imagine you getting transferred."

Manny knew Clara was right but, being right, he felt as if he were trapped. He had almost set a date that day of Willie's wedding but had held back for some reason. That trapped feeling again? Not rising to the level of that feeling he'd experienced at Destiny's Door, but a stifling feeling, nonetheless. In the end, he knew he would set a wedding date and everything would be fine. But for now, he'd take his few hours alone whenever he could.

By the time he had driven back to town, the streetlights had come on with the coming of the night. Manny pulled in front of the apartment the government rented for agents and stepped out of the Toyota truck as Herb Standing Dog stepped from his apartment two doors down. He sat on his stoop and lit a cigarette as he chuckled. "Hey Agent Tanno, if you did more work, they might give you a bigger truck."

"It's just until my own car is done at the shop. Agent Henderson broke it."

Herb laughed again. "No doubt. As big as he is, he's bound to wreck something. How come you're here again? Scuffle with the missus?"

"I'm just too beat to drive up to Rapid. Night, Herb."

Manny held his ring of keys to the streetlight and selected the one for the apartment. As he stepped through the door, he stopped. Looking. *Smelling.* Someone had been in here and it wasn't someone wearing that Old Spice that Shannon liked to drench himself in. It was… different, but Manny couldn't put his thumb on it.

He stepped outside for a moment and just caught Herb Standing Dog before he went back into his apartment. "Herb, have you seen anyone but Shannon go in there?"

Herb took it as an excuse to light another smoke. "Little woman does not let me smoke inside," he said as he flicked his Bic lighter, the flame illuminating his craggy face. "But to answer your question, I have seen nobody. Shannon was here last night, but today… I have been down to Sioux Nation grocery all day helping out. Picking up a few lucky bucks."

"Hear anyone today?"

"What?"

"Have you heard anyone going in here today?"

Herb laughed. "Even if I was here, I would not have heard anybody," he cupped a hand to his ear. "Followed too many buses in my younger days, I guess—do not hear so good. Sorry."

Manny thanked the old man and went back inside. Then, for the oddest reason and without conscious action, he drew his Glock before checking the three small rooms of the apartment. Whoever had been in here was used to entering other people's houses, he was sure—no sign of forced entry. Nothing broken. Nothing moved. But Manny was sure someone had been in here today.

He checked the door lock before pulling off his trousers and shirt and climbing between the covers of his bed. But he left his automatic on the nightstand.

In case someone came in again.

Chapter 18

Manny was knee-deep in the middle of a nightmare where he had waited too long to set a wedding date with Clara. She toasted him *adios* as she drove as fast as she could away from him, Manny running after her as…

The phone—when it rang in the middle of *this* night—was actually welcomed. He grabbed the receiver from the nightstand, knocking his Glock onto the floor. "Suspicious death at the Wakpamni Bed and Breakfast."

Manny swiped the sweat from his face and wiped it on his damp pillow. *What a nightmare it must have been*, he thought, the images fading from him even as he spoke to the Pine Ridge Police dispatcher. "Suspicious, as in, the tribal investigators can't handle it?" he asked. "Batesland is twenty-five miles away."

The voice on the other end wavered, barely understandable.

"I didn't catch that."

"The patrol officers do not want to touch the scene," the woman said. "They want you."

Two o'clock. Why does everyone who gets murdered here get discovered at two o'clock in the morning? "Okay. I'll get dressed. Tell them not to disturb anything."

"They will not."

"Has Investigator With Horn been called?"

"He has not."

"Get him headed that way as well," Manny said, and the

dispatcher hung up, leaving Manny kicking himself in the keister. He needn't tell the patrolmen to leave the scene untouched until he could arrive, yet he had asked the dispatcher to pass the order along as if they needed to be told. Perhaps, he thought, it was because there was such a turnover rate among the police here, no different than most other places in South Dakota, with new inexperienced officers hired nearly every week. *With any luck, Willie will get there sooner than me and make sure the scene is secure.*

Manny dressed hurriedly, slipping his Glock into his belt holster before rushing out of the apartment and into his rental truck.

Across the street, a dog barked at him once before slinking back into its house, and a cat scurried from under the Toyota. Manny hastily climbed in and sped off towards the death call. As much as a four-cylinder mini-pickup can speed.

He drove through town, paying no attention to the stop signs or to one of the two stop lights in Pine Ridge Village that blinked amber, warning Manny of other drivers. *If* other drivers had been on the road, but—at two in the morning—Pine Ridge was as dead as the body Manny would soon meet.

As he passed the turnoff to Porcupine, he reached for his notebook in his briefcase. "Shit!" he said to himself. He had forgotten it in the apartment, and he needed it. Not so much for the notebook, but for the release forms and statement forms that he would need, and he spun around.

As he sped back toward the apartment, he was grateful no other cars were on the road, especially police cars. But then, they were probably clustered around the dead body. As usual. All throughout Manny's law enforcement career, one constant emerged with dead-body calls—every emergency responder wanted to take a look. Everyone wanted to go home and tell the family what they saw that day at work. Everyone wanted to be in the thick of things. Some even wanted to convince their supervisors they were too traumatized from looking at the dearly departed to work for a while.

He slid to a stop in front of the apartment and ran fumbling for his keys. As he inserted the key in the lock, the door swung in—he hadn't locked the door when he ran out. The door opened and he burst through into the room. His hand found the light just as…

…something came down on Manny's head, something hard and sudden, crashing into his skull.

The last thing he saw before he lost consciousness was how messy the apartment had gotten in the few minutes that he'd been headed to Batesland.

* * * * *

Manny felt someone holding his hand but he kept his eyes closed, listening. All he heard was the *beeping* of some kind of machine above his head. After long moments, he opened his eyes and struggled to sit up when Clara eased him back onto the pillow.

He looked about. He lay in a hospital bed while Clara sat in a chair next to him. "What the hell—"

"Just lay back and let your head clear," Clara said. She took his hand once again and a concerned look crossed her face. "Maybe you were right."

Manny's head throbbed and his hand massaged his forehead where a massive headache originated from. "Right about what?"

"A transfer," Clara answered. She grabbed onto a Styrofoam cup of ice water with a straw jutting out the top and held it to Manny's lips. "Seems like you get attacked more than any agent in the office."

"Attacked…" Manny paused, recalling running into his apartment for his briefcase. Remembering the way the apartment looked right before someone… "Who hit me?"

"Pee Pee is processing the scene now." Lumpy walked into the room and wiggled himself into another chair at the foot of Manny's bed. "But a certain Hot Shot FBI man is going to be recuperating while his head mends."

Manny's hand went to the bandage pasted on the side of his head. "How many stitches?"

"Six," Clara said. "The doctor said you were lucky."

Manny took a long sip of the ice water and handed the cup back to Clara. "I don't feel particularly lucky," he sat up. "I would wager there was no suspicious death in Batesland?"

"What're you rambling on about?" Lumpy asked. "Must be that local anesthesia they shot you with before the stitches."

"I got a call that there was a suspicious death at the Wakpamni Bed and Breakfast—"

"If you got a call like that, you were duped," Lumpy said. "Happened to me once, but just once. Seems like you get duped more often than us lowly tribal cops do."

"Just tell me what you know."

Lumpy reached over and grabbed a pastry off Manny's tray. "Since you're in no shape to eat it—"

"For God's sake, tell me what you found in that apartment," Manny said, the headache growing the longer he had to deal with Lumpy.

"Trashed," Lumpy said between bites. "But there was no sign of forced entry. You sure you locked the door when you left?"

"No," Manny answered. "I'm not sure. I ran out to get to Batesland as quick as I could and forgot my briefcase. If I forgot that, I might have forgotten to lock the door."

Lumpy laughed. "What's left of your briefcase, you mean. Seems like that—and the entire apartment—had been gone through. Tossed. Have any idea what they might have been looking for?"

"The map," Manny said without hesitation. "They were looking for the Crazy Horse map."

Lumpy stood and walked to the sink for a paper towel. "They might have found it, as thorough as they were."

"Did they tear down the ceiling tiles?"

Lumpy paused, apparently thinking. *If that were possible.* "They didn't. Why?"

"Because that's where I stashed the map I found on Hanson Becker's body."

"Now you're confusing me," Lumpy said. "I thought you found the Crazy Horse map in amongst Everett's magazines and such in his study?"

"I did. But I hid the one I found on Becker's corpse above the ceiling tiles."

"Then where's the one you found at Everett's?" Lumpy asked.

"Safe," Manny said. "In the holiest of places."

Chapter 19

"You sure you want to do this?" Reuben asked as he turned up the heat in the truck. "You're still a little bit loopy from that head injury."

"I've been vegetating around home for the last two days. I need to get out of the house before Clara asks me one more time about the wedding date. Besides, this is the only way I might really learn about what happened to Becker and Everett."

After they turned off Highway 18 onto South Dakota 385, they drove straight south to Chadron before cutting over to Crawford, Nebraska. By the time they pulled into town, Manny could hear Reuben's belly grumbling as much as his own was. "I heard Stabb's has pretty decent chow," Reuben said.

"Sounds as good as any," Manny said, "soon's I see a man about a horse."

He drove into a small gas station and followed the sign to the restroom around back, returning within minutes.

Reuben rolled his window down and said, "What, you don't have to pee so bad now?"

Manny walked over to the truck. "I need to get a key. Why the hell do gas stations lock their bathrooms anyhow?"

"Guess they're afraid someone's going to stop by and clean them," Reuben answered. "I'll go when you're finished."

After they had relieved themselves of the coffee they'd drunk on the trip down, they pulled into Stabb's small restaurant. Two pickups with Nebraska plates sat parked at the drive-in, their owners jawing amongst themselves when they stopped and stared at the tiny truck. One driver said something to the other and they both snickered as they watched Reuben climbing out of the passenger seat, putting first one arm out and grasping the door before pushing himself off of the seat with the other. They stopped their laughing when they saw Reuben stand up to his full height and glare at them.

The two locals drove out of the parking lot and motored down the road before Reuben could push the issue. "They left just when I was feeling... frisky."

"That's what I was afraid of," Manny said, "being witness to a seventy-three-year-old man kicking the hell out of a couple youngsters."

Manny followed Reuben to the sliding window to order lunch. A kid opened the window and stuck his head out. "What'll it be, old timer?"

Reuben looked around, but Manny nudged him. "Kid's talking to you, *old timer*. What're you ordering?"

"Old timer," Reuben muttered under his breath, then said to Manny, "Is the government paying for this?"

"Of course."

"Then, *boy*, I'll take two double burgers and a large order of fries. And while you're at it, you folks still have sundaes?"

"Sure, old—"

"Don't even repeat it," Reuben interrupted the counter kid.

"Sure, sure," the kid said, brushing purple bangs out of his eyes. "We do have sundaes. Best in Nebraska."

"Then I will take the large with extra chocolate syrup," he nodded to Manny, "compliments of the U. S. government."

Manny ordered a single burger, a small fry, and a diet soda —in case Clara The Calorie Nazi grilled him about what he'd had for dinner that wouldn't spike his blood sugar. When he asked for a receipt, the kid had to go into another room to grab a handwritten paper and then slid it through the window. Manny would turn it in at the end of the month along with his other personal expenses and hope the Senior Agent didn't question why so much food had been purchased with a government credit card.

"Want to set in that outdoor arena and eat?" Manny said.

"Even as cramped as your rental is, I'd rather be warm right now while we… dine," Reuben answered. He walked to the truck as he unwrapped the paper around his burger. By the time they climbed back into the truck, Reuben had finished one burger and started on the other.

Manny turned the heater fan on high and they sat eating when Reuben said, "Have you thought about who might want the map, and which map?"

Manny had thought of nothing else on this trip down to Nebraska. Maybe it was the stitches causing his head to throb, or the headache that had plagued him since he started thinking about all of it, but he had no positive answers, no provable theory. "When Willie and I took that initial report the night of the burglary, I thought anyone in that house could have wanted the map stashed in Everett's safe. If it proved to be authentic, it could bring in a small fortune. But with the Twins inheriting the bulk of Everett's estate, they wouldn't need the money. Certainly not enough to risk getting caught.

"Unless," Manny said as he finished his burger, "they knew Everett intended changing his will. I can see either Tantra or Jimmy taking steps to ensure that the old man never completed the new will."

"Then anyone in that household could have staged the theft and sliced the brake lines," Reuben said.

"Don't know about that—Mary didn't know that she was going to inherit a dime until Mellis read the will." Manny wiped catsup off the corner of his lip. "I am more inclined to think the Kramers were involved. They had access to the safe during the course of their remodeling job—"

Reuben wiped mustard off his chin and said, "But Mary said Everett never left it open."

"When he was not there, he kept it locked. Mary said Everett would often keep it open for convenience when he was doing business in the next room. That could afford some sneaky bastards like the Kramers the opportunity to slip into his study and steal the map, with no one the wiser."

"Then sneak back and slice the brake lines of that old International." Reuben polished off the second burger and eyed the drive-in menu posted outside like he wanted to go back for round two.

"Tell me," Manny said, "how long would it take for brake fluid to leak out if someone cut the lines?"

"That cut was so small," he sipped his soda, "if the truck sat there for a week—providing no one drove it or mashed on the brake pedal—it might not drain out... ah. You're thinking this was planned for some time?"

"If it was, they would have had to disable Everett's new Ford, otherwise the old man would have taken it rather than his beater truck." Manny shrugged. "I just don't know enough to make a judgment right now. It could have been planned for a while."

They finished their lunch and continued the two miles west to Ft. Robinson. They entered the campgrounds, long ago purchased by the State of Nebraska to turn it into an historic state park.

"Unk took me here when I was just seven," Manny said, "not too long after the folks died."

"I know," Reuben said.

Manny stopped adjacent to the museum and turned in the seat. "How do you know when I was here? I hardly recall you coming around back then."

"I came around, all right," Reuben said, "checking up on you. Making sure no one on the rez messed with my little brother. You just didn't know it."

"Why would anyone have wanted to bother with me and Unk?"

Reuben stared out the window for a few long moments before he turned back. "If you knew your reservation history, you'd recall that AIM was pretty active on Pine Ridge back in… '69 when you were just a kid. We didn't always have the support of the people on the rez, and I didn't want you involved because—"

"Because you were their main enforcer…" Manny held up his hand. "Didn't mean for it to come out like that."

"You have every right to be bitter even after all these years, me catching a twenty-five-year hitch in the state pen and not having anything to do with you or Unk. Though Uncle Marion preferred it that way—he didn't want me influencing you the wrong way."

"No," Manny said, "you more than paid your dues. We know all about that homicide you were charged with."

"That was a couple years later. When you and Unk made your field trip down here to Ft. Robinson, I was with other American Indian Movement *injuns* taking in all the 'pleasures' to be had as we occupied Alcatraz." He shook his head. "Some vacation spot that dump turned out to be."

"Then let's say this is the trip we should have made together years ago," Manny said.

He opened his briefcase and took out some notes. The tourist season was long over before the first snow hit two months ago, and Manny knew there wouldn't be any Q & A with the park rangers. So he had downloaded the official map to Ft. Robinson State Park, and now turned that map as he squinted against the sun reflecting off the snow.

141

"What 'cha looking for?"

Manny picked up his notes and said, "Crazy Horse was being led to the Fort Adjutant's office the day he was killed… I think it's somewhere over—" He pointed to rustic buildings on the other side of the highway that split the state park.

"There." Reuben pointed to the southwest. "Past the fort Veterinary Hospital, then turn east. It'll be next to the guardhouse."

Manny looked over the top of his notes. "You've been here then?"

"Many times, after I served my time in prison," Reuben said. "And many times, I have felt the effects of the sacred man." He tapped his chest. "I like to think Crazy Horse resides inside here."

Manny laid his notes on the seat. "What else do you know about the events leading to Crazy Horse's death?"

"Just what our oral history teaches us. That *Tasunka Witko* was being led to the Adjutant's Office. He thought he was going to talk to General Bradley and Indian Agent Lee about being moved to the Spotted Tail Agency to be closer to his family. Touch The Clouds and several of Crazy Horse's warriors—including the young Black Heart—waited with him. Three Stars Bradley and Agent Lee were to meet with Crazy Horse—"

"Bradley never did," Manny said, "and Indian Agent Lee sold him out."

Reuben turned in the seat as best he could and said, "How do you know this? Have you been studying Indian archives?"

Manny rubbed his forehead, the migraine coming on having nothing to do with his head injury, but from a recent memory. "Things are coming back to me. I saw the last days of *Tasunka Witko* in my vision when we were in the *initipi* cleansing our souls. *Wakan Tanka* must have singled me out to receive this vision and, believe me, I will have words with him one day about it."

"Your visions, *misun*, are a blessing from the Great Mysterious.

Where I have mere faint visions now and again, *Wakan Tanka* has blessed you with… vibrant ones."

"I don't feel very blessed."

"You are. But what else do you remember?"

A dizziness overcame Manny and he fought his headache to explain to Reuben that the vision of Crazy Horse's death would never leave him. Never stop influencing him.

Until he solved the murder of the ancestor of Black Heart, the kid who had remained with the sacred man when others abandoned him in death, he would keep remembering the murder of Crazy Horse.

Chapter 20

"Manny!" Reuben said.

Manny blinked in time to avoid another handful of snow being smeared across his face, and he knocked Reuben's hand aside. "What the hell…" A moment ago he *felt* as if he were here. At Ft. Robinson. Walking beside Crazy Horse. But now, he sat in the tiny pickup while Reuben stood outside. "What you doing outside the truck?"

"You pulled to the side of the road for some reason. Next I knew, you were talking gibberish." Reuben dropped the rest of the snow in his hand. "Needed to do something to make you come around. Musta been the head injury you got in that apartment attack because you were saying some scary things."

"What things?"

"Warning Crazy Horse not to go into the Camp Adjutant's office. Then screaming for him to stay away from the guardhouse. 'I couldn't help him,' you yelled."

Manny wiped the sweat dripping down his cheeks despite the zero-degree weather. "I *couldn't* help him…"

Reuben laid his hand on Manny's shaking shoulder. "Perhaps that rap on your head did loosen your recollections of your vision. Sit back and catch your breath." He took the top off his soda and gave Manny a drink. "You're *sure* you want to go through with this?"

Manny wiped sweat off his chin with his shirtsleeve. "The only way I'll be able to find out about Everett's murder is by following his map."

"And there's no other reason?" Ruben asked. "Like finding out who Manny the Lakota really is?"

Manny straightened up in the seat. "Of course not. I'm an FBI Agent and I do this because it's my job," he said, doubting his own voice even as he spoke. "Let's head for the Adjutant's Office."

A park ranger along the parade ground gawked at them, while two tourists willing to brave the wind and the biting snow just to walk where Crazy Horse had walked only gave them a passing glance.

They entered the Adjutant's Office, restored to the way it was that fateful day in 1877, and Manny opened his new briefcase, slowly slipping out Everett's map. He laid it carefully on the floor and turned the map so that he could orient it to the guardhouse. "Everett's map is accurate in that it starts right *here*."

"The map you took off Becker' body does, too," Reuben said.

Manny opened his phone and pulled up the photo he had taken of the Becker map and laid the phone beside the Everett-map. "It does, actually," Manny said. He walked outside and stood looking at the lay of the fort. "The Becker map shows a line from the Adjutant's Office to the guardhouse just like the Everett map. But," Manny stepped outside, "this map shows Crazy Horse being taken away to the west after his death. Whereas," he went back inside and squatted beside Everett's map, "this one shows Crazy Horse taken northeast for burial."

Manny carefully folded Everett's map and slipped it back into the folder and into his briefcase. "I'm not sure which one I want to follow first."

"What does your gut tell you?" Reuben asked. "You always did have pretty astute cop instincts."

Manny rubbed his temples, that dizziness coming over him once more. He fought it off as he looked about, his gaze falling on large bounders in front of the old guard shack as if seeing them for the first time. And for some inexplicable reason, he *knew* the rocks would guide him.

He started walking toward the boulders, four large granite rocks with a fifth larger than the others, all set in concrete, when he stumbled. Reuben caught him and said, "You don't look so good, little brother—"

"The stones," Manny managed to get out as he stopped in front of the largest one. "These... these stones. They align," he rubbed his temples again as he looked about, "precisely with the four directions."

Manny squatted beside the largest boulder and ran his hand over the cold, rugged granite texture. "This has to represent Grandmother Earth."

Reuben knelt beside Manny. "Yes. *Unci Makha*, little brother. You have remembered some of the teaching of the Old Ones."

Manny used the stone to stand, wobbly on his legs, as he said, "Do you have tobacco? For an offering."

Reuben eased Manny onto the stone. "Stay right here. I have tobacco in my daypack in the truck. You gonna be all right?"

Manny looked about. The fort buildings shimmered as if it was a hot day, while he struggled to stay alert until he could offer prayers and tobacco to the four winds. Until he could ask *Wakan Tanka* for guidance in determining which map was the proper one to follow.

*   *   *   *   *

"I'm putting my trust in Everett's map," Manny said, his vision fading fast from his memory. But knowing his vision—as they always did—would guide him in life. And sure it had guided him toward the right map. "That is the one that I *know* shows the proper way."

146

"Good choice," Reuben said. "Because if that is Destiny's Door where Becker was found dead, it is right where we figured— northeast. Around Slim Butte. Just like the Old Ones told me when I was a youngster."

They drove out of Fort Robinson and headed back towards Chadron. Manny had a glorious notion that he and Reuben would be able to follow the map overland to exactly where Crazy Horse's parents took him after he was murdered, a notion that lasted until the first barbed wire fence prevented them from going any farther.

"Sign says this is Mabel Round Tree's property," Reuben said. "She'll never let you cross her land... for *any* reason."

"How do you know that?" Manny said, standing by the fence as he grabbed his briefcase and began taking the Everett map from the folder. "All I want to do is drive across her pasture. There aren't even any cows in there."

"Mabel Round Tree," Reuben said, "hates law enforcement. Especially FBI."

"Can't recall her being in any kind of trouble."

"She was in AIM when I was involved. One of the Old Ones from Minneapolis."

"There you have it," Manny said. "You both were AIM—she ought to have some solidarity with you."

"Remember that little occupation of Alcatraz? Mabel was there and we... made her do the cooking for all of us while we partied. Believe me, I am certain that she would hate me even more than she does law enforcement."

"Then I'm screwed if I want to follow that map."

"*Misun*, are you not issued a survival kit in case you're stranded?"

"We are," Manny said, "but how did you know?"

Reuben hesitated, then said, "oh, what the hell, the statute of limitations has run out anyway. We used to break into agent's cars on the reservation and grab what we could. Sometimes we got guns. Most times, all we managed to find was their survival kit."

"What's that got to do—"

"Just grab your bag and let me see it," Reuben said. "I promise I won't take it."

Manny reached behind the seat of the pickup and retrieved the small black, canvas bag, containing some energy bars and an emergency radio, first aid supplies, and a sealed can of water. "What do you want with the bag—"

"Just hand it here." Reuben fished around inside it and came away with a compass. "Ever use one of these?"

Manny shook his head. "Unk used one, but I never."

"Even in the Army?"

"My squad leader during infantry training always manned the compass. Beats me how it works."

"We used them a lot in 'Nam," Reuben said, as he turned the lensatic compass to face magnetic north and looked through the viewing glass. "They were a whole lot better quality than this one the government bought from the lowest bidder, but it'll do."

Manny chuckled. "But we're not lost."

"Didn't say we were," Reuben said before holding out his hand. "Give me that notebook you never write in. And a pen that actually works."

Manny reached for his notebook and found a working pen in his briefcase that he gave to people when they needed to fill out statement forms. "What do you need these for?"

"To jot the precise direction that the map leads us."

"We know where the map says Crazy Horse was taken," Manny said. "It takes us straight through Mabel Round Tree's property. We don't need a compass for that."

He took several readings, aiming at different landmarks before scribbling on the note pad and handing it to Manny.

"Keep this handy. Once we get back to Pine Ridge, we'll shoot a back azimuth to where the map said the wagon with Crazy Horse was supposed to have traveled."

"Crap," Manny said. "Why didn't I think of that?"

Reuben smiled and hitched up his jeans. "Because, Mister Agent Man, I am a former criminal. And we had to be on our game to keep away from the likes of you."

Chapter 21

Willie stopped Manny before he entered the interview room. "I know I ought to be objective, but those two peckerwoods would be good for Becker's murder."

Manny had thought so, too, recalling the fine red dust that had gotten caught in the tread of his boots, possibly picked up from Destiny's Door, as he recalled the slippery red rock underfoot causing him to nearly lose his balance. "I want you to be right. I want to pin Becker's murder on those two boobs, along with Everett's. But I'm not positive about the connection between Becker and the Kramers. We'll soon find out. How long before that hunter found Becker's body were the Kramers seen in that area?"

"Nanny Jill saw that rat trap of a work truck not two hours before the victim was discovered," Willie answered.

"She's certain it was the Kramers?"

"She's sure. She said you could spot the Kramer's old Dodge a half-mile away just by the smoke. And I believe her. When I followed them here, I almost lost sight of them in the black cloud. That truck of theirs is like one of those mosquito foggers we use here in the summer, it smokes so badly."

When they entered the interview room, Buddy was sitting where he had before, wearing the same clothes as he had last time. Sporting the same green-tinted teeth he had before, he blurted out, "What the hell is this, Agent Tanno, some kind of railroad job? My attorney's going to hear about this!"

"Good," Manny said as he sat across from the Kramers. He dug his cell phone out of his pocket and slid it across the table. "I urge you to call him."

Buddy stared at the phone before sliding it back. "No thanks, I can handle this myself."

"Because you don't have an attorney," Willie said. He turned a chair around and sat backwards, hanging his beefy arms over the chair back. "You don't have an attorney because you spend all your money on booze and dope," he nodded to Bobbie who—as if on cue—began picking at a fresh scab on his face.

"We don't need no lawyer." Buddy sat back in his chair, a smug look crossing his florid face. "'Cause we didn't do whatever the hell you're fixin' to accuse us of."

Manny waited for a moment, quiet as he often was while the target of his interview vented. Sometimes they incriminated themselves. This time, however, Buddy Kramer did not. "I have here a soil sample taken from your shoes that matches the soil where Becker's body was discovered," he lied. Manny was sure—from the position of the body and so little blood—that Becker had been killed somewhere else, his body transported to where the hunter found him. "And your work truck—to use the term loosely—was seen less than an hour from when Becker's body was found."

"We heard that fat bastard was kilt," Buddy said and nudged his son. "Didn't we hear it down at Big Bat's?"

Bobby only nodded and resumed picked at his sore.

"But of course we were headed… where and when did you say?"

"On Highway 41, just past the Oglala Lake. On Thursday."

Buddy took off his grease-impregnated *DEKALB Feed* cap and scratched his balding head. "We were driving down to Chadron for a job. Right, Bobbie?"

Bobbie looked up but did not meet Manny's eyes. "We sure was. Had… a remodel on a kitchen down thataway."

Manny took out the pen that worked and said, "Good, then all we have to do is call the lady. Or the man, whoever hired you guys up for the job. What's the number?"

"I don't have to tell you," Buddy said defiantly.

"Don't *want* to tell us, you mean, because you actually had no job down in Chadron that day?"

Buddy—practiced liar that he was—couldn't control an involuntary micro *tic* that tugged at his eyelid for a split second, and Manny knew the man had no job there. "We hardly knew Becker," Buddy blurted out. "Why would we kill him?"

"But you did know him?"

"Sure," Buddy said. "We talked a couple times when he came to Everett's house to see Tantra. That's who you oughta be looking at for Becker's murder—Tantra Black. Becker argued with Everett both times he was there when we was working, but he *really* tore into Tantra that last time."

"Tore into her about what?"

"How the hell should I know?" Buddy answered. "Have you talked with her yet?"

Manny hadn't. Until just now, he didn't know Hanson Becker had even been to the Black Ranch house after that one time Everett put the boots to him. As much as it pained Manny, he had to cut the Kramers loose. *Perhaps next time I can slap cuffs on your filthy wrists.*

Chapter 22

While Manny drove the Black's long driveway, two ranch hands worked a sorrel gelding in a corral to one side of the dirt road, gentling him, Manny could see. One cowboy led the horse around the arena by a halter, and Manny speculated the horse didn't meet the Black quality, being gelded and soon to be sold as a saddle horse. *Ouch!* Manny felt solidarity with the horse, for surely Clara would soon geld *Manny* if he didn't set a wedding date.

On the other side of the drive a man sat atop the seat of an old Farmall H, the tractor leaking hydraulic fluid as the man scooped manure into the bucket and pivoted to where a flatbed truck awaited the load. "Cheap bastard," Manny said to himself. "As much money as Everett had and he still operated seventy-year-old machinery." Manny knew it took a real artist with a wrench to keep those old tractors operating.

He parked in front of the porch that spanned the length of the front of the house and that wrapped around to the side, and he climbed out, arching his back. Stretching. Looking over the house. The corrals. The bunkhouse that he passed a moment ago. Someone had cut Everett's brake lines and elevated themselves to a murderer. That such a person would not hesitate to kill again—perhaps an FBI Agent on the hunt for the killer—was in the back of Manny's mind as he walked to the door.

"Did you come back just to have another piece of my pie?"

Mary asked. She emerged from around back of the house, her winter coat pulled tight around her, fresh eggs cradled in her apron. "Of course, you'd have to have breakfast first, if you're hungry."

"As a matter of fact," Manny said, "Big Bat's was out of their breakfast burritos I usually get, and I admit I'm famished."

"Then follow me into the kitchen."

"Can it wait until after I talk with Tantra... that is, if she's awake?"

"I actually heard her on her treadmill this morning. Early for some reason." Mary chuckled. "Maybe she's giving up the booze *and* men at the same time. But by now she ought to be knee-deep in her painting. Feel free to go on upstairs—her studio is at the far end of the hallway. When you're done talking with her, come on down and you can sample a couple of these eggs."

Manny entered the house—the tools and dry wall implements gone, the floor spotless—walked up the stairs, and followed the hallway to the end. The door was shut, but Manny heard sounds coming from the room and knocked.

"I told you to leave me be when I'm in here working!"

"You never told me," Manny said loud enough that Tantra could hear.

She stomped to the door and flung it open. "What the hell—" she stopped when she saw Manny. She pulled hair on the side of her head behind her ear and said, "Agent Tanno... I didn't know it was you. Please come in."

She shut the door behind him and waved her hand around the room. "You caught me—doing my best to make up for what my dear old Dad forked out for those four years at the Paris Art Institute." She chuckled. "I think the only French I learned over there was *me donner de la cocaine.*"

"'Give me cocaine' were the only words you learned in four years?"

Tantra dropped her head. "So, you know some French?"

"A little," Manny said. "But just the illicit words. Like cocaine. Comes with the job, I suppose."

Tantra picked up a bottle of Perrier and held it high as if in a toast. "That was the old Tantra. The new Tantra just drinks mineral water and imbibes now and again in Johnny Walker Black. But just occasionally."

"Like when you wanted to forget about your father's death?"

She shook her head and sat on a stool in front of an easel. "More like a celebration, I must admit, and I'm not even ashamed of it, either. My father treated us like servants. He was so damned controlling. But now I can do whatever the hell I want, when I want." She dipped a brush in paint on a palette beside the easel. "Painting *native* scenes. Father hated me to paint anything Lakota, unless *he* wanted me to. But now I can indulge myself and I don't even care if I sell any, what with the inheritance coming whenever Mellis gets his head out of his... but you know what I mean."

Manny walked around and stood looking at the canvas Tantra was working on. For wasting four years in a cocaine-stupor while she was an art student, Tantra painted like a professional. She had depicted a battle scene with four Lakota warriors sneaking up on three Crow overlooking a butte on the prairie. In the background, their horses were hobbled beside clumps of sage, war paint smearing their lathered necks. "That's really quite good."

"Think so?" Tantra asked.

Manny nodded. "But I'm curious as to why you keep paint in a baby food jar." He motioned to a dozen jars lined up on a shelf beside the aisle. "Shouldn't your paint come in tubes, or are they too expensive?"

"These paints," she gestured to the pallet and paint tubes in a rack hanging off a table, "cost a small fortune. These," she motioned to a cluster of baby food jars on a shelf under the table, "cost me little. Free, actually."

Tantra caught Manny's raised eyebrows and she said, "I see you don't believe me. But here—I'll give you a quick lesson in native pigments."

She motioned Manny to the corner of the room where dirt lay in divided boxes. "I make my own paint." She pinched a small bit of dirt. "Hold out your hand."

Manny did so and Tantra sprinkled the light-yellow dirt in his palm. "That's sienna umber, and I can get French ochre from friends I still have in Paris." She tapped another box labeled *burnt umber.* "I use this when I need to paint anything a reddish color, and that in your hand—"

"Feels like limestone or something?"

"Silica in the soil gives it that texture. I even manage to obtain some manganese ore here on the reservation that gives me deep purple and blue colors when I need it."

"You collect these yourself?"

"All by my lonesome. Here." She turned to a mesh screen and explained. "First I collect the soil and dry it on burlap. Then I sift it through this wire mesh and—because I'm a stickler for native methods—I want it even finer. So I sift it again through a flour strainer before grinding it with a mortar and pestle. And, *voila,* I have paint pigments."

"You *do* know another French word," Manny said with a smile.

Tantra smiled. "You are so right."

"But how do you get it this… consistency, like paste, to stay on the canvas?"

"Beeswax and turpentine," Tantra answered. "Just like they did back in the day when they had to make their own pigments. The Old Ones didn't have the luxury of going into an art store and buying paints off the shelf."

"But turpentine isn't 'period.' Even though some of our

ancestors worked in the early days on the manufacture of turpentine, it certainly wasn't widely available."

Tantra shrugged. "So I cheat on one little aspect. I started out using the beef tallow we get when we butcher, but it took weeks to dry and remained tacky all that time. But I still use cactus juice after the piece is finished."

"Cactus juice for what?"

"To set the pigments. I hike out to any of our pastures and cut some prickly cactus and bring it back here. I slice it in half and milk the juice into a jar, then pat it over the painting with a rag. It's just like what the old timers used back in the day, and when it dries, the paint is impervious to moisture."

Manny looked over Tantra's process, impressed by how she stuck to only native ways of harvesting pigments, but wondered... "I have to ask: why paint Indian scenes? When we were in your father's study the other night, you sounded as if you wanted nothing to do with the old ways, just like Everett shunned Indian ways."

Tantra shrugged. "I always was more... attuned to our Lakota culture than Father. He just hated it displayed around the house. But he's gone and," she waved her hand around the room, "I can paint Indians all day if I wish."

"But why the different paints—those you buy as opposed to those you make yourself?"

Tantra downed the last of her mineral water and tossed the bottle into a garbage can beside the drying boxes. "Those I collect myself are for a *different* kind of painting. When I paint native scenes for native customers, I use only traditional methods. But I would bet you didn't come here to get a crash course in Indian painting."

"You are so astute," Manny said and dug out his notebook, flipping blank pages. "You're acquainted with Hanson Becker?"

Tantra's face flushed crimson. "That has-been? He made his

reputation by spotting and reporting on fine art, specializing in native artwork. But his business has gone downhill these last twenty years."

"Actually," Manny said, "he slid down a hill by Slim Butte a few days ago. Someone murdered him."

It took a moment for it to sink in, but a smile finally crossed Tantra's face. "Good riddance."

"I take it you disliked the man?"

"Disliked? I loathed him! Here, look at these." She led Manny to a side closet and pulled on an overhead chain dangling from a swaying light bulb. Leaning across a back wall were five paintings of Indian life. Unlike the scene she was currently working on, these looked almost *abstract,* each depicting a facet of Indian life a hundred years ago. But they lacked the definition of her other work. They looked—in short—like many scenes painted on leger art that Manny had seen in museums. "These are what I use my own pigments for. I am one of the only artists replicating the old methods. Father hated that. Becker loved it. At one time."

"I hear a 'but' in there somewhere."

Tantra shut the closet door and went to a small refrigerator. She took out two bottles of Perrier and uncapped them before handing Manny one. "When I returned from Europe twenty-odd years ago, I needed some guidance. Actually, I was a mess. Just getting clean from drugs. I hadn't exactly spent the four years at the institute learning anything useful, when Becker showed up at the house to talk with Father one day. He gave Becker a tour of my studio, and he saw my work. From there, Becker... seduced me, in a manner of speaking. He told me we could do great things as a team—me painting, him reporting on it. I'd get tremendous exposure, he said. 'Keep painting *native,*' he said, 'and we'll both make a fortune.' The fat ass did nothing but string me along. Every time I had an opportunity for a gallery, he said I wasn't ready yet."

Tantra slid a stool out from under a counter and sat. "That was my ticket away from dear old Dad," Tantra answered. "I thought I was so good that no one could paint as the Old Ones did but me. But my opportunities came and went. So now," she nodded to her current painting, "I am forced to do *that*."

"I'd say it looks pretty good."

"Folks at the Prairie Edge in Rapid think so. They'll buy whatever I bring them."

Manny thought of the times he dropped in to the Prairie Edge, where he could get a glimpse of what native life was like a hundred years ago and more. Local artists displayed everything from artwork like Tantra painted to buffalo hides to scenes made entirely out of paper, all for sale. He always told himself he didn't stop there to connect deeper with his Lakota roots. But then, it wasn't the first time he had lied to himself. "I don't understand the problem," Manny said. "If they'll buy and display your paintings—"

"Because they're not *native*. Oh sure, they look native, but that's just because few people know the difference." She rubbed her temples as if she were rubbing a headache away. "But let's cut to the chase—you want to know where I was when Becker was killed?"

Manny opened his notebook. "I do. Two days ago his body was found by Slim Butte but I am not sure exactly where he was killed."

Tantra threw up her hands. "Then that's my alibi."

"How's that?"

"I couldn't have killed him—Jimmy had the Tahoe that day, somewhere sleeping off a bender, no doubt."

"I don't follow you."

"The Tahoe," Tantra said, "is the only automatic on the ranch. Father was too cheap to buy anything other than stick shifts, but I can't drive one. He finally acquiesced and bought that Chevy with an automatic transmission for when I said I needed to get into town."

"For clarification," Manny said, "Jimmy was gone from the ranch that day?"

"He was…" she stopped and a smile crept across her face. "He was gone the *whole* day. He could have gone to Slim Butte with no trouble."

"You almost sound as if you want him to be Becker's killer."

Tantra shrugged. "It would make administering the results of Father's will so much simpler."

* * * * *

Manny didn't have to know where Mary's kitchen was—all he had to do was tip his head up and the luscious odor of bacon and eggs drifted past his nose. He entered the room where Mary was tossing out eggshells into the garbage.

"Was the queen civil when you talked with her?" Mary asked as she turned over strips of thick bacon sizzling in the pan. "As you already saw, she can be quite unpleasant when she wants to be."

Manny hung his coat and hat on the rack beside the door and sat at the table. "She was, actually. She was knee-deep in painting an ambush scene—"

"She has been working on that for weeks. I think it is very good."

"She says she has no trouble selling them."

Mary flipped eggs and six strips of bacon onto a plate and set it in front of Manny before catching a piece of toast as it shot out of the toaster. "She loathes *modern* paintings. But it is what sells, not that she needs the money now. Her native depictions might be historically accurate, but they have such a limited audience, she will never sell them all."

Manny sliced through an egg and speared a piece of bacon. "She tells me Hanson Becker refused to sell her native paintings, even though he let on that he intended to."

"That pompous ass refused because he knew he would have to tell the world what a fine artist Everett's daughter was. And he did not want to give Everett *any* positive press."

Manny wiped egg yolk that had dribbled onto his chin and set the napkin down. "I take it Becker and Everett were... adversaries?"

"They despised one another."

"If they did, why did Becker visit Everett the day of the accident?"

"The painting," Mary said. "Becker demanded the painting he claimed he had paid for, but Everett said he lost any interest in ownership years ago."

"What painting?" Manny asked, closing his eyes for a moment to visualize Everett's great room where numerous paintings hung on the wall, none that depicted anything remotely Indian. "Was it one of those paintings hanging on the wall of his great room that Becker demanded to have?"

"All I know is that it was some painting that Tantra was working on," Mary said. "But it was not the first time Becker came around wanting 'the painting'. That last time, last year, Everett lost his temper and kicked Becker all the way from his study out the door."

"Were the tribal police called?"

Mary nodded. "Becker wanted prosecution. Miraculously, the tribal judge refused to sign an arrest warrant and Everett was never charged." She sat at the table across from Manny and poured each a cup of coffee, wringing her hands as if memories of her late employer and friend brought frustration. "Everett could be a most unpleasant man. Actually, as he grew older, he became near unbearable." She laughed nervously. "He even

161

kicked me out of the house about a dozen times, but I never left. After a couple days, he would cool off and deposit a bonus into my checking account."

"You said Everett claimed that Becker lost ownership in some painting. Did Becker buy part ownership from Everett and just not pay him?"

Mary stared into her coffee while she dissolved a lump of sugar with a spoon. "All I know is that Everett had one of Tantra's paintings that Becker was obsessed with. Everett finally agreed to sell—at an exorbitant price, if I heard their arguments right. Becker made payments to Everett, who claimed that Becker had stopped with the payments after a time. Refill?"

Manny shook his head and Mary refilled her own coffee cup. "The last time Becker came by here was when he and Everett really got into it. That day when the cops were called."

"But that wasn't the last time," Manny said. "The last time was the day before Everett's accident."

Mary nodded, the wringing of her hands resuming. "It was. Becker was not here for long as their argument was so brief. But intense. I would dearly like to know what they talked about."

"But you don't know what painting Becker had his eye on?" Manny asked as he finished the last strip of bacon and stood.

"I do not."

"Perhaps you could look around… see if there's a painting gone that Becker might have taken that last day. Maybe Tantra has an idea."

"I will look around. But I do not think that Tantra knew what painting Everett was selling to Becker under her nose."

As he donned his coat, he asked Mary, "Tantra said Jimmy had the Tahoe the day Becker was found murdered. Do you recall that?"

Mary's eyes looked up as if figuring out days in her mental calendar. "He took it that day, but do not ask me where. Since the reading of the will, Jimmy has been avoiding me like the plague."

"That's all I needed to confirm that Tantra was on the ranch that day."

"What makes you say that?"

"The Tahoe is the only automatic transmission on the ranch— the only vehicle that Tantra can drive."

"She told you that?" Mary asked.

"She did."

"I suspect," Mary said, "that one of the ranch hands taught her how to drive a stick shift many years ago. I suspect she could hop into any of the trucks and SUVs on the ranch and drive off the place like she was born to it."

Chapter 23

Manny paused before knocking on the door. *Once I go in there, that man might suck all the intelligence right out of me*, he thought, recalling the times he'd talked with Phil "Philbilly" Ostert. Philbilly's folks had breezed through Pine Ridge one fall, returning to Arkansas from picking lettuce in Oregon, and stopped for gas at Big Bat's. When they left, they forgot—or did so on purpose—their little Philbilly, and so, the teen had had to make his own way in the world. But not without pulling some real boners. Phil managed to convinced Willie to let him cater his wedding with Phil's new food truck, Sizzling Hot Indian Tacos pasted across the side.

His next venture yielded even less customers, few wanting to buy cut beef from someone advertising, "You Can't Beat Phil's Meat." He was a living, breathing example that no one is ever too old to do something stupid. Manny cringed as he could only imagine what Philbilly was up to now or what vital information he might have for him. As Manny entered the room, he steeled himself, as the last time he talked with Philbilly, he could have sworn that he heard the sound of the ocean coming from the man's head.

When Manny knocked on Phil's apartment door, Willie opened it. "I woulda had him come to the justice building, but he doesn't have a running car."

"That's a blessing," Manny said. "Where is he?"

"At his computer writing more letters to the National Weather Service."

"He's not still trying to get them to name tornadoes again?"

Willie nodded. "'Fraid so."

Ever since last summer when Phil got caught up in a small twister that touched down by Manderson, he'd been on a crusade to convince the NWS that tornadoes ought to have the same dignity as hurricanes. He felt they should be given a name. And he volunteered to let the service use his name for the first twister. *Hurricane Philbilly. Does have a ring,* Manny thought.

He stepped around the Christmas tree—the one that Phil kept up year-round for "special occasions." At St. Patrick's Day it was Phil's Paddy Tree, and he'd hang pieces of shamrock candy from the limbs. At Easter it was Phil's Easter Tree, decorated with chocolate Easter bunnies. All because Philbilly was too lazy to take the tree down after Christmas. *Hell,* Manny thought, *Philbilly was so lazy that he even bought toast in the frozen food aisle.*

Phil sat hunched over his computer, banging away with one hand while he tore into a piece of toast like a coyote after deer guts with the other hand, the sound of ill-fitting dentures crunching down making Manny wonder if he'd borrowed Pee Pee's teeth. Philbilly looked up and turned his chair to face Manny. "Manny," he grinned, his hand going out to shake.

Where the hell's the hand sanitizer? he thought as he shook Phil's mitt, sticky with jelly. "I hear you have some information for me."

"I do," Philbilly said. "Is there a reward being offered?"

"The FBI offers rewards for information leading to the capture of a Ten-Most-Wanted fugitive. If you have that kind of information…"

"Not *quite* that big," Philbilly answered. "But information that might solve the break-in of your apartment."

"This time Phil's info might pan out," Willie said to himself.

Manny sat on the coach across from Philbilly and took out his notebook as if he intended writing in it. "Let's hear it."

Philbilly sat looking up at the ceiling as if lost in thought, which was unfamiliar territory for him. "Okay," Phil said at last as he wiped his mouth with his shirtsleeve. "I was walking over to visit Herb Standing Dog… he has that apartment a couple doors down from that one you feds stay in now and again." Philbilly sat back as if that pearl of information was all Manny needed to find out who broke into his apartment. "'Twas 'bout two o'clock in the morning, if my memory serves me right."

"You were going to wake up Herb at that time?" Manny asked.

Philbilly shrugged. "I had nothing else to do and figured Herb didn't neither."

"Please," Manny seemed to plead, "continue."

"Ok, here's the juicy part… my old Pontiac broke down and I was walking towards Herb's when this truck even more beat up than mine damned near ran me over. I'm here to tell you there are two kinds of pedestrians—the quick and the dead, and I was near one of them dead 'uns."

"Did you get a license plate number?"

"He did," Willie answered when he saw Philbilly had another mouthful of pastry. "But it came back registered to a car and not a truck."

"But I got the number right," Phil said as he tapped the side of his head. "You know me—I got a pornographic memory."

Manny let that pass and asked, "What did the truck look like?"

Phil leaned back and said proudly, "I not only saw it, I knowed the driver. It were a rusty blue Dodge that smoked like one of them mosquito foggers that come around in the summer time."

"Tell him who was driving," Willie said.

"It were that Buddy Kramer. Bobby was riding bitch. They sped away from where your FBI apartment is like they was scared of something. Or because they'd just done something bad."

"Can Officer With Horn come by and have you fill out a statement form this afternoon?"

Philbilly shook his head. "I have to make it to Rapid City this afternoon. Martha, my girlfriend's, fixing to undergo surgery." He lowered his voice as if there were someone in the room besides Willie and Manny. "She's having a triple mastectomy."

"You mean double?" Willie said.

Philbilly waved his hand. "One of them. Point is she's going to be really sensitive about it."

"Understood," Manny said.

He thanked Philbilly for the information and was first into the fresh outside air just ahead of Willie. Manny leaned against the fender of his rental truck and shook his head. "Times like these I wish I smoked cigars to drown out the odor in there."

"It was worth it if he can place the Kramers near your apartment at the time of the break in."

"Just one more little piece of evidence, but not enough to put the squeeze on them."

"I know," Willie said. "I'd just like to put the cuffs on them and lead them to the hoosegow."

"And I wouldn't? Be pure heaven to see the smile wiped off Buddy Kramer's face." Manny popped a piece of gum and offered one to Willie. He passed as he grabbed the can of Copenhagen from his back pocket and stuffed his lower lip.

"Maybe it was just a coincidence that the Kramers were in the area of your apartment when you were responding to the fake homicide call."

"Might be," Manny said, "but you know I don't believe in coincidences. I'm thinking they were after the Becker map."

Willie spit tobacco juice into the snow. "If they snooped into Everett's safe while they were working there, they would know about it."

Manny thought back to the dust that he had seen inside Everett's open safe. Dust he was almost certain was drywall dust. "We'll have to talk with the Kramers again. We need to find out how well they really knew Hanson Becker."

Chapter 24

Reuben shielded snow from Manny's compass as he stood outside sighting along the green-colored device before climbing back into the Toyota and closing the lens cover. "If we follow that ridge line," he pointed through the windshield, "keeping that downed cottonwood just to our right as a landmark, we ought to be right about where the map shows."

Reuben assured Manny that, if he shot a back azimuth from where they ended their route at Mabel Round Tree's fence line earlier, they would be close enough to the map location on the Pine Ridge side that they could tweak it. Manny thought back to when he and Willie entered what they thought was Destiny's Door and said, "Will that bring us to those spires where the hunter found Hanson Becker's body?"

"Can't say," Reuben said as he popped the top of the cooler on the seat between them. He took out a hoagie and peeled the plastic wrap back. "I've never hiked this part of the rez. All I can say is it'll be close to that area where that hunter found the body."

"What if your compass direction leads us into Destiny's Door? Will you go with me?"

Reuben smeared mayo on his sandwich and stared out the side window for a long moment before he said, "I didn't feel so good the other day when we were there. And I was more than a hundred yards from the *door*. But you're my *misun* and I'm sure not going to have anything happen to you. Besides, a sacred man just might get you through it unscathed. If it leads us there."

Manny remembered he and Willie approaching the "Door." Even with Willie offering prayers and smudging them with sage, they still nearly didn't get through—he and Willie had faced one another with hands on their gun butts as if an unseen puppet master were pulling the strings. If the same thing overcame Reuben, Manny wasn't sure he could handle his much bigger brother.

Manny drove toward the ridge line as far as they could go in the deep snow. He stopped and called Willie while he still had cell service. "Any luck?"

"Wait a second," Willie said, and Manny heard a door slam. "I can talk now. Man Mountain Mike just went into Big Bat's for more donuts. To answer your question, I've shook down all my sources, and we haven't had any luck finding the Kramers."

"All right," Manny said. "Keep on it. We're fixing to head towards where the Everett map shows. I'll call when we're back into cell range." He hung up and put the truck into four-wheel drive, heading toward the ridge line that Reuben pointed out.

* * * * *

Manny pulled his stocking cap down around his ears and stomped his feet for circulation while he watched Reuben take another reading. "I think we're headed in just the right direction," he said before wiping the snow off the compass and pocketing it.

"I hope to hell we come onto some landmark that we can orient this map to," Manny said. "It's colder than—"

"Colder than the dickens," Reuben said and slapped Manny on the back, jarring his teeth that were already clicking together like Pee Pee's dentures. "The Old Ones would be out in this kind

DEATH THROUGH DESTINY'S DOOR

of weather for days and never complain."

"But they had horses to ride. They didn't have to hike the fields."

"I told you we could have borrowed that junk-yard horse of Crazy George He Crow's. Lord knows I've 'borrowed' it enough whenever I need to get somewhere."

Manny stopped and faced Reuben. "I've seen you atop that old swayback. Poor thing could hardly move with your big butt on top of it. I can only imagine how far we'd get with both of us weighing it down."

"Got a point," Reuben said. "Let me see the map." He turned it and faced the direction he'd just shot a reading from. "It's hard to tell distances with this—the Old Ones thought differently than we did about it. But... there!" He pointed to rolling hills another half-mile down the shallow valley where the tips of two sandstone spires jutted up from the frozen ground. "I'd say that looks like where Becker was found dead but from a different angle."

"All right, then," Manny said. "Let's get this over with."

"We don't have to do this, you know."

"I keep telling myself the same thing," Manny said. *Am I trembling from having to go back through Destiny's Door, or from the damn cold?* "A part of me wants to turn around and head for the nearest warm café. But something keeps assuring me it will help find Everett's killer if we go in there. And now Becker's."

Reuben draped his heavy arm around Manny's shoulders. "Or maybe this is more about finding out who *you* are?"

"Don't give me that lecture again about finding my Lakota roots."

Reuben smiled. "But you have been on a journey to do just that since you came back to the rez. You just don't know it."

Manny shook Reuben's arm off and started down the snow-covered prairie. "Can we just get this over with, please?"

They hiked the half-mile in silence. Manny's legs buckled and

171

he stood shaking.

"What is it?" Reuben asked, snaking his arm around Manny's waist and holding him up.

"I'm getting that dizzy feeling I got the other day when I came upon the Door."

"Want to sit somewhere?"

Manny stood and looked around. "I could either sit on cactus or sage brush, either one wouldn't be very pleasant. I'm ok now. Did you bring sage?"

"Of course," Reuben answered. "When we get closer and the feeling is stronger, we will have to pray and smudge ourselves before entering."

Manny carefully took out the map and shielded it against the snow, turning his body so the features somewhat matched what he looked at. It was so hard to tell—terrain could change from year to year. Time had surely altered the face of the landscape in the hundred-fifty years since Black Heart drew the map. "I think this is where we found Becker," Manny indicated.

Reuben reverently took the map and turned it. "The grave marked 'NOTCH' ought to be another quarter-mile past Becker's murder scene..." he paused and looked again. "The map is off. After a hundred years, it's off."

"Or course it's off," Manny said. "The land changes with the weather—"

"I mean Black Heart's map is *way* off... look," Reuben said and pointed down a narrow gully. Not more than a hundred yards away, they saw the distinct impression of an anomaly in the prairie, of the ground giving way. Ground shaped like a person's grave.

Manny put the binos to his eyes and glassed the site. Even though Reuben had Manny by fifteen years, his eyesight was so much better. After a minute, Manny finally spotted an outline in the ground where the soil had sunk in.

Reuben looked at the map once again and said, "I don't know what it is, but I'm almost certain it's this NOTCH notation." He slipped the map back into the Ziploc and closed it against the snow. He started once again toward the Door when the glint of something on the hill overlooking them caught Manny's eye. He stopped just as that dizziness overcame him again and his legs gave way. He dropped to the ground a heartbeat before a shot echoed off the hills, the bullet kicking up snow where he'd stood a moment before.

He felt strong arms yanking him behind a thick clump of sage brush as another shot just missed him and Reuben by inches. "Hundred yards up on that hill just to the right of that stump of a tree," Reuben said as Manny jerked his gun out of his holster. He fired... three times. Then the fourth shot hit a cactus fifty yards in front of the shooter, and Manny fired again, missing by another ten yards.

"Give me your gun."

"What?"

"Your gun!" Reuben said. "You haven't even come close to hitting that shooter up there, but then you never were much of a shot. Give it to me."

Manny handed his gun to Reuben who said, "Get another magazine ready and spot me."

Reuben moved sage brush aside and rested his gun hand on a rock while he let out his breath, and fired.

"Right and low about ten yards," Manny said.

Reuben fired again, pieces of the tree flying, and Reuben fired again.

"You got the range," Manny said and Reuben fired again. And again, until the gun was empty. Manny handed him a fresh magazine and Reuben quickly dropped the old one and inserted the fresh one into the butt of the weapon. He kept up a steady firing, each time shards of the tree on the hill above flew into the snow.

Reuben stopped when the gun was again empty, and inserted yet another full magazine.

"Look." Manny pointed to a plume of smoke from a truck as it sped away. "That was either a diesel or a truck needing new cylinder rings."

After a long moment, silence replaced the gun shots and the sound of the truck driving away.

"Let's go have a look-see what our shooter left up there," Manny said, and held out his hand for his gun.

"Maybe I ought to keep it. As you saw, you can't hit anything with it."

"A felon with a gun—"

"Then arrest me."

"Our shooter is long gone. Besides, I don't have cuffs big enough for your wrists."

Manny stood and holstered his pistol before starting up the hill to where the shooter had lain in ambush.

"Shouldn't we see if that is a gravesite down that ravine?" Reuben called after him.

"We can come back and look at it later. Right now, I want to see what kind of evidence the shooter left for us."

Chapter 25

M anny leaned over the front seat and said to Willie, "We just don't have enough to arrest the Kramers for that ambush, but we damn sure have enough to bring them in for questioning."

Willie flipped on the Expedition's wipers and looked into the rear-view mirror. "I still think we do. Haul them in and let them stew in the pokey for a night, and I bet little Bobbie spills his guts. As bad as he was tweaking the other day, think how bad he'll be if he sits all night without a hit of crack. What do you think?"

"I'm all for arresting them," Shannon said from the passenger seat next to Willie. With the two of them taking up the cab, they looked as if they were sitting right next to one another. "Like you said, Agent Tanno, you did find a roofing nail beside that tree where your shooter hid. And the exhaust smoke… you know how that beater truck of the Kramer's smokes, if you believe Phil Ostert."

Manny did believe Phil, even down to recalling the license number correctly. That the Kramers had slipped a stolen plate on their truck, Manny had no doubt, and he could see either one winging rounds down toward Manny and Reuben. Still, a black plume of diesel smoke and a single roofing nail didn't make much of a case against them. He suspected the U.S. Attorney would require something more like evidence before he went to a grand jury.

They drove along the Black driveway, a ranch hand sitting atop the sorrel Manny saw him gentling earlier. He rode the horse slowly, heeling him now and again to get him used to the snaffle bit.

On the other side of the road, another ranch hand lay on the ground beside the manure pile he was working on the other day. An open toolbox lay at his feet while he repaired the hydraulic line on the old Farmall tractor.

"I'd know those feet anywhere," Shannon said as he pointed to a set of legs sticking out from under a Ford Power Stroke truck parked in front of the porch. "Hobart's boots are near as big as mine."

Willie parked to one side of the truck just as Hobart scooted out from under it. He stood and brushed snow and dirt off his trousers before walking to Willie's Expedition and sticking his head in the window. "Thought I'd seen the last of you," he said to Shannon. "Come around to help me fix this old truck of mine?"

Shannon opened his door and wrenched himself free of the seat belt. "What do I know about mechanics?"

"Probably more than you know about football," Hobart laughed.

Shannon's face flushed red with anger and Manny was quick to hop out and step between them. Again. "Reuben's pretty comfortable turning a wrench. I doubt he's doing much right now except watching *Days of Our Lives*. I could call him and see if he could help."

Hobart stepped back and shook his head as he looked at his truck. "I'll get it eventually. I had to replace the glow plugs last week. Now it's the CPS sensor. Stopped dead in the middle of an intersection in Rapid yesterday. This," he slapped the fender of the truck, "is why you ought never buy a vehicle you can't push. I'll figure it out eventually."

"Like I said, if you need help, I'm sure my brother can pitch in," Manny said, then asked, "is your mother inside?"

Hobart grinned. "Do all you lawmen time it so's you stop by at meal time? She's inside getting lunch made. Just go on in."

Manny thanked him and led Willie and Shannon into the house. "Wonder if that truck smokes?" Shannon asked under his breath.

"Why?"

"It's a diesel. Just like the one you saw fleeing the scene after your attack."

Manny shrugged. "That's just it—I *didn't* see the truck. Only heard it. Most diesels pretty much sound alike unless you have a mechanic's ear. And most of them smoke, too, so I can't ID the truck just by that either."

Manny knocked on the door before stepping inside.

"Saw you boys coming down the drive," Mary called from the kitchen. "Lunch is not ready yet, but I have coffee going."

They started down through the entryway into the hall leading to the kitchen when Manny stopped. Fresh sheets of eight-foot drywall had been hung, the seams mudded only recently, the drywall compound cool to the touch, giving off a slightly musty odor. "So, the Kramers finally came back and finished their job," Manny said as he, Willie and Shannon stepped into the kitchen. "Looks pretty good, too."

Mary was bent over the cookstove. She straightened and tuned around while she nibbled on a carrot stick. She stopped and stared up at Shannon, his head inches away from the ceiling fan. "The Kramers did not finish that drywalling," she said. "Hobart did. He called yesterday and I filled him in about the will and that I got possession of the house. He said since I am the owner now, he would come help out around here until school started again after the break." She laughed. "I am glad those fool Kramer boys left their tools so Hobart could finish the job. Sit."

Manny and Willie hung their Stetsons on the coat rack and

sat at the table. When Shannon remained standing, Manny motioned to one of the chrome chairs situated around the table. "Even *you* won't break one of these."

"You don't look the worse for wear," Mary said to Manny while she set three mugs on the table. "I heard about you and your brother getting shot at."

"How did you hear?"

"Moccasin telegraph," Mary answered. "Even this far out, we hear things. But you did not come here wanting to tell me about that."

"We didn't," Willie said. "We need to talk with Jimmy. And Hobart, as soon as he's finished fixing his truck."

"Hobart? What on earth do you need to speak with him about?"

"I'd rather wait until he comes in."

"Fair enough." Mary turned back to the stove and said over her shoulder, "you'll have to go into Rapid City if you want to talk with Jimmy." When Mary turned around again, she was kneading her hands together and her mouth was downturned into genuine sadness. "I think that Jimmy is trying to get guardianship over his sister."

Manny remained quiet and put his finger to his lips as he glared at Shannon about ready to speak. He needed to learn some folks just take their own time telling their story. "Tantra fell off the wagon last night in Hot Springs, and she started drinking. Then she found someone to give her drugs. Her kind always seems to know just where they can get their hands on them, don't they?"

Manny nodded. "They do. I'm sorry to hear that, but where is she now?"

"She was at the Fall River County Jail. After she got high last night, she was stopped driving that new truck of Everett's. Got arrested for DUI and started fighting the police. Punching them. Kicking them." Mary sat at the table. "Jimmy sent a couple of ranch hands over to pick up the truck." More hand-wringing. "Mellis called in some favors and got Tantra transferred to the rehab in Hot Springs. Jimmy's meeting with Mellis to make sure she's kept in rehab. Says he needs to take care of his sister so she doesn't hurt herself even more. I am afraid if Jimmy manages to become her guardian, it will show her incompetence to manage her own affairs."

Mary dropped her head and stared into her coffee cup for many moments before Manny asked, "There's something more to it?"

Mary nodded. "I fear Jimmy is working with Mellis. If they manage to get awarded guardianship over Tantra, Jimmy will be free to cut her out of the will."

"He could do that," Shannon said, holding his silence no longer. "We studied motives in the Academy."

"Altering a duly executed will is near impossible. But petitioning the court for guardianship. Brilliant," Manny said. "Mellis is smarter than I gave him credit for. He might not get Everett's will altered, but he could pull off the guardianship stunt, and the only money Tantra would receive would be what her guardian felt like giving her, that guardian being Jimmy."

"And if he gets awarded guardianship of his sister," Mary said, "I am next. I can only imagine what Jimmy and Mellis would use to get rid of me."

"So much for brother-sister love among twins," Willie said as Hobart came into the kitchen. His hands were damp from scrubbing grime off them, and he took off his outer sweatshirt and dropped it just outside the room.

"Want to buy a good truck?" he asked Manny. "At least until something else breaks down."

"Thought you'd be driving that nice old Crown Victoria we saw you in the other day."

Hobart poured coffee into a Bugs Bunny–shaped mug and sat at the end of the table away from Shannon. "I trailer my cars

179

when I go to shows that are very far away, and that Ford truck of mine has gobs of power. When it runs. But I know you *three amigos* didn't come all the way out here for Mom's coffee and to find out about my classic cars."

Manny nodded to Shannon who took out his notebook and flipped pages.

"That your playbook you never used in the NFL?" Hobart taunted Shannon.

"No," he answered. "It's the playbook of Hobart Comes Flying… sorry, I forgot you are going by Black now."

Hobart shook his head and leaned back. "Let's have it. You must think you have something on me."

"All right then," Shannon said, squeezing the notebook in his big hands. He breathed deeply to calm himself as Manny had told him, keeping his composure even when suspects piss him off. "The day Hanson Becker was found dead by Slim Butte, you were—"

"Leading a group of kids to the mammoth dig at Hot Springs—"

"With another teacher." Shannon turned his notebook to the light and squinted. *No wonder he never got on the field,* Manny thought. *He probably didn't see it any better than he can his notes.* "Beverly Janek. An archeology teacher as well."

Hobart's jaw muscles clenched, and he blurted out, "What the hell, you came to my school and nosed around?"

Shannon smiled. "We did."

"What Agent Henderson means," Manny said, "is that we have to verify the whereabouts of anyone who might be involved with Becker's—"

"Involved how? I only talked with him once when I was here visiting Mom. Besides, I was in Hot Springs when he was found. With my kids."

"Forty miles away, you were," Shannon said and flipped to

another page. "Ms. Janek said you told her to take over the tour of the mammoth dig as you... 'had an errand to run.' And it appears you came back a couple hours later." Shannon closed his notebook. "More than enough time to drive to Slim Butte and dump Becker's body."

"This is more than a little ridiculous," Mary said as she heaped stew into bowls for each of them. "Hobart left for a while—"

"I'm not sure they even deserve an explanation after that accusation." Hobart picked up his spoon and dipped it into his stew. "I was bringing Mom a case of vinegar she asked me to get for her. Figured since I was close to the rez, it'd save me a special trip."

"And I already used most of it," Mary added. "I wanted to can some tomatoes that I grew in our greenhouse and found out I ran out of vinegar. Some of the same tomatoes I kept back to put in that stew you're eating."

"We had to ask," Willie said to Hobart, "as much to eliminate you as a suspect as anything else."

But in Manny's mind, Hobart *wasn't* eliminated. He could have concocted that story about needing to deliver vinegar to Mary, and Mary could have sensed that and gone along with it. Or their story could be prearranged. But what Manny didn't want to do—just yet—was ask Hobart how he picked up that red dust that seemed to stay on one's shoes forever. The same type of red dust native to the region where Becker's body was found, and that had flaked off Hobart's boots just now as he had entered the room.

Chapter 26

Manny passed on the wafer-thin, cold pizza that Lumpy placed in the middle of the conference table. Instead, he opted for a ham and turkey on rye from the Wheel of Death vending machine that dispensed week-old sandwiches. He patted his shirt pocket: the Imodium capsule was still there in case the sandwich had been in the machine longer than a week. Either way, it was more appealing than Lumpy's pizza, so hard and thin you could prop up a short table with it.

"Are you too good to eat what we eat?" Lumpy said, his shirt front already stained with a drop of pizza sauce. "This being a working lunch, I figured the least I could do was provide lunch."

"The *very* least," Manny answered, noting that Pee Pee had speared a slice and took out his teeth to gum it. "But no, I am not too good… I'm just trying to cut down some," he said as he patted his belly.

Lumpy chuckled. "That's what you get for being a hot shot FBI agent—soft. Now if you would have stayed with the tribal police like me all these years, you might be in some semblance of shape."

Some shape. As Manny watched Lumpy polish off one slice of pizza and grab for another, he figured that Lumpy was so happy with his first double chin he decided to add a second. "No luck locating the Kramers?"

"None," Lumpy managed to say with a full mouth. "I put out

a BOLO, but we're just a little shorthanded—by about thirty-one officers, to be exact. We've been up to our asses in alligators with family fights and thefts that looking for the Kramers is secondary. But our units are keeping an eyeball out." He wiped sauce off his chin and said, "You're pretty hot after the Kramers."

"Right now, they're at the top of my list. Especially after what Shannon found out."

"Where is your trainee?" Lumpy asked.

"Out looking for the Buddy and Bobbie."

Lumpy reached for another slice of pizza, but Pee Pee was quicker and snatched it from the jaws of death. Lumpy glared at Pee Pee—gumming the crust, making more noise than a hair-lipped cowboy trying to whistle—and turned to Manny. "What did your trainee find that's so important?"

"Stolen plates, for one thing," Manny said, gnawing on his sandwich that was only slightly less crunchy than the pizza, "from Crawford, Nebraska. Car plates. The same plates that Philbilly saw speeding away from my apartment the night I got that phony homicide call."

"And this connects how?" Lumpy asked, turning to watch Willie burst through the door. He stooped to the pizza box and—when he saw it was empty—turned to the Wheel of Death to take his own chances with Montezuma's Revenge. "I haven't eaten all day."

"I wish I had your will power," Lumpy said.

Willie fed the machine coins until a sandwich *thunked* down on the bottom of the plastic door. "Will power has nothing to do with it. Just been too busy to eat. I've been trying to trace the Kramers' tracks to find out if they are the ones who killed Hanson Becker. After Shannon got word of the stolen plates in Crawford, I met one of the Dawes County deputies at the state line. They had a bunch of wire stolen from a rig site in their county a few miles out of Crawford. A rancher found the burn pit on his land where the thieves scorched off the insulation. The deputy's pretty sure it's the same two who sold the wire to a salvage yard in Chadron."

"The yard hands get a name?" Manny asked.

"They don't ask questions," Willie said, peeling the bun back and squirting packs of mustard and mayo on to kill the stale taste. "But they got a description... two guys. One did the talking while the other one stood picking at a sore on his cheek. The salvage dude described the younger one as... mentally challenged. Quiet. Didn't look him in the eye the whole time. They drove up in a faded blue Dodge that smoked more than the yard hand did."

"Enough for a felony warrant?" Lumpy asked.

"With the amount of wire they sold to the salvage yard, the deputy said there'll be enough for one. He's going to file that warrant application today."

"And based on them being suspects in the wire theft about the time Becker was found, you think they killed him?" Lumpy asked.

"It's not just that," Pee Pee said. "Manny found a roofing nail where the shooter was perched while ambushing him and Reuben. And the Kramers were on a roofing job, according to what they told Mary Comes Flying."

Lumpy threw up his hands. "Then by all means, Hot Shot, get your murder warrant based on *that.*"

Manny sipped his Coke and said, "I didn't say we had enough for a warrant. I said we had enough to bring them in again for questioning."

"For what motive?"

Manny looked at Lumpy polishing off his slice of piece of pizza. *I'd like to leave you with an idea, but I'm not sure you'd have anywhere to put it.* "The map, of course. It's always been about the map."

"And you think they have it now?"

"If they did and it was authentic, those fools would be driving around in a new seventy-thousand-dollar truck."

"Which reminds me," Lumpy said, "where is Everett's map?"

"As safe as it can ever be."

*   *   *   *   *

"Chief Looks Twice has a point," Willie said as they pulled out of the Justice Building lot. "We're focusing too much on the Kramers."

Manny hated to admit it, but Lumpy *was* right. His bright idea of looking at other possible suspects was beginner's luck for the Chief. "About the time Clara brought me a piece of her apple pie for desert last night, I started thinking about Hobart. With his mechanical skills, he would know just where to cut the brake lines of Everett's truck. And the day he was escorting those students on the field trip to Hot Springs he was within miles of where Becker was found. Barely a thirty-minute drive from there to the murder site."

"But why set the old man up for a certain accident? I know Hobart and Everett didn't get along, but why would he risk it? Hobart wasn't going to get much from the estate... unless he didn't know," Willie said.

"You mean unless Hobart thought Everett intended giving him a sizeable amount in the *original* will and—"

"And he figured he was about to be cut out of the new will if the old man lived," Willie said.

Manny watched out the side of Willie's SUV, hoping for a glimpse of the Kramers' beat-to-hell truck. He wasn't convinced that they were involved in Everett's death and that of Hanson Becker, but he wanted a chance to eliminate them as suspects if they were not. Or cause them to float to the top of the suspect heap. "It still brings us back to the map of where Crazy Horse is buried. That alone would fetch mega-bucks for the genuine one."

"Or even that second map stolen from the safe." Willie stuffed Copenhagen in his lip and brushed the excess off on his pant leg. "Why would Everett even have that map, unless it was *the* genuine one?"

"It isn't," Manny said, thinking back to the vision he had at Ft. Robinson. "I'm thinking the one in the safe was a decoy in case anyone intended to steal the authentic one. Everett told whoever would listen that he had the only true Crazy Horse map. But I am still convinced the one we found sandwiched between those magazines *is* authentic."

"Where do you think Jimmy fits into all this?" Willie said. "He had as much access to Everett's room as anyone. He had the opportunity to notice when the old man stepped out to the crapper or left the room with his safe open. He could have snuck in and grabbed the cedar box containing the map."

"I don't know. Jimmy is a drunk and a spoiled brat, but would he know enough to surgically cut Everett's brake lines?"

"Since he was raised on a ranch," Willie said, "he would have had to pitch in with keeping the machinery running at some point in his life. Everett would have made sure he worked for his supper. My guess is he is more familiar with trucks and tools than he first appears. He's just too damned lazy to help around the ranch. And now, he'll be too damned wealthy when the estate money comes rolling in."

Willie drove slowly through Crazy Horse Housing, his head on a swivel looking for the Kramers. "Becker had to have stolen the map that night, but he must have had help in the scheme. It could have been anyone in the house, but I'm putting my money on the Kramers. I just want to find them and ask them, face-to-face, where I can watch their reaction—"

"Shush!" Willie said and turned up the volume on his police radio.

Manny cocked his ear to the speaker mounted under the dash. Lumpy's voice screeched across the radio. Needing help. His voice breaking. Out of breath. Chasing Shannon who was in a foot pursuit of the Kramers bolting out of Big Bat's.

"The other units are way the hell out on calls," Willie said, skidding the Expedition around, tires slipping, running over a curb as he floored the accelerator. "Buckle up."

Willie barely slowed through the intersection, now four blocks from Big Bat's when he heard Lumpy on the radio calling for an ambulance two blocks south of the convenience store. "Damn... hope the Kramers didn't open up on the Chief and Shannon like they did on you and Reuben."

"We'll know soon enough." Manny pointed to one side of the alley. "There. Shannon's down and Lumpy's clutching his gut. Shit!"

The Expedition slid sideways in the snow as Willie frantically fought for control of the wheel. He stopped a few yards from the downed lawmen.

Manny bailed out the door and ran to Lumpy, still holding his gut, still bending over Shannon, the big man moaning in pain. Manny squatted beside Shannon. He held his leg, and pain was etched on both of their faces. Manny asked Lumpy, "Was this the Kramers' doing?" He looked them both over but saw no blood. "They shoot you guys?"

Lumpy tried standing, but bent over once again, a grimace crossing his jowls. "It was the Kramers... in a manner of speaking."

The sirens of the ambulance approaching reassured Manny they would be all right and he pressed Lumpy, "Where did they nail you—"

"The Kramers didn't shoot either of us," Lumpy blurted out

187

loudly to be heard over Shannon's wailing. "Your clumsy trainee here ran out the back after those two peckerwoods." Lumpy winced in pain as he kept holding his gut. "I was a dozen steps behind him. He was gaining on them, arm out to grab that Buddy Kramer, when he stepped in a pothole. He wrenched his knee something terrible by the sounds of him."

"But what happened to you?"

"Did you ever try to help a three-hundred-pound man to his feet," Lumpy answered. "Don't. Or you'll get a hernia like I just did."

"Boss," Shannon managed to say just as the paramedics stopped their ambulance close to the two injured men, "don't send me back to the field office in Rapid City. They'll... tube me out. Shit-can me from the program."

"You'll have to get your knee fixed—"

"It's not broken. Just twisted it something awful. I had this happen once before... on the field. Wrapped it with ice and it was good in a few days. Please, boss, let me stay in the apartment. Just for a few days. Until I can walk again."

A woman paramedic set her jump box beside Shannon and her eyes widened. "Radio for more help," she yelled over her shoulder. "And a stronger back board."

Chapter 27

Manny slid into the curb with a jar as he parked at the rehab center on Jennings Avenue in Hot Springs. He climbed out and nearly slipped on the ice, which worried him. The last thing he wanted was to wrench *his* knee and end up in the government apartment with Shannon until they both mended. He turned his back to the wind that had picked up in the last hour, pelting his face and neck with hard frozen sleet. He pulled his collar up tight while he entered the rehab facility.

He stomped his feet on the entry mat and walked to the reception desk where a stoic sixties-something lady looked up at him over half-glasses, clutching the current edition of *Good Housekeeping*. "I would like to visit Tantra Black."

Unblinking, the woman said, "I can neither confirm nor deny that she is a patient here," and went back to looking at fall recipes.

"Oh, she's here all right. The sheriff's department transferred her—"

"I said," the woman interrupted as she stood to her five-foot height and took off her glasses, "that I am not at liberty to say if she is a patient."

Manny took out his FBI ID case and showed the lady. "It is official."

She shrugged. "Since when does being arrested for drunk

driving and fighting with the cops become a federal offense?"

"It's not," Manny said. "I just need to talk with her."

"I am under very strict orders not to allow anyone access to patients in their first thirty days—"

"So, you admit she is here?"

The woman's face flushed, and she glared at Manny.

He took out his pocket notebook and pen and asked, "What is your name?"

The lady looked warily and backed up a step as if Manny intended to arrest her. "Why do you need to know my name?"

"I need to know who to put on the complaint—"

"Complaint of what?"

"Denying a federal officer access to a witness. Now what is your name, and where is your supervisor?"

The lady backed into her chair and said, "I suppose it won't hurt for a federal officer to visit Ms. Black. This way." She stood and led Manny down a well-lit hallway to a row of rooms, each with a patient number on the door but no name. "Wait here," she said and disappeared through the doorway. She emerged within moments and said, "Ms. Black does not want any visitors, but I told her it would be in her best interest to see you."

"Very good," Manny said and waited until the receptionist had started back down the hallway to her desk before entering the room.

Tantra sat at a small table, her legs curled underneath her. Gone was the precisely applied makeup accentuating her round eyes, makeup that would hide her high cheekbones of the Lakota. She glanced up at Manny through red-rimmed eyes and covered her face with one hand, the other holding a piece of charcoal. "Don't look at me. I'm a wreck. They won't let me have any makeup in this place."

"I'm not here to look at you *or* criticize you for what you did to land you in here."

She set her charcoal down on top of the drawing she had started and uncurled her legs. "I messed up," she said.

Manny didn't answer, letting Tantra tell what she would in her own good time. "If I just hadn't taken that first drink with Jimmy—"

"You were drinking with your brother?"

She hung her head and brushed hair out of her eyes. "He called me into Father's Great Room and sat with his legs propped up on the desk. 'Have a little celebration toast,' he said, and set a whisky sour on the desk for me. My go-to drink when I was on the sauce."

"'What's to celebrate?' says I, and he laughed long and hard at that. 'I'm celebrating because I have asked Mellis to apply for an emergency court date to grant me guardianship over you.' 'What the hell are you talking about?' I asked, and he said, 'Because you are an addict and cannot manage your own affairs. Especially now that we know you will have access to more money to feed your addiction.'"

"I haven't been on the sauce or taken any drugs for years," I told him.

"'Once an addict, always an addict,' he said. 'You could relapse at any time.' He laughed at that. 'But don't worry, little sister—I will ask Mellis to make sure you have a stipend every month. Enough to buy your paints and maybe just enough to go into town for a lunch now and again.'"

Tears formed in Tantra's eyes and she grabbed a Kleenex on the table. "Agent Tanno, I have to tell you, I got hot. *Real* hot. I demanded to know how he intended doing that with Father's will on file. He got his usual shit-eating smirk on his face and told me Mellis assured him anything is possible with the right judge."

She wiped her eyes again. "I'm not ashamed to say I got mad enough to kill him. I just walked behind that big mahogany desk where Father used to *work* and knocked Jimmy right out of the chair." Tears slowly cut tiny rivulets down her cheeks and she brushed them aside with the tissue. "But all he did was laugh as he picked himself up off the floor. 'See you in the poor house, little sister,' he said, and waltzed right out of the room, laughing all the way."

"Leaving you alone with the liquor cart?"

Tantra nodded. "Before I knew it, I was schnockered-up and I thought to hell with it—if I'm going to be tricked into losing most of my portion of the inheritance, I'm going to get me some good dope while I still have the money." She scooted her chair closer to Manny and he resisted the urge to drape his arm around her, to console her. Even sporting no makeup and wearing loose-fitting clothes, she was still a beautiful woman and he didn't trust himself. Especially with images of Clara at home popping into his mind. "I must have drunk way too much before leaving the house, though I don't remember. I scored a dime bag from an old... friend here in Hot Springs, and the next thing I remember, the law stopped me."

"I hear you put up quite a fight before you were corralled."

"Don't remember that either, but it's what the jailer told me when he transported me here. I should be grateful for Mellis Considine—he managed to call in some markers and get me sent here rather than the county jail."

"Hate to break this to you," Manny said, "but he did you no favors. By getting you committed here—and later for an indefinite period if he can get a judge to sign off on it—it will go a long way to show you are incapable of handling your own affairs."

Tantra groaned. "Then I'm screwed. I'll see no money from the estate." She held her head in her hands. "What can I do?"

"You can start by telling me about the map."

Tantra abruptly stopped her wailing and looked up at Manny.

"I don't understand."

"And neither did I for the longest time," Manny said, pausing, thinking of the best way to win his bluff. "There was dust inside Everett's safe—"

"Drywall dust," Tantra said. "Mary told me."

"But it wasn't drywall dust like I thought. It was pigments of a light tan color. Just like you grind to make your native paintings."

"That's just ridiculous."

"Is it?" Manny asked, upping his game. "The light pigment was mixed with a fine red colored dust that I thought at first was scoria dust. Picked up in many places on the rez. But it wasn't. Once again it was red pigment like the type you grind for your paintings."

Tantra stared into Manny's eyes so long he thought she'd not heard when she broke and blurted out, "I was in Father's safe, if that's what you want me to admit!"

Manny remained silent, waiting for her to explain. "That night of Father's accident, I had just heard him yelling that he had been robbed and caught a glimpse of him running out the door yelling, 'call 911!' I started down the stairs when I heard Mary on the phone calling the cops... though I'm not sure what she told the dispatcher. I could hardly call for help—you saw how that part of the rez has no cell service so I... took advantage of Mary being on the phone and Father running out the door like a crazy man to go into his office, thinking he probably had no chance to throw the door shut on his safe. I was right—the safe was standing wide open and it gave me the chance to look around in there."

"For the map?"

Tantra nodded. "But it was already gone." She looked at Manny again. "Plumb gone. Whoever my father chased after stole the map."

"Mary told me he never showed it to anyone. How did you even know about the map?"

"Because I painted it."

Chapter 28

Manny pulled alongside Willie in the back parking lot of the Sinclair station on Highway 79 and rolled down his window. "Where's *my* hoagie?"

Willie stopped long enough from devouring his Subway sandwich to answer, "I thought Clara had you cutting down on calories."

"That doesn't mean cutting *out*. Don't you beat all."

"I got a Moon Pie in the console if you want it."

"How long's it been there?" Manny asked.

Willie shrugged. "Since last summer is all."

"I'll pass."

Willie waved the air with the rest of his sandwich, his mouth full, unable to speak. "Just tell me what Tantra said when you interviewed her," he managed to get out.

Manny explained that she had admitted to painting the map they found on Hanson Becker's body. "Everett would bring the genuine map to her studio under wraps and tell her what to paint. He wouldn't let her see it, just told her what he wanted. He claimed he wanted a duplicate in case the original one Henry Black Heart painted was stolen or destroyed."

"Everett had her copy the map from the original?"

Manny opened the pack of rice cakes Clara had packed for him and eyed them suspiciously, hoping he had enough coffee left to wash them down. Debating between the rice cakes and

Willie's stale old Moon Pie. "She said Everett was unusually secretive about the painting sessions, meeting in Tantra's studio once or twice a month until he said the map was complete."

"He must have thought she was something special to entrust her with copying the map," Willie said.

"The old man told her she had genuine talent for modern techniques, though he encouraged her to paint only one native piece—the map. She figured it was because she was the only one Everett knew who painted traditionally like the Old Ones did. But, she never actually saw the map in its entirety."

"I don't understand."

"Everett never allowed her to look at the original map. He would stand off to one side while she painted, telling her what to put onto the parchment paper. She only glimpsed the actual map a couple times but could recall nothing except what her Father told her to paint."

"There has to be more to it than needing a copy if something happened to the original one."

A piece of rice cake stuck in Manny's throat and he quickly took a swig of coffee. "She suspected that the old man intended to sell the map she painted as genuine. She'd sneak into his office and check his computer, but he never put it on the market for sale."

"Or maybe he intended to sell it to Becker, not offering it in the open market," Willie said.

"She thought that, too. Becker came by the house the night of the accident. He got into an argument with the old man when he showed the art critic her map," Manny said. "At least from what she could hear through the vents. When Becker demanded the map that he'd already paid the old man for, Everett wanted more money. When Becker tried to insist, Everett lost it and put the run on him. She figures Becker came back later and stole the map."

"Then how does she explain that the map we found on Becker's body—the one that she painted—had the directions nearly opposite where they took Crazy Horse after his murder. Opposite of where he is supposed to be buried?"

"Because Tantra painted just what her father told her to paint. To this day, she doesn't know how accurate her map is to the original, as I did not show her the one Everett had hidden in plain sight in his reading room."

"You believe her when she told you she didn't take the map that night?" Willie asked.

Manny tossed the rest of the rice cake in the trash bag. "I sat right in front of her and asked her that very thing. There was not the slightest tic. Not the least little tell that indicated she was lying."

"You think she could have been in cahoots with Becker if he was the thief?" Willie said.

"That's possible," Manny answered, "but unlikely. I'm leaning on someone else who might have known it was in Everett's safe."

"That leaves us with the Kramers. They worked there enough that they might have known about it. And Jimmy and Mary 'cause they live in the house."

Manny ran his suspect list over in his mind. Everyone living in the ranch house was a suspect, as well as the Kramers for being in the house when Everett surely left the room for moments. But were there others—perhaps some ranch hand with good enough mechanical skills to slice the brake lines cleanly and who knew about Everett's map? The old man never covered up the fact that he possessed *the* map, often bragging about it as if it were just another status symbol.

"There's one other possibility," Willie said as he wiped mustard off his lips, "that Everett knew portions of *his* map were wrong, and he wanted Tantra to paint one reflecting what he thought was true."

"How would he know? There's nothing written down about the map or the directions it had in regards to where Crazy Horse was taken after his death. For damn near a century and a half, it's been unknown where he was buried."

Willie smiled. "We Lakota—indeed, all our Plains tribes—had their history passed down orally. Things told as we gathered around the smoke holes on cold winter nights in our teepees. It could be that Everett had just enough tradition in him that he listened to his father when he talked about Crazy Horse. Listened just enough to know the map Henry drew had some things wrong. If that's the case, we still don't know which map is authentic."

"Guess that's what makes it a mystery," Manny said.

*   *   *   *   *

As Manny walked into Mellis Considine's office, the receptionist looked up over her computer and smiled. Unlike the receptionist over at the rehab center who had looked as if she were annoyed that Manny had interrupted her reading.

This receptionist—tall, lithe like Clara, and in her early forties, he guessed—said something that Manny couldn't understand over the music piped into the office. "Can you turn the sound down a mite?" he asked.

The woman reached beside her desk and cut the volume to "Coward of the County." "Kenny Rogers is—was—my favorite singer. Since he died, I guess I can't get enough of him." She stood and smoothed her pleated grey skirt. "You must be Agent Tanno... Mellis is expecting you. First door on the right," she laughed. "It's the *only* door on your right, we being a one-attorney office."

Manny thanked her and rapped lightly on the only door past the receptionist.

"Come on in, agent," Mellis said, and Manny stepped into a neat—almost compulsively neat—office. Books on shelves were lined up by subject, then by dates, then by size. Four pens lay lined up in a row to Mellis' right, a legal pad to his left, and he motioned to a chair in the room sitting squarely in front of Mellis' desk. "You were... cryptic when you called for an appointment. What is it I can do for you?"

"Everett Black's estate—"

Mellis held up his hand. "You know I cannot discuss his will."

"I understand that. But you *can* talk about Everett's state of mind prior to his death." Manny leaned closer. "Surely you want to catch the man who staged that accident as much as I do?"

Mellis remained sitting upright as he nodded. "What would you like to know, Agent Tanno?"

Manny took out his notebook and his non-working pen and asked, "Did Everett and the Twins have some major fight just before he died that would cause him to change his will?"

"It was no new argument. Just the same one he and the Twins always had—get off your dead butts and make something of yourselves."

"So the new will would have left them with nothing?"

"No comment," Mellis said, "except to say the new will would meet Everett's wishes—that Jimmy and Tantra make their own way in the world or starve. He didn't much care which during the last few months of his life."

Manny flipped to another blank page, his pen poised above the paper as if he intended to write down what Mellis said. "The original will that you read last week leaves the Twins pretty well off."

"It does. Everett didn't have a chance to finalize the new will before his death. We had been working on that for months—"

"I get that," Manny said, "but what I don't get is Tantra being involuntarily committed to the rehab center in Hot Springs."

Mellis brushed a pen with his arm and set it back in line with the others on his desk. "It was either rehab or she face multiple state charges from drunk driving to assaulting a peace officer. I… pulled some strings with the judge and got her transferred."

Manny sat back and watched the colored strips attached to a wall vent, flapping as the air passed over them. "If Tantra is committed to this rehab facility for an extended length of time—"

"Then she may get the help she needs. She had a serious substance and alcohol abuse problem in her past, and that was the best place for her."

"I understand that, too. But if she is in rehab for that extended length and is unable to fight the guardianship order—"

"What order?"

"Come now, counselor, you know very well Jimmy hired you to see that he is awarded guardianship of his sister. Resulting in Tara receiving whatever monthly pittance Jimmy deems appropriate. He even admitted that to her."

A *tic*. Just an almost imperceptible *tic* at the corner of Mellis' eyelid told Manny he was lying when he said, "My intention is only to make sure she gets the help she needs."

"Giving Jimmy sole control of the estate. If the judge approves?"

"Nonsense!" Mellis burst out. He stood abruptly and said, "Get out of my office. I don't need to be accused of tipping the scales."

"Ok," Manny said, "but does that also include a sizable fee if you can persuade the judge to give Jimmy sole control?"

That telltale *tic* once again.

Mellis *would* earn a sizeable amount if Jimmy wrestled control of the estate from Tantra.

Chapter 29

"I wonder if Jimmy knows his sister painted the Becker map?" Willie asked.

"I doubt it," Manny said as he unbuckled his seat belt. "I would doubt even Mary knew about it by the way Tantra said Everett insisted on secrecy." He stared through the windshield of Willie's Expedition and pointed. "Is that Jimmy actually getting his hands dirty under that tractor?"

"Damned if it isn't." Willie stopped a few yards from the old Masse Ferguson, the gold colored engine and transmission housing chipped with only specks here and there to indicate it was ever painted.

Jimmy craned his neck from underneath the tractor and spotted Manny walking toward him. "I'd even welcome the feds here today." He pulled himself out from underneath and brushed snow off his trousers and jacket. "Can you just believe the old man—keeping damn near seventy-year-old machinery running when all he had to do was buy a new one."

"Is that what you're going to do after Everett's will is executed, buy all new equipment? After you get control of the estate?"

Jimmy snatched a shop rag from his back pocket and wiped his hands. "I hear an accusation in there somewhere. Maybe we ought to go inside and talk where it's not so cold and windy."

Jimmy led them up the steps and into the entryway. He took off his coat and motioned to a rubber mat beside the door. "The new Queen of the House insists we take off our boots now. We're on a ranch, for God's sakes, can you believe it? She says now that Hobart's gotten the drywall and painting done, she intends to keep the house looking nice. Slip yours off and I'll see if Queen Mary has coffee on."

"Can Willie use your telephone?" Manny asked, cell phone service lost five miles before reaching the ranch.

"Sure," Jimmy said. "Use the one in the old man's study. You know the way by now."

"When you talk to Shannon, tell him I don't want him leaving that apartment," Manny told Willie as he struggled to take off his boots. On the way to the Black Ranch, Manny had gotten a text from Shannon. *I found out something about that map*, it said. *Tell you when you get back to town.*

Willie started toward the study, while Manny sat on a hall tree that nearly touched the twelve-foot ceiling. When he slipped his boots off, he set them on the mat besides Willie's before following Jimmy down the hallway, both in stocking feet.

"I think that woman's trying to drive me out of the house," Jimmy said. "Hell, I know she's trying to drive me out—she didn't even start a pot of coffee before she left."

Manny suddenly realized Mary wasn't home. Every other time he'd been at the house she had been there, greeting him, usually tempting him with some goody or meal, and Manny was sorry she wasn't there. "She leave the ranch this afternoon?"

"For Rapid City. Said she had to get away from me and the house before she lost her mind. Like Tantra."

Manny took off his hat but didn't hang it on the coat rack. He figured this conversation wouldn't last long enough to get comfortable. "Let's talk about your sister. When I visited her in Hot Springs—"

"No one was supposed to have access to her!" Jimmy blurted out, his whisky breath seeming to fill the kitchen even at this early hour. "How the hell's she supposed to recover with you bothering her?"

"Just as important," Manny said, "is how she fell off the wagon in the first place."

"She got knee-walking drunk and scored some dope," Jimmy said. "What's to say?"

"I say you set her up. Made a nice whisky sour for her, knowing that was her preference back in her drinking days. And it pushed her over the edge when you said you intended tasking Mellis Considine with filing for guardianship."

"You make it sound as if I *wanted* my sister to fall off the wagon."

"Didn't you?" Manny said. "If she's deemed incapable of managing her own affairs, you could get Mellis to judge-shop, and get control of the estate. Might even kick Mary off the ranch."

Jimmy forced a laugh. "That old bat can stay right here. Even when… *if* I gain guardianship over my sister, Mary can stay in this rat trap, for all I care. I'll be building myself another place well away from here. Now if there's nothing else, I have a tractor to fix."

Manny donned his Stetson and faced Jimmy. "Where were you two days ago?"

"What?" Jimmy said. *Stalling.*

"You heard me."

"I was a lot of places. Where specifically?"

"On that road to Slim Butte. Someone shot at me and my brother as we were walking the grasslands."

"Did you see your shooter?"

"No," Manny said. "Just heard him drive away in a diesel truck."

"Lot of diesel trucks on the rez." Jimmy smirked. "Dad's new Ford is a diesel."

"That's my point."

Jimmy grabbed a tin of coffee and began dumping grounds into the dripolator, stalling once again while he thought of some answer Manny would buy. "I was right here working. You saw what condition the ranch machinery is in." He faced Manny. "When you have something linking me directly to your attack, feel free to come back." He turned on the burner to start the water boiling. "Now make sure the door is shut against this wind when you leave."

Manny was right—the conversation didn't take long. But then, he had completed his goal—Jimmy was on the defensive and wondering just what Manny had on him concerning Becker's murder, and the assault that day at Destiny's Door.

Willie and Manny walked outside and buttoned their coats against the driving wind. Snow pelted Willie's cheek as he began telling Manny about his phone call with Shannon when Manny motioned to Willie's Expedition. "Let's sit in there and get some heat on us," he told Willie.

When they were seated inside and Willie put the heater on high, Manny asked, "Now what did Shannon have to say?"

Willie stuffed Copenhagen into his lower lip and smiled as he handed Manny the can. He grabbed for it when Willie said, "Not on your life. You'll just toss it out."

"I would and do you a favor. But what did my trainee say."

"NOTCH," Willie said. "That name on the map that we thought might be the name of a member of the party who took Crazy Horse's body away that night after he was killed. Shannon searched the tribal archives back to when they were first recorded—"

"How did he get to the tribal office—limp all the way?"

"He said some nice feller who was visiting Herb Standing Dog saw Shannon hobbling away from the apartment and gave him a ride in his old Plymouth. A *real* nice feller, he said. Some guy with a thick *Okie* twang."

"Not Philbilly?"

"The same." Willie spit tobacco juice out the window and started down the long drive toward the tribal road. "Phil claimed he just came from the hospital where his girlfriend was scheduled to have that triple mastectomy." Willie held up his hands. "Philbilly's claim, not mine. I'm still trying to figure that one out."

"At least Shannon didn't have far to ride to the tribal office."

"He wasn't so lucky. Philbilly hung around to give Shannon a ride back after he was done with his research. On the way back to the government apartment, Shannon mentioned NOTCH might be the name of a cavalry trooper during Crazy Horse's time, and off they went on another road trip—this time to Crawford, Nebraska. Shannon researched old Army records but could not find any trooper named Notch."

"So it was a wasted trip for The Animal?"

"Not wasted at all," Willie answered. "He got the pleasure of spending hours with someone as *mentally* clumsy as he is *physically* clumsy."

* * * * *

Manny unfurled the sheet and Reuben helped him put it on the bed in his spare room. "I don't blame you one bit," Reuben said as he performed a hospital tuck in one corner of the sheet. "I wouldn't trust anyone to sleep in the same apartment with me either—you being the exception. I don't figure you're going to injun-up and slit my throat."

"I don't figure Shannon would, either," Manny said. "It's just that the man snores so loud, it sounds like Crazy George's horse baying at a full moon."

They finished making the bed and went outside to Reuben's new screened-in porch where he had the barbecue grill going.

He put on a heavy coat and tucked his braids under a thick stocking cap while he took the lid off the meat pan.

The man would grill in any weather... even on a day as cold and blustery as this. "I'll need to go out to Destiny's Door again," Manny said while he wrapped an itchy, green Army blanket around him. "At least the area we figure is Destiny's Door."

The steaks sizzled when Reuben plopped them onto the grate and he stepped back away from the smoke. "You need to go there to do what—help you figure out who killed Everett?"

Manny nodded.

"And not to help you figure out who Manny Tanno—the Lakota—is?"

"Don't start with that again," though he knew there was some validity in Reuben's argument as he always tried to steer Manny towards his Oglala roots. Perhaps through Destiny's Door he would find himself. Just like Reuben hoped.

"Still like your meat rare?" Reuben asked.

"I do. You still like yours charred?"

"I do."

"Well, we *Lakota* like ours very rare," Manny taunted Reuben, "like our ancestors preferred their meat, being hunters and all."

Reuben smiled and reached for two ears of corn to lay onto the grill. "I've had my feelers out around the rez for the Kramers like you asked but not one sighting of them."

"They're not from the reservation," Manny said. "They could have fled anyplace."

"But they've lived here so long, this is their home." Reuben took up a large fork and speared Manny's steak. "And folks hereabouts always come home." He set the plate in front of Manny. "Just like you did."

Reuben left his steak on the grill for a few more minutes before taking it and the corn off and sitting across from Manny. Wind whipped through the screens, sending flakes of snow onto them and their table, but Reuben paid it no mind. "You sure you want to go back to that area?" he asked as he smeared butter onto corn. "Last time we went there I got a… bad—no, *intense*—feeling that our ancestors were warning us away from that place."

"I felt it, too." Manny turned his back to the wind. "That's why I still think the answer to Everett's murder is there. And Becker's as well."

"I've been pondering that as I take in this fresh air." Reuben waved his hand around the porch. "I am certain that fat-ass Becker didn't hike to where you found him. I've seen enough shot men to know there ought to have been blood. But Hans lying there just looked kind of peaceable. In a fat-assed kind of way."

"That was my thought as well," Manny said. He reached for the saltshaker, but the thought of Clara scolding him for using it and possibly upping his blood pressure, and he left the shaker alone.

Reuben, however, had no such qualms as he shook and shook and shook salt onto his corn and steak. But then, few things bothered Reuben. "That's why I'm thinking it was the Kramers. It'd take a couple strong men to haul Becker across the prairie like that."

"Or one very strong man," Manny said. "You could have carried Becker."

"I could have," Reuben said.

"And Hobart Comes Flying could have—he is nearly as big as you. He could have carried Becker down that slope. All for what he thought was a genuine map."

"I pondered that as well," Reuben said, waving the air with a piece of steak on the end of his fork. "When you're alone you *ponder* a lot. Even though your vision told you the map Everett kept between old magazines is the authentic one, the map you found on Becker *could* be. You going to eat the rest of your French bread?"

Manny shook his head, and Reuben snatched it from Manny's plate. "We just don't know which one is real for certain, even though I still think it's the Everett map. But what it looked like to me was that someone got spooked the closer they got to the Door, and just left Becker's body there and fled. I told you how it affected me and Willie as we got closer, just like when you and I went there."

"The ancient ones warning us," Reuben said, slicing into his T-bone.

Manny gnawed a row of corn off the cob and said, "Maybe it's just the power of suggestion. We figured we would feel something spiritual if that spot is actually Destiny's Door."

"Then why do you keep referring to that place as Destiny's Door?"

"Until we find another place we know that the map referred to," Manny said, "that's as good a reference as any."

Reuben put his fork down and looked across the table at Manny. "When you go again, *misun,* I will go with you. As powerful as the feelings I got in that short time the other day, you'll need a sacred man to get through it."

"I just hope that sacred man doesn't snore like Shannon does."

Reuben put his hand over his heart. "Not me—I sleep like a baby. You know that."

"I know," Manny answered, washing his meat down with hot tea. "And what do you and babies do every hour? They wake up and make a fuss. I just hope you don't tonight—I have an early meeting at the Justice Building tomorrow."

Chapter 30

Lumpy opened the door and yelled down the hallway, "Did anyone see that big trainee of Hot Shot's?" When no one answered, he shut the door and waddled back to his chair. He eased himself into it, his outpatient surgery to repair minor stomach tears not even a day old. "We're going to have to start without him." He held his stomach gently and glared at Manny. "Every damn time I get the FBI involved, I have trouble."

"Not my fault he's late," Manny said, checking his watch. *Thirty-five minutes late. A new record for Shannon.* "Guess he just won't earn a happy face for today. Let's start and I'll fill him in later."

"Willie," Lumpy said.

Willie grabbed a white board leaning against the wall and turned it so the rest could read it. In one column was a list of suspects, in the other column numeric numbers assigned to each name. "Shannon explained it last night, so I think I know what he was trying to accomplish here."

Lumpy leaned over ever so slightly and examined the board before turning to Manny and saying, "Is this crap what your trainees are taught at the Academy?"

"It's some new system," Manny answered. "Supposed to help one filter out non-suspects and help us concentrate on those that are more likely. Came from the profilers."

"It all looks like a bunch of gibberish to me." Lumpy nudged

Pee Pee as he picked at his teeth with a pocketknife. "It's nonsensical to you, too, isn't it?"

Pee Pee slipped his teeth back in and blew air out to seat them. "Actually, it's an old system developed by a Frenchman named Model and a German by the name of Rodgilier. It uses comparative logic against a set of knowns, then weaves in variables that the analyst deems appropriate—"

"Okay," Lumpy said. "Okay. I get it's some advanced shit. But what does it mean?"

Willie pointed to Tantra's name and said, "She has a low rating on the suspect list, but not because she's currently in rehab. She could have tinkered with Everett's truck anytime it sat at the house, and she knew Hansson Becker so she could have killed him. But she couldn't have carried him into the prairie. Also—if one can believe her—she heard Everett running out the door after the thief."

"What's this rating to the right of the first one?" Manny asked.

"Tantra's rating *after* all variables are factored in. She could have been in cahoots with someone—namely the Kramers—in rigging Everett's brake lines. And she could be in cahoots with them trying to find the map Becker had on him. *If* she knew it was Becker that Everett chased out of the house that night."

"Makes sense," Lumpy admitted. "And it looks like Mary Comes Flying also has relatively the same rating, if one believes the way The Animal's mind operates."

Willie tapped Mary's name and explained. "She knew all the players probably better than anyone. She could have thrown in with the Kramers, just like Tantra could have, and she knew Becker as well. Shannon thinks that if Mary tipped off Becker that Everett often left his safe open while he meandered about the house, Becker could have gotten the map that night."

"Now that *doesn't* make sense," Lumpy said, holding his stomach. "How could Mary haul Hanson Becker out to the grasslands?"

"Again," Willie pointed to an assigned number nearly as high as that Shannon had assigned to Tantra, "she could have been in partnership with the Kramers who could have hauled Becker out to the prairie. Or Hobart. He would do whatever his mother asked, especially since he wanted to get possession of the Crazy Horse map before anyone else could."

"Let's talk about Hobart." Manny stood. He couldn't take any more of Pee Pee picking his dentures, so he walked around the conference room, stretching his calves, tight from his latest hike to Destiny's Door. *Perhaps Clara is right—I need to start exercising again.* "Hobart would have done most anything to ensure the Crazy Horse map never reached the public. After seeing his temper flare that day that Shannon and I spoke with him at the ice cream shop, my best guess is that he'd kill to get possession of it."

"You mentioned yesterday that Hobart had asked Everett for a donation for some heritage center he was trying to get off the ground," Lumpy said, and snapped his fingers. "Grab me a cup of coffee, Pee Pee."

"Do I look like your servant?"

"I'm hurting just a little here. Didn't see you helping me pick up Shannon."

"I'd have been smarter," Pee Pee said as he reached for the coffee pot. "I'd have called a wrecker."

Lumpy said to Manny, "Hobart's charity he wanted money for?"

Manny nodded. "He's been trying to get his Indian Heritage Center up and running for a few years now. He's having a hard time picking up donations."

"But," Lumpy said, rubbing his stomach, "if he sold the map, he would have more than enough money to finance his project."

"Would he trade possession of the Crazy Horse map for

funding for his heritage center?" Willie asked. "That would be a toss-up in my thinking. He *is* all about tradition, which is why Shannon bumped Hobart's number up when he factored everything in."

"Pass me that box of donuts," Lumpy said to Manny. "Hard for me to stand, and I need my strength."

Manny slid the box of yesterday's donuts toward Lumpy, who picked out a filled Long John and said, "I see Jimmy's suspect number is low. He had access to everyone and everything, just like his sister did."

"Here's Shannon's reasoning," Willie began. "Jimmy barely knew Hanson Becker, if at all. Mary said Jimmy had been in a perpetual stupor the last couple years and only left the ranch to go into Hot Springs to buy his booze. She wasn't even certain Jimmy would recognize Becker or the Kramers when they were at the house, drunk as Jimmy gets."

Manny stopped his pacing in front of the board and studied it, "Jimmy ought to be higher, what with him and Mellis Considine scheming to get Tantra cheated out of her inheritance."

"Shannon didn't know that information when he drew this chart up yesterday." Willie leaned the white board back against the wall. "But I still think it all ties back to that map. Which map is still the question."

Pee Pee poured a cup of the sludge that Lumpy had made that morning and said, "Just for shits and giggles, I got on Ebay this morning and typed in Crazy Horse map. I found thirty-four maps from folks who claimed they have the original one. But one was a little different—it's parchment in two pieces and it's missing one corner." He turned to Lumpy "Can I put in a bid on it with the tribal Visa card?"

"Of course not."

"Then maybe I can use your personal card."

Lumpy laughed a moment before he winced in pain and held

his stomach again. "What do you take me for—a fool?"

"But how about if it is *the* map? Just think what profit you could make."

The smile left Lumpy's face as he thought for a moment. "All right, but try not to go too high," he said, and handed Pee Pee his Visa card.

"Keep it," Pee Pee said. "I just wanted to show how even informed people could fall for such a scam."

"Guess he did take you for a fool," Manny said.

Lumpy began cursing Pee Pee when the conference room phone rang. Willie answered it and his face blanched. Like it always did when he was about to meet another dead person. "Man in the FBI apartment is dead. Big man."

"Shannon," Manny breathed.

* * * * *

By the time Manny and Willie and Lumpy arrived with lights and sirens at the FBI apartment, a crowd had gathered around the open door. Herb Standing Dog saw Manny climb from Willie's Expedition and ran over to Manny while Willie walked past him and elbowed his way through the crowd. "Agent Tanno, I am sorry I did not pay them no mind," he blurted out, taking in gulps of air as he looked wild-eyed over his shoulder at the open apartment door. "I was kicking back watching a re-run of the *Price is Right*... I just love Bob Barker. He is from Rosebud Reservation, you know—"

"Damn it, Herb," Lumpy said, "tell us about that dead man in there."

"Him. Sure. Him," Herb said, stalling the telling of something unpleasant he had just seen. "I was watching the show just as the women from Chicago won the washer-dryer set when one of the little Woods boys came waltzing right into my apartment like he often does. 'Dead man couple doors down,' says he."

"What?" says I.

"The kid snatches a banana right off my counter and plops down on the couch beside me. Starts peeling the banana, eyeing the television. 'What dead man are you talking about?' I asked him.

"'That big feller in that there FBI apartment. I think he's dead 'cause he ain't moving.'"

Herb grabbed Manny's forearm and squeezed it uncommonly hard. "I did not believe the little fart... he is prone to lying. So I put the run on him and told him to skedaddle. Damn if he did not come back twenty minutes later just as the woman with that same washer and dryer went into the grand finale, and the kid says, 'I been looking through the door. He still ain't moved any, Herb. And there's blood on the floor.'"

"And that's when you called 911?" Lumpy said.

"No," Herb said. "Not right then. I waited to see if the old bat won the car before I got off the couch and wandered over to the apartment. The kid was right—the feller *was* dead, from what I could see. And *that* is when I called the police."

"I'm afraid to ask," Manny said, "if you saw anyone enter or leave the apartment?"

"No," Herb said, "I did not. I get into this... special place I call the *Price is Right* Zone where I concentrate on the show. I just love watching that Bob Barker."

"Alright, Herb," Lumpy said. "Go back to your apartment. We'll be by later to get a written statement."

Lumpy said to Manny, "See what Willie has while I start asking if there were any witnesses," and walked towards the crowd.

Manny parted the lookie-loos and squatted down beside Willie looking at Shannon's body lying face up in the room, his eyes transfixed in that stare reserved only for the dead, "What do you think?"

"I don't think he'll be hobbling off any football field again," Willie answered. "Besides that, it appears as if Shannon was stabbed. Lot of blood, and by the looks of the apartment, he put up one hell of a fight."

"You do have a way of understating things," Manny said as he stood and leaned inside the doorway. Shannon The Animal Henderson lay atop what had been the small kitchen table in the apartment, broken pieces strewn across the floor beside a chair that had splintered. The door on the apartment's half-refrigerator stood ajar at an odd angle, broken when it crashed to the floor, and the small television set that had once rested on the dresser now lay smashed beside it, broken pieces mingling with Shannon's coagulated blood. "Without examining him closer, why do you think Shannon was stabbed and not shot?"

Since Manny and Willie had started working reservation cases together, Manny did his best to mentor the big Santee Sioux, and Willie was developing into an astute investigator. He stood and rubbed the back of his legs. "I remember you telling me how knife wounds are three times more lethal—statistically—than gun shots."

"They are."

"But that it takes longer, generally, for the victim to succumb to their wounds. I figure Shannon put up a fight while inside he was bleeding out. Musta been some powerful feller to best Shannon like that."

"Do you think it had anything to do with our killer hitting Shannon on the head first, perhaps disorienting him long enough to knife him to death?"

"Hit with what?" Willie asked. He squatted again, looking at the scene.

"Something that matches that round indent on his temple."

Willie pointed to Shannon's head. "I figured he got that when he fell. Probably postmortem."

"Not the way I figure it." Manny looked around the apartment but could not see anything that would make such a mark. "Way I see it is just like I said—the killer hit Shannon, giving him time to lay into the big guy with a blade."

"Then someone must have heard something."

Willie looked around at the crowd nudging one another, vying for a spot to gawk into the apartment. "It's winter. These people were all warm inside their apartments, doors and windows shut, I can almost guarantee. Maybe like Herb—watching their favorite television show with the volume cranked up. Which is another reason I figure Shannon was stabbed and not shot—even with their TVs turned up, these people would have heard a gunshot."

Willie slowly faced Manny. "Weren't you going to stay here overnight last night?"

"I was going to, until Shannon got hurt and I let him stay—"

"Manny," Willie's face blanched. "Shannon wasn't the intended victim. It was *you.*"

"That's just what I was thinking," Manny said, and grabbed his phone to call the coroner, and Pee Pee Pourier.

Chapter 31

After Pee Pee photographed Shannon and the crime scene from every angle, and swabbed debris he thought the assailant might have touched, he leaned against the doorjamb and eyed the coroner's van backing up to the apartment. "I've developed some back problems lately—"

"You're not getting out of this!" Willie told Pee Pee. "You're going to grab onto a part of Shannon like the rest of us when the coroner's ready with the body bag."

"Look at it this way," Manny said, taking off his coat and draping it over the one chair in the apartment that was still intact, "the rest of us are going to have back problems after lifting him onto the gurney, too. Except Lumpy, who about killed himself the last time he tried hoisting Shannon up."

The coroner wheeled his gurney into the apartment and stopped. And stared. "That's the victim?" he gasped.

"George," Willie said, "do you see anyone else leaking blood on the floor with his eyes glazed over. And no, a forklift won't fit through the door. Now put the cart down and grab onto him."

George collapsed the gurney and unzipped the black bag already atop the cart. Each man grabbed an arm or a leg and the grunting began. By the time they had Shannon loaded and zipped into the bag, they were winded and had to pause a moment before raising the cart.

"Wait a minute, George," Manny asked and walked around to

the far side of the body. He unzipped the bag and bent within inches of Shannon's head. "I just realized what that mark might be. Look here," he said to Willie.

Willie squatted and watched as Manny parted Shannon's hair that was matted with blood and dried sweat from the fight. "Now what do you see?"

"Jesa!" Willie said. "Like you figured—something round. Like a hammer, maybe?"

"More specifically, a drywaller's hammer, if I'm reading that checkerboard pattern across the indentation correctly."

Manny stood and zipped the bag up once more before helping George wheel the gurney into the coroner's van. "Send me the photos and what you have," George managed to say right before he left with the body.

"I hope he catches his breath before he arrives at the medical examiner's in Rapid," Willie said.

"I hope we all do," Pee Pee said, arching his back, his hands massaging his lumbar region.

Manny felt that way as well. But—unlike The Animal—he was grateful that he could still feel pain. He shut the door against the onlookers and stood in the middle of the floor.

"By the looks of the castoff from the hammer—if it was a hammer to his head," Willie said, "the blow had to have happened there." He pointed to the far side of the small apartment. "But for what reason?" Willie asked.

Manny looked up at the ceiling tiles dangling where they had been ripped away. He moved the only chair untouched in the room and stood on it under where he had stashed the Becker map. Even before he felt under the ceiling tiles, he knew the map was gone. "Damn," he said. "Some fool got the map," grateful the Everett map was safely stashed at Reuben's house. "After the first time someone—likely Shannon's killer—trashed the apartment and didn't find the map, he must have thought he should have checked the false ceiling. Figured this time he'd find the map under the ceiling tiles as he had checked most everywhere else."

Manny walked around the small apartment, getting down on his knees now and again to examine something on the floor that had gotten broken or knocked off the table during the fight, careful not to kneel in glass or in the blood that had soaked into the carpeting. "Bag those two empty cans of Coke," he told Pee Pee. "With any luck the lab can get DNA off them."

"And the others?" Pee Pee asked of the half-dozen other cans on the floor, some full, some having been crushed in the fight, sticky cola mixing with the blood.

"Only DNA on those you'll find is mine when I stocked the fridge last week." Manny stood and leaned back against a wall. He closed his eyes, picturing himself in Shannon's shoes, as he often did with other victims, visualizing how the killing occurred. "Did Shannon know his killer?" Manny asked aloud and opened his eyes, looking to where the table once sat. "Two sodas opened as if he were offering one to a friend."

"From the few times I talked with Shannon, he was friendly enough," Pee Pee said. "He would have offered most anyone a soda if they came over to visit."

"What friends?" Willie asked. "Shannon didn't know anyone here on the rez except those he talked with about Everett and Hanson Becker's cases, and us, and we weren't here. Unless… he went to the tribal office several times for research. Perhaps he developed a friendship there."

Manny shrugged. "Could be most anyone who knew the The Animal was affable." Manny closed his eyes again for a moment before opening them. "Shannon would invite him—or her—in and, when his guard was down, *bam!* Swing the hammer to the side of his head because Shannon was too tall for the killer to hit the top of his head. The blow might have knocked him to his knees. At least stunned him long enough to slide the shiv into his ribs."

"Only Shannon was tougher than our killer thought," Willie said, pacing the apartment, stepping over broken glass and the splintered table, and the blood that had pooled on the floor. "We know by the looks of the place that he fought hard. The hammer... Shannon would have tried knocking it away as the killer swung it. It probably flew..."

Willie slowly walked around the apartment before he stopped at a faint indent in the wall. He ran his hand over it and picked up a single hair. "Here's where the hammer landed when Shannon surely knocked it aside. But where's the hammer..."

"The killer took it with him," Manny said. "Whoever it is, he wants to make certain we can't connect him to the murder."

Willie snapped his fingers. "It *has* to be one of the Kramers. Neither is tall enough to reach the top of Shannon's head with a hammer. A *drywall* hammer. Just like they use at their jobs... crap. That leaves them out."

"How so?"

"They left their tools at the Black's ranch house."

"Whoa," Manny said. "Just because they left their tools there doesn't mean they don't own others. And it doesn't mean someone else doesn't have the same type of hammer." He turned to Pee Pee. "How many contractors on the rez do drywall?"

Pee Pee massaged his lips where his ill-fitting dentures rode sore in his mouth and said, "Half a dozen. Another half-dozen come in from Rapid City. Three or four from Chadron work jobs here on the rez now and again."

Willie groaned. "Then the chance of finding out who the hell killed Shannon is slim, given that no one saw anyone come or go out of the apartment."

"Willie," Manny said, "has there ever been a case where things went easy for us?"

*   *   *   *   *

220

That afternoon in the conference room, Pee Pee projected on the large screen his crime scene photos for Lumpy and Manny and Willie to examine. "Hot Shot," Lumpy said, "this is another *luncher*. This croaker's going to eat your lunch like Everett's and Becker's deaths are going to eat your lunch. You ain't never gonna solve it." He tapped the screen with a glazed-donut-laden finger. "There's almost too much evidence with Shannon's murder, and somehow, not enough evidence at the same time. You have Shannon getting whacked on the head. Then knifed... how many times did the ME say?" He looked at the autopsy report. "Four deep punctures, any that could have been fatal eventually, with one severing the aorta the most probable one. But you have found nothing that the killer left that could identify him. About DNA—"

"It'll be more than a week before we find out if there's any DNA from anything Pee Pee seized from the apartment—"

"You're putting all your marbles into that one pot you call two Coke cans," Lumpy said, "like you really believe Shannon just invited someone into the apartment. And when he did, offered them a little refreshment? Now you're clutching at straws."

"We have nothing else to go on right now." Manny felt a rising headache, surely a product of talking with Lumpy.

"We're still looking for the Kramers. They were at the top of... Shannon's suspect list," Willie said, lowering his voice as if in respect for the dead. "But like Manny pointed out, if Shannon was first disabled with a drywall hammer to his head, such a hammer could be owned by anyone. Not only a professional drywaller but a handyman or a homeowner as well."

Lumpy stood slowly using the side of the chair while he held his stomach. "Then you better start knocking on every door on the rez 'cause tomorrow's Saturday. With the National Weather Service predicting a cold snap and more snow, a lot of businesses will be closed. Folks picking up firewood. Filling gas cans. Buying extra food in case the roads are drifted over."

Lumpy was right. With only a couple of state roads from Rapid City and Chadron open to bring goods and services to the reservation, road closures were a definite possibility. But Manny would leave Willie to do the knocking. Tomorrow, he and a sacred man had a date with Destiny's Door before the heavy snow arrived.

Chapter 32

Manny put on an extra pair of gloves before slinging his duty rifle over his shoulder and locking the rental truck. He saw Reuben on the other side of the truck eyeing him. "What? After that last time we were shot at, I'm damn sure not taking any chances."

"It's not that," Reuben answered. "But shouldn't I be the one carting that M-16 around? After all, only fifty-percent of us here who could actually hit what they're aiming at."

"That's all I need—the Senior Agent finding out I handed a rifle over to a convicted felon. And a fully-automatic rifle to boot. No, I'll hang on to it. Besides, you're going to be too busy telling us where to go to tote a rifle around the prairie."

Reuben looked skyward and opened the viewing pane on the compass. "Then we better get a move on before that storm hits."

They hiked a quarter mile when Manny stopped abruptly. His legs trembled and his breath came in shallow gasps. "We're near Destiny's Door," he said, and bent over to catch his breath. "I think... now is a... really good time to put that sage and sweetgrass to use."

"I think you're right," Reuben said.

He set his daypack on the ground and grabbed his stalk of sage, lighting it with a Zippo engraved with *1ˢᵗ Marine Division non-traditional*. When the sage caught, he began offering prayers to the four directions, then to the sky and finally to Mother Earth.

Reuben held out his hand and Manny put the beaded lizard in his palm. "That's because this doesn't belong with this woman in the grave," he said, squinting as he examined it. "This is modern beadwork, and it dropped off someone." He handed it back to Manny. "I'd bag that as evidence were I you—it most likely came from whoever opened this grave."

"And whoever opened this grave must have seen Everett's map at one point."

"Be my guess," Reuben said as he scooped dirt back into the hole. "I have just enough time before that snow hits to pray over this woman."

Manny stood and held his hands in front of him as he heard Reuben's lamentations carried high and far with the wind. And deep down inside, Manny knew this was as important as any Christian ritual he had participated in as a youth in the Catholic Church. When Reuben finished, his sage was all but burned down and he put his hat back on. As soon as they returned to Pine Ridge Village, Manny would notify the tribe of the location of the grave and leave it to the discretion of the elders as to whether they wished to move the woman's remains or leave them in place.

Manny took a Ziploc out of his backpack and started to put the beaded lizard inside when he stopped and looked at it closer while he blew more dirt off of it. He had seen such beadwork recently—a lizard earring dangling when he was sitting in the ice cream shop watching Shannon writhe on the floor after he fell. An earring dangling from Hobart's ear lobe.

Chapter 33

Crazy Horse's father, *Waglula*, mourns the murder of his son. Yet there are preparations to be made. Things that need to be accomplished so that the burial place of *Tashunke Witko* will never be found, his grave site never desecrated by souvenir seekers or soldiers bent on defaming the holy man of the Oglala.

Six Indian policemen have followed them since Crazy Horse's body was loaded into the wagon. They will follow—Waglula is certain—and tell others where his son is buried. They will have to be diverted. But not tonight.

Tonight is for grieving.

*   *   *   *   *

Two wagons—one containing Crazy Horse's body, the other a decoy meant to fool the enemies of the sacred man—pull into the camp of Touch The Clouds. While the others remain outside, Waglula goes into his lodge alone where he will mourn the death of his son throughout the night.

When the sun just rises over Mother Earth, Waglula along with others—Touch The Clouds, Standing Elk, Hump Two, the

229

young Black Heart—mount one wagon and head toward the Good River that the *wasicu* call the Cheyenne River, while Black Fox takes his wagon east.

The wagon carrying Crazy Horse follows the bank of the Good River for some miles before meeting with another follower in the trees along the bank. He leads Inyan, Crazy Horse's favorite pony. He lashes the body onto a travois and leads the horse away.

For hours the group led by Waglula trek across the prairie, always looking back for the Indian police. Finding none. Finding that the followers of American Horse and Red Cloud have been deceived.

Except for a lone woman. Waglula has only caught a fleeting glimpse of her before she again melts into the landscape. That she has bad intentions toward his son's body is a certainty, whether to gather belongings that he carried in life and that will be buried with him, or to defile his grave site. If she continues, she will know just where his son is buried, something that cannot be. Something no one can know.

Waglula motions to Black Heart, and he whispers a request to him. Color leaves the young warrior's face and he trembles. But he agrees to do what Waglula has asked.

Black Heart rides off, slipping his war club from his belt as he nears where the woman was last seen sneaking about. And where she'll soon be buried.

Chapter 34

"How could Tantra just walk away from rehab?" Willie asked as he stuffed his can of Copenhagen back into his pocket. "I thought the whole objective of drug and alcohol treatment was to keep someone there until they could get a handle on their addiction."

"Hot Springs is a rehab center," Manny said, "not a detention center. Tantra walked out because she got into a fight with one of the counselors in group therapy. Kind of like when you went to Tobacco Anonymous meetings and couldn't stay off the snuff for even the second session."

"That was different. This," Willie tapped his back pocket, "is legal. But if it's not illegal to escape from rehab, we can't even put out a BOLO on Tantra," Willie said as he turned onto the Black Ranch driveway.

"What would we do if we found her?" Manny asked. "We can't force her to return. We might *suggest* she go back for her own good, but that's about all. And the Fall River County prosecutor already deferred her case, so it's not like they can pick her up."

"Then at least I hope we find Hobart to make this little trip worthwhile."

"Only if you can play back the messages on Mary's answering machine," Manny said. He didn't expect to find Hobart at the ranch, and he didn't expect Mary to give honest answers as to her son's whereabouts—Manny would expect nothing less of a loving mother. But while Manny was searching the barn and other outbuildings as he kept Mary busy looking for her son, Willie would be pulling up messages on her answering machine. They both hoped they'd find one that'd give them an indication where Hobart was, because he sure wasn't at his Rapid City apartment.

They pulled through the yard just as a ranch hand stopped his truck and flatbed loaded with hay bales beside the corral and jumped out. He pulled up the collar of his parka and looked at Manny as if expecting him to help. Manny had worked as a ranch hand up by Interior as a kid for one summer that convinced him he'd rather be shot at now and again than spend every single working day living the hard life of a rancher.

As Willie pulled up in front of the porch, Manny noted Hobart's truck wasn't there, and neither was Everett's new Ford diesel. The Tahoe sat where it usually did awaiting Tantra, who now had no driver's license, and an old Chevy Cavalier Manny presumed was Mary's was parked next to the Tahoe.

As before, Mary met them at the front door and motioned them inside. Manny shook snow off his hat before entering and started slipping off his boots when Mary stopped him. "Leave them on."

"But Jimmy said you instituted a new rule—"

"Never mind that blowhard," Mary said. "I just told him to take *his* boots off from now on just to make him mad. Come, I have hot coffee on—"

"You won't want to give us coffee once you find out what we're here for."

"Oh?"

"We're looking for Hobart," Manny said.

"What on earth for?"

Manny explained that he and Reuben had followed directions on Everett's Crazy Horse map and found an ancient grave. One recently robbed of jewelry and other things the deceased woman had worn in life.

"Does that require the FBI *and* the tribal police to investigate?" she asked as she dried her hands on her apron.

"We think, Grandmother," Willie said, using the term of respect for elders, "that Hobart might know something about the ambush of Manny and his brother the other day as well."

"It couldn't be Hobart—he has been teaching school—"

"The high school said he took a leave of absence for a few weeks. A substitute teacher is covering for him."

Mary sat down on the hall tree, wringing her hands. "He is not here, if that is why you came."

"I believe you," Manny said. "But if I go back to Rapid City and tell my Senior Agent I didn't ask to search the house and outbuildings for Hobart, I'd be the one getting a couple weeks off."

"So you want to search the house for him?"

"And outbuildings," Manny said, "while you accompany us."

Mary shrugged. "Suit yourself. Might as well start upstairs."

She led the way up the stairs, creaking under even her slight weight, stairs that were laid when Henry Black Heart first built the ranch house. They began in the back hallway at Tantra's studio and Mary said, "Rehab called wondering if Tantra was here. That girl is a fool. She should have stayed in Hot Springs and gotten herself clean. Now by running away before she's completed the program, it gives Jimmy more ammunition to have her deemed incompetent."

"Where is Jimmy?" Willie asked, poking his head inside Tantra's workout gym adjacent to her studio. "Last we saw him he was wrenching underneath a tractor."

Mary laughed. "And that will probably be the last time you will see him work. No, Jimmy went into Rapid City. The hearing on guardianship is tomorrow morning and he is meeting with Mellis to prepare for it."

"Kind of soon, isn't it?"

"Jimmy managed to find a judge that granted an emergency hearing. That conniving... man claimed if he isn't awarded her guardianship immediately, she would harm herself. Her escape from the rehab center only helps his case."

They completed looking in the upstairs rooms, and had just finished the downstairs when Manny said, "We'd like to look in the barn and the buildings outback. The bunkhouse, too."

Mary grabbed her coat from the hall tree and began zipping it when Willie said, "Can I use your bathroom?" He held his stomach. "I musta ate something that doesn't agree with me."

"Of course," Mary said. "Go on down the hallway. Use the bathroom next to Jimmy's room. Feel free to stink it up all you want."

"When you finish," Manny told Willie, "find us. We'll be looking in the barn and bunkhouse."

"Sure," Willie said, and headed off down the hall like distress was overtaking him.

When Mary stepped outside she faced Manny and said, "I'm telling you, Hobart is not here," she said. "But I understand that you have to verify it." She forced a laugh. "After all, if he were here, I would do whatever I could to hide him from you. But you know that already."

"I would expect nothing less," Manny said.

They started with the barn where two ranch hands curried horses, another dispensed alfalfa to stalls, while another patched a torn leather bridle with thick sinew. "These are the studs that keep the Black Ranch name at the top of the list of registered horses people want." She shook her head. "And that Jimmy will soon run it into the ground when he takes control of the entire ranch."

"Maybe he will see the light—"

"All he will see is the almighty dollar. Once him and Mellis

Considine get finished carving up Everett's wishes, he will have control of his and Tantra's share of the inheritance. He can't sell the ranch, but Mellis says there's nothing to prevent Jimmy from leasing it out."

After they walked through the barn, they headed for the bunkhouse. No one was inside at this time of day. Twelve bunks sat in a row at one end, a heat stove beside a long table at the other with a pot of coffee on top. There was always a pot of coffee waiting for hands in from the field to warm themselves. "I fix breakfast and lunch for the crew," Mary said. "Up to them to make their own supper. And," she waved her hand around, "as you can see, Hobart's not here."

"I see that," Manny said, but he had not expected him to be hiding here. All he wanted was to stall until Willie listened to the messages on the house answering machine.

They walked out of the bunkhouse just as Willie walked towards them. "I'm done."

"Are you feeling better?" Mary asked.

"A little," Willie lied.

"Perhaps we'd better head for town," Manny said. "Stop at Big Bat's and buy you some Pepto-Bismol."

"Don't you want to check the shop and the chicken coop?" Mary said, a wry smile crossing her face. "Hobart *could* be hiding in there."

"I think we've checked enough to satisfy my boss," Manny said, and walked ahead of Willie to the Expedition.

When they were seated inside and had started the Ford to get the heater going, Manny asked, "Were you able to listen to the messages?"

Willie eyed Mary as she went back in the house and he turned in the seat. "There were eight old messages. Five from Hobart. One," he looked at a date he had scribbled on his hand with a pen, "was three days ago. Hobart left Mary a message saying he

235

suspected the Kramers were the ones that night who had stolen Everett's map and he was hunting them down. 'If they are the thieves, I'll kill the bastards,' he said in his message, 'before I let them blaspheme Crazy Horse.'"

"If Hobart found them," Manny said, "that could explain why we haven't located those two peckerwoods yet."

Chapter 35

Clara set a plate in front of Manny. An egg white and spinach omelet stared back at him along with one slice of gluten free toast. "I know what you're thinking," she said. "You wanted a plate of flapjacks to go with a half-pound of greasy sausage. But you know what that does to your cholesterol and your weight. You do want to look handsome in our wedding photos, don't you?"

As Manny picked at the omelet, wedding photos were the farthest things from his mind. Right now, he needed meat. Preferably fatty, juicy sausage, dripping onto the front of his shirt. After all, he *was* trying to reclaim his Lakota roots. And the Lakota of old *were* carnivores.

"You have thought about a date?"

"I've thought about it," Manny said. *I've also thought about being pestered every day about what I eat, though I know Clara is just looking out for me.* Reuben had never married, and he had offered Manny wisdom that surely didn't come from the Old Ones. "A man is incomplete until he is married," he'd told Manny many times. "Then he's finished."

"I need to pick a date where I am actually available. They have me working so many reservation cases it's hard to pin down when—"

"It's hard to pin down *anything* with you lately."

Manny set his fork down and sipped on his decaf coffee.

"I've been… distracted lately. It's this Everett Black murder that is eating at me. I just can't get a handle on it. There are so many contradictions—two maps, both of which claim to be the burial place of Crazy Horse. At first I thought everyone in the household would want the map—it'd bring a bundle at an auction if one could be authenticated as genuine."

"*Iktomi* is playing with your mind," Clara said.

Iktomi. The Trickster. Able to send one along the path on the promise of fulfillment only to have destruction waiting at the end of the journey. Though Clara was not Indian, she had grown up on the Rosebud Reservation adjacent to Pine Ridge and she knew the legends as well as any Lakota. "I don't think Oglala myth has anything to do with this case."

"Sure it does," Clara said. "*Iktomi* dwells in here," she touched his chest over his heart. "If he is influencing you, things are not what they seem. Just when you think you have something figured out, *Iktomi* steers you in another direction."

Manny thought about what Clara said. From the two maps—both of which were purported to be genuine—to the Twins relationship with one another, their father, and Mary. Everything he thought about concerning Everett's and Hanson Becker's death could be skewed. Not to mention Shannon Henderson's murder in the FBI apartment. Manny needed to sweat. He needed to enter the *inipi,* the sweat lodge, once again. As much as he feared his visions, he felt he needed to go into Mother Earth with Reuben. As soon as he finished at court. "I'm late," he said and pushed his plate aside.

"But you've hardly eaten anything," Clara said. "You'll go into court and your stomach will rumble and—"

"I'll grab a late lunch," he said as he leaned over and kissed her lightly on the cheek. "And I will think hard about setting a date for our wedding."

* * * * *

Clara was right—Manny would be hungry by court time. He mulled over what he would say when he approached the court, while he parked in the McDonald's lot and devoured a Big Mac and a large order of fries. Then, so as to keep his weight and cholesterol in shape, he sipped on a vanilla shake. How *would* he approach the court? He had testified as an *amicus curiae* in a federal case back in D.C. when the target of an FBI probe— whom Manny thought was innocent—reached out from behind prison walls for Manny's help.

But now, going before the court as an intervener on behalf of Tantra, he wasn't sure if the judge would accept his testimony at this late stage. And why should he? But after talking with Tantra at the Hot Springs rehab a couple days ago, Manny was convinced she was neither a danger to anyone—including herself— nor was she incompetent. She was like so many Lakota who had gotten sober and one day fallen off the wagon. It didn't mean she couldn't get right back up and handle her own affairs. Hobart had, and he had remained sober and clean.

"The emergency hearing is set for ten o'clock today," Hazel Watts said under her breath when she called. Hazel had set hearing dates in Federal District Court long before Manny was transferred here. He had called and asked her to keep checking the docket, figuring the guardianship hearing was being held there since Tantra was a resident of Pine Ridge, and his hunch had paid off.

Manny turned onto Ninth Street and debated about pulling into the parking garage of the Andrew W. Bogue Federal Building, then thought better. If anyone saw him driving this little Toyota truck instead of his government car, he'd never live it down. Instead, he parked across the street in front of Murphy's Pub and fished into his pocket for coins to feed the meter.

He walked to the security checkpoint, taking his FBI identification wallet from his pocket and was waved through. *I still don't know just how I'm going to convince the judge to allow me to testify on such short notice.* And he still didn't know exactly what he would say if the judge allowed it.

He stopped in front of the clerk's desk and once again dug for his ID case. "I need to speak with Judge Talbott."

"He is about to convene a hearing in his courtroom," the receptionist said.

"I know," Manny said. "That is why I wish to speak with him. It will only take a minute."

The clerk glanced at the wall clock and said, "Excuse me for a moment," and walked through a door directly behind her desk. She emerged within moments and said, "You can go into the judge's chamber. But you only have a few minutes."

Manny thanked her and walked into Judge Talbott's chamber just as he was donning his robe. "My clerk says you have something urgent you need to see me about." Gruff tone. Demanding a simple answer. Like Manny remembered Judge Talbott. Manny had testified in the judge's court twice before, and the man was fair. But he demanded exactness. He had no time for a person being ambiguous.

"It's about the guardianship hearing Mellis Considine filed representing James Black."

"I'm listening."

"I would like to testify on behalf of Tantra Black," Manny said, tugging at the brim of his Stetson in his hand.

The judge snapped his robe closed. "Why not file a brief as protocol demands? You would have had to file a brief within forty-eight hours of the hearing date. You know that."

"I also know there's provisions for exigencies—like new information coming before the court. I just learned about the hearing late yesterday—"

Judge Talbott nodded. "I heard two days ago that Ms. Black walked away from rehab."

"She did," Manny said. "I talked with the facility manager. Tantra left shortly after the sheriff served her notice of this hearing. She had no time to procure the services of an attorney. And she cannot speak for herself if she is not here."

"You believe you have information pertinent to this case that I need to examine?"

"I do, your Honor."

Judge Talbott paused for a moment before he said, "I will allow it. Mellis Considine will put on his argument first, then I will call you as an *amicus* witness." The judge smirked. "That ought to piss Mellis off. Be good for that pompous bastard—he's pissed *me* off enough times with his shenanigans. I will see you in Courtroom One."

Manny left the chambers and walked past the clerk's desk to the courtroom. He cracked the door and peeked inside. Mellis sat at a table with Jimmy Black beside him. A large white board on an easel stood beside the table as the two whispered among themselves. Manny entered the courtroom and coughed loud enough that Mellis turned in his seat.

"Agent Tanno… what are you doing here?"

"Same as you," Manny answered, walking past rows of empty pews to sit in the front row. "Seeking justice."

"How's that?"

"Tantra," Manny said, "cannot defend herself. Somehow you got this emergency hearing and she has no one to speak on her behalf. So I am here to speak for her."

"What! That's nonsense—"

"All rise," the court officer announced, cutting Mellis off as Judge Talbott entered the courtroom. He bent and talked briefly with his court stenographer before seating everyone and reading the civil intention of the hearing. "Call your first," he said as he looked over his glasses at a list, "and only witness."

Mellis called Jimmy to the stand. Under oath, Mellis asked Jimmy questions they had obviously rehearsed before the hearing, in an attempt to make their answers support their case. If Manny were an attorney and if he were not here as an intervener, he would have had a field day with the cross examination. But his role here was so limited in scope, all he could do was sit and listen.

Throughout his testimony, Jimmy emphasized Tantra's addiction, pointing out that she had been enrolled in rehab programs some years before her short stint in the Hot Springs rehabilitation center. "She is incapable of minding her own affairs," Jimmy said. "She has slid so far downhill that she dresses like a tramp despite having money to do otherwise. And she perpetually looks like she's on a week-long bender without sleep. Without food. Not paying any attention to her hygiene or how she looks."

"That's not true! I ate this morning."

Manny turned in his seat to stare at the door as did Mellis and Jimmy. Tantra *glided* into the courtroom wearing a glistening gray business suit and a beige scarf that encircled her neck. Perfect braids hung on her chest, each held by a beaded turtle. Despite Jimmy's claim that she didn't care about her looks, Tantra was a walking, breathing contradiction that made Manny draw in a quick breath when he saw her. For a woman nearly Manny's age, she looked twenty years younger, her makeup applied in exacting layers.

"Are *you* Tantra Black?" Judge Talbott asked.

She walked through the swinging quarter doors and stood straight and proud in front of the judge. She looked up at him and said in a strong voice, "I am."

"Take a seat there," he pointed to a table next to where Mellis sat scribbling furiously on a legal pad. Judge Talbott took off his glasses and looked at Jimmy slumped in the witness chair. "Ms. Black appears not at all like the impression you just gave the court."

Jimmy remained silent and the judge said, "What is your explanation? And it had better be a good one."

Jimmy sat up and looked over at his sister. "She might look like she is composed and has the ability to… function. But I am telling you, she is a basket case. I am willing to take responsibility for my sister to ensure she does not harm herself."

The judge turned to Mellis. "Are you finished with your witness?"

Mellis nodded. "I am, your Honor."

"You can step out of the witness seat," Judge Talbott told Jimmy. He used the edge of the railing to steady his wobbly legs as he made his way to the table. He dropped into the chair next to Mellis as the judge ordered Tantra sworn in.

For the next hour, Tantra told how she had been taunted by Jimmy that night in Everett's study when Jimmy had said he intended to file a petition to name himself as her guardian, and how he had conveniently fixed her favorite drink to help shove her off the wagon of sobriety. Tantra doodled on a piece of paper in the witness box as she told how she had been so enraged—knowing Jimmy would then control her portion of the estate as well as his—that she had drank herself into a stupor before hopping into Everett's new Ford truck and driving to Hot Springs, only to get arrested. "I don't believe that I will take another drink, your Honor."

"Mellis?"

Mellis Considine dipped his head and whispered to Jimmy before saying, "We have nothing else. I believe Jimmy Black's testimony will stand. And the fact that Tantra has been doodling on that paper the whole time she was on the witness stand shows that she does not take this hearing seriously."

"I just have one question, young lady," Judge Talbot said. "When *was* the last time you fell off the wagon that you were admitted into a rehabilitation facility?"

"Twenty-one years ago, your Honor. I was... younger then. Foolish." She glared at Jimmy. "And would never have taken another drink if my *loving* brother had not angered me so."

Judge Talbott sat back and thought for a moment before he said, "Agent Tanno, Counselor, approach the bench."

Manny walked through the swinging doors just ahead of Mellis and they both stood as if at attention. "Agent, you have come before me twice on federal cases and I've found you to be truthful and levelheaded. What is your professional opinion as to Ms. Black's competency?"

Manny paused for effect before answering. "Ms. Black has obviously struggled with addiction, as we all have with something. I did with my smoking some years ago. Hers happens to be alcohol. If she were able to stay on the wagon for twenty-one years, I would bet my reputation that it'll be another twenty-one years before she falls off it again."

Judge Talbott leaned over and said to Tantra, "I am inclined to believe Agent Tanno, and to take in the contradictions between what your brother testified and how you present yourself today. But... doodling while sitting there this last hour leads me to believe that you *might* not be taking this seriously."

"I wasn't doodling, your Honor," Tantra said, and handed Judge Talbott a pencil sketch of the judge, the courtroom, Manny and Jimmy with Mellis beside him. An accurate depiction down to the small mole behind the judge's ear.

"This is remarkable," Judge Talbott said. "You could make a fine living with this talent even if you were not to receive a portion of your father's will." He took off his glasses and rubbed his eyes before putting them back on and squinting at the sketch. A broad smile crossed his face before he said, "I am denying your motion, Mr. Considine. Do not come before this court again with such a flimsy case."

Mellis and Jimmy stood abruptly. Jimmy glared at Manny, before fixing his stare on the judge. "This is bullshit. Just bullshit."

"Counselor," the judge said, "do you concur with your client?"

"I do. This ruling *is* bullshit and I intend to appeal it."

Judge Talbott smiled again, this time there was a slight chuckle in his voice as he said to the bailiff, "Take both men to the county jail. Two days for contempt I think will change their attitude." He looked at Mellis and the smile waned. "This will give you time to work on your appeal."

After the bailiff escorted Jimmy and Mellis to their weekend home-away-from-home, the judge said to Tantra, "Give the clerk out front your contact information. I intend to contract you to do a portrait of me and my wife, if that's agreeable."

Tantra grinned. "It is."

"But only if you don't do this," he tapped the sketch. "That wouldn't be good, would it Agent Tanno?"

Manny picked up the sketch and immediately spotted what Judge Talbott was referring to. Tantra had sketched Mellis and Jimmy hunched over at their table, and Jimmy discreetly held his middle finger to the judge.

*　　*　　*　　*　　*

"I have to meet up with the Pine Ridge Police this morning," Manny said as they walked across the street to his car. "I could give you a lift, if you wish."

Tantra grinned at him and laid her hand on his forearm. "I appreciate it, but I have to meet friends here in Rapid City."

"Fair enough," Manny said. "But I'm curious as to how you got from Hot Springs to here."

"This isn't an official interrogation where I could be charged with lying to a federal agent, is it?"

"No," Manny said. "Just something that's piqued my curiosity. If I were a journalist, I'd say it's a question off the record."

"Fair enough." Tantra took Manny's arm and led him away from in front of Murphy's Pub. "Just to take the temptation away."

"Understood," Manny said.

When they had walked to the end of the block, Tantra stopped in front of a Plymouth station wagon. "They haven't made these in years," she said.

"I know," Manny said. "What's your point?"

"My point is the owner is sure to be looking for it."

"You know the owner?"

"No," Tantra said, "but if you run the plate, it'll trace back to somebody in Hot Springs. Coincidentally, only two blocks from the rehab center."

"You stole it and drove down here?"

Tantra held up her hands as if in surrender. "I didn't say that. All I'm saying is that somebody in Hot Springs has surely filed a police report on it." She winked at him. "And I'm certain if you run that plate, you'll get credit for recovering a stolen vehicle. Oh, and I suspect the thief wiped down all prints. Just an educated guess."

Manny understood. Tantra did the only thing she could after being served the notice of the competency hearing.

"If you speak with the owner, tell them I suspect the thief will reimburse them the price of the gas and use of their car once the thief gets some money. She hasn't any now."

"I will do that," Manny said. "I'd also tell the thief to be more careful shoplifting clothes to attend a hearing."

"How's that?"

Manny reached around Tantra and snatched a tag still left on the suit jacket. He held it to the light. "Karma Boutique. I would wager money they'll come up missing something just like this from their inventory."

"And you can wager that the thief will reimburse them for their loss as well. Just as soon as she gets her inheritance."

Chapter 36

M anny and Willie sat alone in the conference room. Lumpy had to actually take a domestic call as they were too short handed, and Pee Pee couldn't make it because he was collecting evidence from a vehicular fatality on the road going to Rapid City. With Lumpy gone, Manny had taken the liberty of making a *fresh* pot of coffee before he sat down. "Still nothing on the Kramers?"

"Nothing. It's as if they dropped off the face of the planet."

"Or Hobart found them and squeezed the life out of them because he thought they had the map. Has anyone seen *him*?"

"Nothing on Hobart, either." Willie stood when the coffee was finished and poured each a cup before opening the fresh box of donuts. He grinned. "I would have given a month's pay to see the look on Jimmy and Mellis' faces when Tantra walked into that courtroom."

Manny broke a Long John in half and put the other half back in the box. He'd come back to it in a moment, he was sure. He'd read somewhere that if you divided your food up into portions, you would consume fewer calories. Something that Clara would have been proud that he just did, although he'd never tell her he was snacking on a pastry. "I have to admit it was priceless sitting there seeing Jimmy and Mellis squirm."

"What're Tantra's plans now? Where is she going to live?"

"At the Black Ranch, of course," Manny said.

"But that's nuts."

"Tell me about it. If I'd have known she was crazy enough to go back there and stay in the house with Jimmy, I would have told Judge Talbott she *is* nuts."

"That ought to be interesting for her, living under the same roof with the brother that tried to have her committed." Willie broke off a corner of a Bismark and gnawed on it. "Think of the bright spot," Willie said. "You got credit for recovering a stolen car."

"Some bright spot. We're no closer to solving Everett's homicide—let alone Hanson Becker's *or* Shannon's." Manny set his cup down and asked Willie, "You're a student of Margaret Catches, what does she teach you about *Iktomi*?"

"Trying to get a handle on your Indian roots finally?"

Manny shrugged.

Willie stood and paced in front of the conference table, gathering his thoughts. "*Iktomi* is one to be wary of. Avoided at all costs. One should never take what he says literally, and never heed his advice or it may destroy you. Why?"

"That is essentially what Clara said to me when she saw me struggling with figuring out these murders. 'Contradictions' is how she put it, and that got me thinking about folks. Tantra, for one. Her Tahoe is usually parked in front of the porch—"

"Cause she can't drive a manual transmission."

"Then how did she manage to drive Everett's new truck to Hot Springs? A truck we know Everett specifically ordered with a stick shift. And that car stolen two blocks from the rehab—it was a stick shift on the column."

"Jesa!" Willie snapped his fingers. "You're right. She could have been the shooter that day you and Reuben were ambushed, driving Everett's diesel. And she would sure know about guns—every ranch kid knows how to handle guns. But why would she?"

"I thought of that as well, and the only explanation is that she knew I had the authentic map that day, using it to find Destiny's

Door. Knowing it could bring in as much as she would inherit with her portion of the estate would be a good motive."

"I put all my chips on Hobart," Willie said. "With his passion—and I do empathize with him—for preserving Lakota history and the sacredness of it. What if he thought that map Becker had was the authentic one. Hobart might not have known you had another map besides the one Everett kept in his safe. I can see him killing Becker to get it, and Hobart is damned sure strong enough to carry Hans across the prairie."

Manny picked up the second half of the donut and then dropped it back into the box, proud of his willpower. "You forgetting the Kramers working in Everett's house?"

Willie tapped his finger on the table. "Shannon *was* struck with a drywall hammer—"

"After he had a Coke with a friend..." Manny stopped abruptly and snatched his cell phone from his pocket. When Pee Pee answered, he said, "Did you get anything back for prints from those two cans of Coke in the FBI apartment?"

"I rolled Shannon's prints at autopsy," Pee Pee said. "Like you figured, none of the prints I lifted from the cans were his. I sent the latents to the state DCI and FBI to see if the prints were on file, but the results are not back yet. All I can tell you is that there were two separate people handling those cans."

Manny thanked him and hung up when Willie asked, "Is there something else about the cans with those prints that interests you?"

"They were Coke cans," Manny said.

"Ok," Willie said. "So, they were Coke cans."

"Shannon didn't like Coke. He was strictly a Pepsi man. He told me several times. He never touched the Coke I stocked in the fridge at the apartment. Two other people were in the apartment when he got murdered. Two other people that Shannon didn't invite in—his prints were not on the cans at all."

"Makes sense," Willie said. "It'd take two people to bring down a man as big as him. So, we're looking at two people teaming up… has to be the Kramers. They had to kill Shannon to be able to search the apartment."

Manny thought of them as well and he recalled once again the tales of *Iktomi*, the trickster. Making people contradict themselves. Clouding their judgment. "If we're so focused on the Kramers, we're forgetting Hobart. Being a fervent supporter of preserving Lakota history, he would have an even greater desire to get his hands on the Crazy Horse map. He just may not have known that the one Becker had was actually the bogus one Everett kept in his safe as a decoy."

"So we're back to Hobart knowing the combination to the safe and sneaking in there, only to be caught by Everett," Willie said.

"We're back to a lot of suspects," Manny said.

Willie stood and walked to the Wheel of Death, swiping his debit card and being rewarded with a hoagie at least as hard as the stale doughnuts Lumpy usually supplied in the conference room. Willie peeled off the wrapper and bit the end off a mustard packet as he looked over at Shannon's white board with his analysis still on full display. "He put a lot of thought into that."

"He did," Manny said. He turned in his seat and looked it over. "Here's what we have: the Kramer's are top of the suspect list. If they had possession of the genuine map, it'd make them more money than they had ever made in their miserable lives."

"Hobart's not far down the list," Willie tapped his name on Shannon's board. "He meets all the criteria, according to Shannon—the motive as well as the opportunity to steal the map. He's knowledgeable enough to have cut the brake lines on that old International Everett drove that night, along with disabling Everett's Ford."

"So you're thinking Hobart planned to have Everett chase him, knowing he'd have to take his old truck, knowing the brakes wouldn't last but a few hard pumps?"

"I'm just saying Hobart could have sneaked in and opened the safe and taken the cedar box with the map anytime Everett was away. If Hobart was the thief the night of the accident, I am sure it wasn't by mistake the old man was set up for that wreck," Willie said. "And he was strong enough to have carried Becker's body to where that hunter found him. If he's attuned to the Red Road like I figure he is, Hobart might have gotten spooked enough the closer to Destiny's Door he got, and he might have dropped Becker's body where the hunter found him."

"And then we have the Twins," Manny said. "Both had reason to want their dear ol' dad dead before the execution of his new will, which would have cut them out of their inheritance. I know Mary said Tantra *suspected* a new will was in the making, but she may not have known for sure. She might have heard more than she let on, listening through the vents. And both her and Jimmy knew enough about mechanics to have staged the accident."

"You might be on to something," Willie said before washing down the last of his hoagie with his coffee. "But I can't see the Twins teaming up to kill and drag Becker's body to Destiny's Door any more than I can see them getting along good enough to kill Shannon."

"But remember, we figured Shannon let his 'visitors' in. Probably told them to help themselves to Cokes in the fridge. Casual like. He must not have been intimidated by them. And the Twins showing up to talk about the case with their father would have sent no alarm bells off in his thick skull." Manny stood and stretched as he glanced at the wall clock. "You're about done for the day?"

"I am," Willie said. "Why?"

"I need a ride into Rapid City. The body shop called, and my Crown Vic is repaired."

"What about the little truck?"

"Enterprise in Hot Springs is sending over a guy to pick it up. I'm parking it in front of the FBI apartment," Manny answered. "And none too soon. With my back giving me fits driving that around, I'll probably kiss my Crown Vic's new door when I pick it up."

Chapter 37

"Can't you just let the tribal police handle this?" Clara said. "After all, it is just a traffic accident."

Manny wolfed down the rest of the lasagna made with vegan noodles, and wiped his mouth with the floral print napkin, just wishing he could stay around for seconds. Thankfully, he couldn't. "Willie said this is a traffic accident like Everett's murder was a traffic accident."

Clara dropped her napkin on the table and began gathering dirty dishes. "Just this once I'd like to be able to sit down with the man I love and have an uninterrupted meal."

"I'd love that, too."

"Are you sure you can't let someone else—"

"The driver who was run off the road was driving that mini-truck from Enterprise the Bureau rented for me."

Clara's face blanched and she sat back down in her chair. "Your truck... then that means whoever caused the accident meant for you to be the victim?"

"I'll soon know. But given what Willie told me, my guess is that's just what happened."

*   *   *   *   *

Robert Hollow Thunder was wrapping up his traffic investigation as Manny stopped his Crown Vic beside the police cruiser. Robert collapsed his *QuikMap* laser that would diagram the accident later and stowed it in the trunk of his squad car before walking over to Manny.

Robert watched the wrecker slowly winch the totaled Toyota truck up from the ravine and said, "Before you even ask, I will tell you this is more than just vehicular homicide. This was *deliberate* homicide. I wouldn't have asked Willie to call you all the way out here from Rapid."

Manny zipped up his coat and shoved his hands in his pockets. "Give me the headline version, Robert."

"Headline is that someone deliberately rammed that rental truck of yours and shoved it into that ravine. Driver DRT. Dead Right There, for you federal guys."

Many smiled. "I worked the street a time or two when I was on the force here. I know some of the lingo. But how do you know it was rammed deliberately?"

"There is an eyewitness," Hollow Thunder said. "He's sitting in Willie's Expedition."

Manny thanked Hollow Thunder and walked to Willie's vehicle. Manny shook snow off his hat and stomped his boots before he hopped in the back seat.

Willie turned and said, "This is Malcom Frazer. Feller who rode to the rez with the victim to pick up your rental truck. He's calming down a little so's he can write a statement in a little bit. Sit up front and talk with Malcom… I'll help Robert finish up with the accident."

Manny climbed out and walked around to sit behind the wheel. He introduced himself and said, "Tell me what happened. Don't be afraid to go into as much detail as you can recall—Officer With Horn will ask you to do the same as soon as he's done here."

Malcom—a big twenties-something kid with his hair dyed blue on one side, green on the other—looked at Manny through red-rimmed eyes accented by piercings on both lids. He brushed his hand across his eyes and wiped tears onto his jeans. "I never seen a person die before. Chad. He was there one minute. Following me. And then just *gone*. Pushed into that ravine." He looked down at the floorboard. "I'm ashamed to tell you but I hightailed it away when I saw it happen." He looked up at Manny and the tears flowed again. "Does that make me a coward?"

Manny laid his hand on Malcom's shoulder. "No. It just means that you decided on self-preservation. And good thing you did, or you might not be here talking with me. Now tell me about the vehicle that pushed your friend off the cliff."

"Okay," Malcolm said, taking a deep breath. Calming himself. "I drove Chad over here to pick up that rental from in front of an apartment building…"—he started digging into his pocket—"I have the address here somewhere…"

"Not necessary. I know where the truck was parked. Go on," Manny said, gently prodding Malcolm to relate the terrible thing he saw. Just like Manny did for a thousand other witnesses to horrific events during his career.

"Okay. Okay. I dropped Chad off… if I was a little smaller, I'd have driven the truck and it'd be me the coroner hauled away. But Chad… he fit into the Toyota better." Malcolm paused before continuing. "I dropped him off at the apartment like we planned. He was following me off the rez… maybe back a block or so, when this truck came up behind him and rammed him. And then rammed him again."

"Did you see what kind of truck?"

Malcom shook his head. "I didn't. Like I said, I only seen it happen in my rear-view mirror. But it was a diesel truck, that I know for sure. Gas trucks don't spew that black shit like diesels do."

* * * * *

"Are you sure you're safe to stay in the FBI apartment tonight?" Willie asked. "Whoever killed that kid tonight is probably the one who ransacked your apartment after that fake call the other night. You could be targeted again."

"Those contractors from Chadron installed a steel door and jams that a truck couldn't ram through. They replaced the window with bullet-resistant glass. And the restoration company took up all the carpeting and wiped the blood off the walls."

"But they're not done working in there yet," Willie pleaded with Manny.

He waved the air as if to brush the worry away. "They've taped and mudded the new drywall where the hammer flew into it, and they'll be back tomorrow to sand and texture." He chuckled. "At least the bedroom is livable."

"You could come home with me. We have a spare bedroom—"

Manny shook his head. "And endure the wrath of Doreen? Since Clara has been getting on *Doreen* to get on *you* to get on *me* about setting a wedding date, she would be absolutely charming to me, I'm sure. I'd be lucky to get out of your house without being beaten to a pulp."

"You know about Clara and her talking?"

"After that fake call sending me on a non-existent homicide, the office installed a recording device on my home phone—"

"That Clara doesn't know about and that you check now and again?"

"So, I'm human," Manny said. "Point is, I'll be just fine at the apartment."

Manny waited around until the wrecker had winched the Toyota up from the ravine and stopped it at the rear of the rollback. Chad Dains was barely visible inside the crumpled cab of the truck, pinned inside, the steering wheel tight against his crushed chest, a thousand shards of glass stuck into his lifeless face. Pee Pee took additional photos before stepping back and allowing the firemen access to it. Two men hooked the Jaws of Life to the steering column and pulled it off the body. The top had crushed downward onto the driver, and the fireman used the Jaws to cut the top off. Two others helped Manny and the coroner wiggle the victim from the cab and lay him on the open body bag atop the gurney.

"I'll have the photos in a PDF file by the morning for you to look at," Pee Pee said.

Manny thanked them and drove away, thinking about what kind of person could run a kid off the road, knowing he would die after tumbling down such a steep embankment. But that person wasn't trying to run a *kid* off. The person was running someone off the road who fit the cab of that Toyota like Manny fit the cab. Willie was right—*Manny* had been the target, and he was cautious as he circled the apartment, looking for vehicles that didn't belong. Looking for people who didn't belong.

The streetlight shone bright illuminating the new steel door, and lights from apartments on either side of his leaked through the curtains. The dog across the street barked at Manny every time he drove past the apartment, while at the end of the block, a man leaned across the fender of his truck, shop light flooding the engine compartment as he worked on his car. Normal.

With no hint of anything out of the ordinary, no hint that danger waited for Manny, he pulled in front of the FBI apartment.

He yanked the cover off the dome light before taking the bulb out and then opening the door, his hand close to the holster on his hip. He paused for a moment and looked around. Quiet. Except for the dog and its occasional yapping, and the man cursing when his hand slipped off a wrench, it was quiet.

Manny drew his pistol while he inserted the key into the new lock and cracked the door. He waited until his eyes adjusted to the light before entering the apartment and button-hooking around the open door to stand with his back against the wall. Listening. Breathing deeply.

Nothing.

After he closed and locked the door, he flicked the light on, taking deep breaths, berating himself for being so jumpy. But whoever had come by the apartment to search for the map had killed Shannon when it ought to have been Manny staying here that night. And Chad driving the rental truck had been killed because someone thought Manny sat behind the wheel. Thought that Manny had the map in his possession.

He looked inside the bathroom—he had seen too many movies where the victim was killed in the shower—and then the bedroom before relaxing completely. But should he relax completely? He thought of that as he lay on the bed that night, trying to force the homicide cases out of his mind. Praying to *Wakan Tanka* that he got a decent night's sleep. For once.

Chapter 38

Banging reverberated on the steel door, and Manny swung his legs over the edge of the bed. He grabbed his pistol from the nightstand and went to the door, peering through the peep hole. Willie reared his big fist back to bang again when Manny threw open the door. "For God's sake, it's six o'clock," Manny said, "Don't you ever sleep? 'Cause *I* sure would like to, now and again."

"Patrol found the Kramers there," Willie blurted out. "Hop in."

Willie entered the apartment and closed the door while Manny grabbed a clean pair of jeans from the hanger above the bedroom door. "Where's there?"

"Right about that hill overlooking where you and Reuben were ambushed that time," Willie said as he helped himself to a Coke from the new fridge. "But in this weather, they'll be just fine until we get there."

"I don't understand—"

"The Kramers are dead. One knifed through the heart, the other shot with his own gun."

"Hobart?"

"Be my guess," Willie said, and held the door for Manny. "He damn sure was hunting them as hard as we were."

Manny grabbed his electric shaver for the road and climbed into Willie's SUV. "Any sign of Hobart?" He turned the rearview mirror so he could see to shave.

"We gave the description of Hobart's truck again to our patrol units and to Nebraska State Patrol. Dispatch called Fall River County folks in Hot Springs, and Rapid City PD sent a squad car over to stake out Hobart's apartment, but he hasn't shown yet."

They pulled out of Pine Ridge Village and headed west as fast as Willie dared go in the snow. "Pee Pee's already cordoned off the crime scene and erected a tent over the… victims. I'm reluctant to call them that since they've been shysters for as long as I've known them."

As they started out of town towards Oglala on Highway 18, Manny asked, "Who found them?"

"Mel Platte. He was flying over that area hunting coyotes—"

"He that feller who bought that rickety old plane of yours?"

"Clementine," Willie nodded. "My plane's name was Clementine. Not that it cost him much. That tightwad could have bought any beater car on the rez and it woulda cost him more than what he gave me for that old Cessna."

Manny was just glad Willie sold that airplane. The few times he'd been up with Willie, Manny had prayed nearly the whole time that the Cessna 150 would hold together. It didn't help that the duct tape pasted over the wings kept coming off and flapping as if waving goodbye to the world below. If Doreen hadn't insisted Willie sell it, he would still be coaxing it into the air. "Mel Platte," he pressed.

"Sure. Mel. He was running a coyote. Fixing to ventilate him when he spotted a pickup way down in a deep ravine. Turns out, it was that junker Dodge truck of the Kramers. But they weren't in it. They were lying on that hill we talked about."

Manny rapped on the dash, "And by now they are as hard as this if they've been laying out in the cold for any length of time."

Willie slowed as he drove around a paint pony pulling two young boys riding precariously atop a discarded car hood.

Another boy riding the gelding laughed as he whipped the horse faster along the icy road, paying the SUV no mind. "Did anyone check the Black Ranch?" Manny asked. "Mary would let Hobart hide out there for sure."

"Chief Looks Twice squealed when I asked for a round-the-clock surveillance there, but he put an officer on it anyway. Especially after Hobart became a suspect in the Kramers' deaths," Willie said.

"Let's not assume that Hobart killed them. He might be at the top of our list, but we still don't know enough at this point. Unless you have something specifically pointing to Hobart?"

"I'll let you look at the scene and you tell me," Willie said.

Manny finished shaving and looked out the window. Ice houses dotted Oglala Lake, and he wished he were there dangling his line through a hole in the ice rather than going to another homicide. Perhaps Clara was right—perhaps it *was* time for him to retire. Get into something... normal. Clara's brother had offered Manny a sales position at his appliance store in Rapid City. *I could to that. I could intimidate some old couple into buying the newest and greatest washer and dryer combination. Might even earn eighty to a hundred bucks commission for the sale. Just what I want—to put the muscle on old folks to buy something they don't need.* Suddenly, responding to another homicide with Willie didn't seem so bad.

They turned onto BIA 41 heading toward Slim Butte, neither man speaking. Neither wanting to say, "I can feel it." Willie said at last, "Something... is warning us away from here. From Destiny's Door." He glanced at Manny. "You feel it, too, don't you?"

Manny did, but by saying it aloud, whatever spoke to him and Willie might just materialize right there between them, so Manny merely nodded.

The tension broke when Willie's cell phone buzzed. "We're

just about to the crime scene," he said into the phone. "Tell him I'll call him just as soon as we've cleared… when I can get on some hill again where I have cell service." He hung up and said, "Chief Looks Twice wants me to call him. He's gotten information on Hobart from the Nebraska Patrol. It can wait until we're done."

After they had driven another fifteen minutes, they topped a hill overlooking the valley where Reuben and Manny had been ambushed. And right atop that hill where the shooter had fired down on them, Pee Pee Pourier sat in a lawn chair under a wall tent he'd erected over two bodies partially covered by snow. In the two hours he had been here waiting for Manny and Willie, the windshield of Pee Pee's van was already covered, and the center of the tent sagged from the heavy wet snow.

Willie stopped beside the tent and climbed out. Pee Pee looked up from his sack lunch and wiped his hand across his mouth to drag sandwich crumbs away from his scraggly whiskers. "Your friends are over there," he chin-pointed.

"I can see that," Manny said. Bobbie Kramer lay with his own knife sticking out of his chest, one hand clasped around the bone handle as if he had tried pulling it out before dropping to his death.

Buddy Kramer lay several yards away from him, the side of his head gone from a bullet's exit wound, black blood staining the snow. The butt of a blued revolver rested against a clump of sage, and Pee Pee said, "Thought you wanted to do the Perry Mason thing where you stick a pencil in the barrel and pick the gun up to gawk at. So, I just photographed it and left it while I had lunch."

Manny walked a tight circle around the two bodies, squatting now and again to look closer, brushing snow away where he thought evidence may lurk beneath the powder. He arose and began following faint tire tracks toward the edge of a steep gully where the sun glinted off a truck's mirror forty yards down. A grey Dodge pickup lay overturned beside a large bounder that it had struck on the way down. Side glass and gloves and tools lay strewn along the gully like the wreckage trail of the Titanic.

One again, he squatted and let the angle of the sun contrast highlights, his eyes picking up differences in the snow. He used his glove to brush powder from the ground until he finally spotted a single boot print pointed toward where the bodies were. Pointing *away* from where the truck had gone off the cliff.

He stood and soon picked up another impression darker than the surroundings: another boot print, confirming the direction the person had walked.

"What 'cha see?" Willie asked.

"After our killer took care of the Kramers, he drove the truck up to the edge of that gully. Pushed it over, would be my guess. Once we get the truck up, I wager it'll be in neutral... you did call a wrecker?"

"Does a fat baby fart?" Pee Pee answered. "I called the wrecker from Hot Springs but the operator said he didn't have enough cable to reach all the way down there. I ended up calling one out of Rapid City. It'll be a while before the truck's recovered. You seen enough?"

Manny nodded. "You finished with your photos?"

Pee Pee stood. "I am and ready to load our friends into the coroner's van once he gets here."

"Good," Manny said. "While you're waiting, cast those two boot prints."

Pee Pee groaned. "Do you enjoy making extra work for me?"

"Only if it leads to a case being solved," Manny said, and turned to Willie. "Now let's go find a high hill and see what Lumpy found out about Hobart."

Willie switched the Expedition into four-wheel-drive-low and slowly crawled up the icy slope. When they reached the

264

DEATH THROUGH DESTINY'S DOOR

top, Willie checked his phone, shook his head, and drove another quarter mile north until he had bars. "Boss, it's Willie." He talked for a moment before he said, "Chief wants to talk to you," and handed Manny the phone.

Lumpy told him that Scottsbluff stopped Hobart last night and he was in their county lockup. "I told them not to ask him any questions," Lumpy said. "They said he started to talk when they shut him up in isolation."

"Good," Manny said. "It's too late now to go down and interview him, but this will work out just right. By the time I finally make it down to talk with him, I suspect he'll be more than willing to tell me what happened."

"I was wondering if you were going to drive to Scottsbluff tonight," Willie said. "And I'm glad we're going tomorrow. Doreen said she wanted a real sit-down talk with me when I got home today."

"About your little swimmers?"

"Yeah. She insists we consider a fertility clinic." He checked his watch. "But I already have to go to Rapid City. They picked up Jamie White Cloud on our BOLO."

"For those burglaries over by Kyle?"

"Yes," Willie answered. "The detective says she's singing like a bird and I'd better get there while she's still in the vocal mood."

"Welcome to the wonderful world of investigations," Manny said, closing his eyes. Just for a moment, he felt the fatigue of the last week ever so slowly leaving him. Just for the briefest of moments…

"We're here at your apartment."

Manny sat up with a jolt. "Where—"

"In front of your apartment," Willie said. "You were cutting zzzs big time. You better get some rest."

"I'd say the same to you, but you got a drive up to Rapid City ahead of you."

"But I'll be ready to go to Scottsbluff in the morning with you. Goodnight, and don't forget to double-check the apartment when you go in."

Chapter 39

Wakan Tanka was not smiling on Manny like he hoped when the ringing of his cell phone woke him from a fitful sleep. "I need you to come to my place tonight," Reuben said.

"Do you know what time it is?" Manny asked. "Just what do you need me there for at two in the morning?"

"Just come on out here, Manny. Please."

"Where'd you get a cell phone..." but the line went dead.

Manny stared at his phone for a long moment before hanging up. The call was odd. Strange, and he just couldn't put his finger on it. Like the strange call he got that night from someone claiming to be the police dispatcher luring him to Batesland for a homicide that wasn't... *that* call was off. Was not at all like people talk now on the reservation, and a suspect popped into his mind. A suspect that should have topped the suspect list long ago.

Manny speed dialed Willie, but Doreen answered, her voice groggy, barely discernible. Until she heard Manny asking for her husband and then she came alive. "Just what the hell do you want him for?"

"I need him to... go someplace with me tonight."

"Willie got a motel in Rapid City. His interview with that burglary suspect took longer than he thought it would," Doreen said. "He told me he'll leave to come back to Pine Ridge in the morning just in time to go to Scottsbluff with *you*," and she abruptly hung up on him.

He quickly dialed the Pine Ridge Police dispatcher and asked for any available unit to respond with him. "We're just a little overwhelmed tonight," the dispatcher said, while another barked orders into the radio in the background. "Even Chief Looks Twice had to take a couple calls," and Manny thought he detected a snicker from the woman. "At least as many as he could hobble to. He's still not healed up—"

"Put him on the phone."

"Can't. He checked out for the night an hour ago. He might still be up if you call him, but he was plenty pissed he even got called out earlier."

Manny thanked her and hit speed dial. "This had better be good, Janice—"

"It's not Janice," Manny told Lumpy. "It's me. I need your help."

After Manny explained that Reuben had called and wanted Manny to drive to his place, Lumpy said, "What's so suspicious about that? That ex-felon brother of yours cons you into coming out to his place all the time."

"But he called from a cell phone."

"Of course he did," Lumpy said. "The man's too cheap to have a landline."

"But he doesn't *have* a cell phone. He was just talking about getting a TacFone this week. If he did, he would have told me."

"Go to sleep," Lumpy said. "I'm not going out to Reuben's this time of night on another of your flimsy feelings."

"He called me *Manny*."

"No shit, Hot Shot. Last I ran your driver's license that *was* your name."

"That's not the point," Manny said. "He hasn't called me by my first name in years. He always calls me *misun*."

"That's because you *are* his little brother."

"I'm telling you," Manny said, slipping one leg through his

trousers as he held the phone, crow-hopping across the floor to stick the other leg in, "there's something wrong. Now are you going to back me up and ride out there with me?"

"Shit," Lumpy said. "If I didn't go with you, you'd probably trip over some log or something in the dark at Reuben's and hurt yourself. Then the tribal council would be on my ass because another FBI agent got hurt on the rez. I'll park on the side of Big Bat's. Pick me up there."

* * * * *

Manny doused the headlights before he drove off the dirt road onto Reuben's long driveway. "I don't know how this is going to go down," Manny said, "or even *what's* going to go down. I'm thinking you let me approach the house first. Wait until I've made it around back before you come. But walk carefully—with that stomach operation you just had, I don't want you falling and ripping your stitches out."

"Staples," Lumpy said. "They stapled me like I was some kind of piece of paper or something." He gently massaged his stomach. "Damn it, if you hadn't gotten me so spooked on our drive here, I'd still be convinced you were being a drama queen."

"Even you admitted there was something wrong with Reuben's phone call."

"I did," Lumpy said. "Reluctantly. You may just be right. *This* time."

Manny used the emergency brakes so as not to engage the brake lights, and coasted to a silent stop twenty yards from Reuben's trailer house.

"You sure he's not going to start shooting, us creepin' up like we are in the middle of the night?"

"A felon, in possession of a firearm?" Manny said. "You know Reuben is a regular Boy Scout now."

"Just the same, I don't trust him."

Manny took the bulb out of the dome light again. "I'm not sure I do fully."

He grabbed his flashlight beside the seat and stepped out of the car a moment before Lumpy did. Manny eased his door shut and paused, his eyes adjusting to the night devoid of any moon as he stood still. Listening.

Silence.

Until the patter of hooves approached: Crazy George He Crow's junkyard horse had heard them. The swayback trotted over to the fence to see what had disturbed him this night, and Manny prayed the horse would not sound the alert as he was usually wont to do.

Manny's prayers went unanswered as the horse brayed loudly, echoes from George's barn answering back. "We'd better hustle before that damn horse wakes everyone on the rez," he whispered to Lumpy, standing with his Glock clutched tightly in his hand.

Lumpy held back while Manny walked the remaining few yards and stood at the corner of Reuben's trailer. A gentle wind whistled through the cedar trees on three sides of Reuben's house. This was one time Manny wished the wind were howling to mask the noise of his steps.

He drew in a deep breath to calm himself before inching toward the back. The lights normally illuminating the porch were off, and Manny squinted, staring, at someone sitting in the dark.

He pointed his pistol at the form thrashing about in a lawn chair and said, "I don't know who the hell you are, but do not move!"

"I would tell you the same thing," a voice behind Manny said, only slightly louder than the cocking of a gun inches from his head. "This old Winchester don't hardly shoot straight, but from here I can't miss. Drop the gun and get on in and join your brother."

Manny dropped his gun and said, "Do not shoot us, Mary."

The old woman lowered the rifle to Manny's back. "Just get on in there," she said, poking his back with the barrel.

He stepped onto the porch just as Mary flipped on the light switch. Reuben sat on a lawn chair, his hands handcuffed behind him, duct tape pasted across his mouth. A rope encircled his legs lashed to the chair, yet still he was trying to wriggle loose.

"Do not bother taking Reuben's tape off his mouth," Mary said. "He did not have anything useful to say when I first got here."

"What's this all about?" Manny asked.

"You ought to know," Mary said. "The map."

"You gonna kill us over the Crazy Horse map?"

"Not if you give it to me now."

Manny forced a laugh, looking around the porch for anything that he could use as a weapon, cursing himself that he did not have an Onion Field gun tucked somewhere away. "I'm not so dumb as to think you'll let us walk once you have the map. So far, you have killed no one, and all I could charge you with is conspiracy to commit murder. With your age and being a woman factored in, you might be out of a federal lockup in only a few years."

Mary motioned with her rifle for Manny to sit on a chair while she leaned against the porch railing. "No one will ever know I was involved."

"No? I've already filed my report requesting the U.S. Attorney charge you with conspiracy in Everett's death as well as Hanson Becker's," Manny lied. "You just made too many obvious mistakes."

Mary aimed her gun at Manny's head.

He winced, expecting the worst.

"I ought to kill you right now for lying like that," Mary said. "No one knows I am involved—"

"Easy with that thing," Manny said, and Mary lowered the muzzle slightly. "First off, I finally recognized the beaded lizard we found in that grave just inside Destiny's Door. It was modern, not buried with the body a hundred-fifty-years ago."

"There was no lizard—"

"Yes, there was. One that looked just like the one you and Hobart wear, just like the one you were beading in your kitchen that first day we were called to Everett's death. You must have dropped it when you were down rooting around in that grave you thought was Crazy Horse's. Did you actually think it was Crazy Horse buried there?"

"Didn't you?" Mary asked. "I saw you scooping dirt away from the skeleton."

"Were you the one who shot at us from the hill with that thing," Manny nodded to the rifle, "or was it the Kramers? Did you come along hoping they would succeed in killing us and getting the map?"

Manny looked at Reuben squirming to get out of the handcuffs, seeing he would be no help in disarming Mary.

"You know nothing about the Kramers—"

"Don't I?" Manny asked. "The Kramers were the ones doing your bidding. What was their price—a cut of the sale of the map after you helped them get it?"

"I have done nothing."

"I think you did. That fake call to Batesland that night to get me out of the apartment so they could ransack it looking for the map... that was *you* who called me claiming to be the police dispatcher."

Mary started to object when Manny said, "The voice was muffled, but the woman caller spoke... like elders speak. Plain. Using no contractions. Like you do."

"There are other elders here on the reservation," Mary said. "Your U.S. Attorney will not believe your report. He will look at others more likely—Jimmy and Tantra. They were the ones standing to lose if Everett filed a new will cutting them out." She raised the rifle again. "Now tell me where the map is!"

Manny caught sight of Reuben's eyes darting to the side of the heat stove away from Mary, to where a stout-looking piece of firewood lay. "I'll tell you where the map is after I have some answers. Surely, you have the decency to give me answers before you cap me," Manny said, inching his chair closer to the firewood, wondering what was taking Lumpy so long to sneak back here. "Let's talk about that new will—how was it that you knew Everett was drawing up another one... one that cut you out?"

"I overheard him and Mellis talking about it from Everett's study," Mary said. "They started drawing it up months ago."

"So you figured you'd better set up Everett to be killed before Mellis could complete it and file it. I'm just trying to figure out how you talked Hansson Becker into stealing it."

"That damned fool," Mary said. "I did not talk him into it. He knew Everett kept it in his safe. He had tried to buy it from Everett. When Becker stole it, *that* was not planned."

She motioned Manny away from the stove. She put another log into the fire and closed the door. "I could not have set up Everett's accident any better than Becker did for me."

"Setting up Everett for an accident was the plan—the map was merely an afterthought?"

"I guess you do have some things figured out," Mary said, her finger white on the trigger of the rifle. "Bobbie sliced the brake line and disabled the computer in Everett's new truck the afternoon before Becker came to the house. Buddy and me thought the next time Everett went into town, he'd have to take his old truck. Drive like a crazy person, as he always did, and that would be it. We never counted on Becker stealing the map that night when he visited Everett. Never counted on him running out with Everett right behind him in that old International truck. Until that happened, the only thing I wanted the Kramers for was to ensure Everett had a fatal accident before he could file a new will. But the theft of the map was… icing on the cake."

"But Becker stole the false map."

"I did not know that at the time," Mary said, "and neither did he."

"Did you throw in with the Kramers because of Everett's will?" Manny asked, knowing that was just why she had. He kept the piece of firewood in his peripheral vision as he inched painstakingly closer to it. *If I can keep her thinking and talking…*

"Damned Everett," Mary breathed. Her face flushed red, anger growing in her voice. "Soon after I moved in as his housekeeper when Hobart was a little guy, Everett and me became… intimate. But he never wanted another wife and—as the years dragged on—we grew apart, like a lot of couples do. I knew that his original will—written not too long after I'd moved in here—left me sitting pretty. But listening to him and Mellis discuss the provisions of a new will that cut me short, I knew the new one would have left me out in the cold. Literally."

"But you didn't know that Mellis never filed the new one, did you?" Manny said.

Mary shook her head. "I thought that he had not, but I was taking no chances. If Everett was killed in that wreck and the old will stood, I would be sitting good. If he was killed and the new will *had* been filed, the only thing I could do was steal the Crazy Horse map. Recoup all that I would lose by being cut out of the will."

"Except Becker beat you to it."

"That's when I called the Kramers back again—to get the map back from Becker. And by the time Mellis came here and read the new will to us, I was in too deep with the Kramers to look back."

"But why Shannon Henderson?" Manny asked, carefully scooting his chair closer to the heat stove. And the piece of firewood lying next to it. "He was just my trainee. The man never hurt anyone except himself."

"The Kramers... those idiots thought they did not search your apartment good enough the first time. I warned them not to go back but they did. They sweet-talked themselves into the apartment and killed that poor man. Buddy told me afterward they didn't expect anyone to be in the apartment after they listened to the police scanner, knowing you were out. All they had to do was come up with some story to tell Agent Henderson to get him off his guard long enough for Buddy to hit him with a hammer. 'Staggered him,' Bobby said, but then he stuck him with that knife of his. A shame, like you said, as he had done nothing wrong except being clumsy."

"And the Kramers helped themselves to Cokes after they killed him. Cold. Pee Pee Pourier identified their prints. Another reason we can link them to you."

"How can you connect me with them being the killers? You can't."

"No?" Manny said, pointing to Reuben wiggling against his restraints. "Those are Hyatt handcuffs—the same make that I carry. The same that most agents carry. The same that Shannon Henderson carried, and now the same ones securing my brother."

Mary shrugged. "Those two fools came to me after they killed the big man, whining that they still hadn't found the map."

"Of course they didn't find it," Manny said, "or they wouldn't have run that Toyota truck with that Enterprise kid behind the wheel into the ravine thinking it was me." He wiggled the chair closer to the wood and said, "If they had it, they wouldn't have gone back to the apartment the night Shannon was killed. When did you come into possession of the map Becker stole?"

"I never had it," Mary said. "I told them two fools they did not search your apartment good enough the first time and they said they would go back and do it again. I heard the apartment was trashed good that second time, and so, I was certain the Kramers had it. They denied it and I was sure they double-crossed me, intending to sell it on their own."

"You knew the map Becker had was a fraud," Manny said, eyeing the firewood, keeping Mary talking, "'cause you said the one I showed you—the genuine one—was a fake to throw *me* off."

"To be honest," Mary said, "I cannot swear which map is real. I knew Tantra had painted one based on Everett's directions. When she paints native, it is near impossible to tell from the way the Old Ones did. Can you imagine how much *the* map will bring? Give it to me!"

Manny shoved his hand in his coat pocket. "I'm likely to crush this delicate old canvas map unless you tell me if you and Hobart were together in your dirty little scheme."

"You have the map on you?"

"I do," Manny said, "and I will destroy it unless you tell me. It is so brittle—"

"Hobart was not involved at any level," Mary blurted out, the muzzle of the rifle drooping ever so slightly. "When Hobart stopped by the house, I told him I suspected the Kramers had the Crazy Horse map that at the time I thought was genuine. I knew he would squeeze the information out of them. All Hobart knew was that the ancient map showing where the sacred man was buried was in the possession of the Kramers."

"If your son gained possession of it—"

"Then it would be an easy matter for me to slip by his apartment one afternoon as he was teaching and take it."

Out of the corner of his eye, Manny caught movement. *Lumpy.* Was he waiting until Mary told the full story before he made his move, just being a good witness as she ranted?

"It surprised me when Hobart killed the Kramers. I could see him beating the information out of them, but killing them?"

Mary's mouth downturned as sadness crossed her face. "Hobart came to me right after that. He *was* after the map. It ate at him that it would fall into the hands of those two idiots for sale to the highest bidder. But he did not know I was working with them to do just that. That would have broken his heart."

Mary leaned against the porch and the weight of the rifle lowered the muzzle a little bit more. "He found the Kramers trying to find Destiny's Door on that same hill we... they... ambushed you and your brother," she mentioned, with the gun toward Reuben, who continued struggling against his restraints. "Might as well stop, big man. I double-locked those cuffs myself."

"So Hobart just outright murdered the Kramers?" Manny asked, as much for his information as Lumpy's ears. *If* they got out of this mess with Mary, another witness to her story would prove invaluable in court. "Then left them in that ditch after he pushed their truck down that ravine. How did he ever think their truck and bodies wouldn't eventually be found?"

"Because Hobart did not *murder* them," Mary said. "He killed them in self-defense."

Manny scooted the chair closer to the firewood and Mary raised her rifle once again. "Set right there and do not do anything that would set this here gun off."

"Why?" Manny asked. "Does admitting Hobart murdered them make you jittery?"

"Killing in self-defense is not murder," Mary said. "Hobart was beside himself when he came to the house afterward and I had to patch him up. That pup... Bobbie sliced Hobart across the chest when he confronted the Kramers. Hobart reared back far enough that the cut was shallow. When the kid came after him again, they fought for it and Hobart wrenched the knife away and buried it in Bobby's chest.

277

"Then Buddy pulled a gun and they got into a wrestling match over the revolver when it went off. But you already know that if you examined the scene atop that hill. Now this little tale has gone on long enough," Mary raised the rifle and sighted down the barrel.

Things went into slow motion for Manny as they often did when his life was a hair's breadth from being snuffed out.

Mary's trigger finger whitened. She aimed the rifle as...

Lumpy stumbled around the corner of the house, his own gun raised. Mary's head jerked around when she saw him and swung the muzzle of the rifle toward Lumpy.

Manny lunged for the piece of firewood but...

...Reuben threw himself forward, reaching it first. Clutching the wood. Swinging it hard. Crashing down on to Mary's forearm.

She howled in pain.

The rifle's muzzle—deflected toward the floor—discharged, the sound louder than Manny would have imagined it could be as Lumpy reached her. He grabbed the gun and snatched it away from Mary. She stepped back into a corner of the porch, holding her broken forearm, eyeing the three men like a cornered mountain lion eyeing baying dogs that had treed it. "How'd you get lose?" Manny asked Reuben.

Reuben ripped the duct tape from his mouth and said, "When you've been handcuffed as many times as I have by the cops, you learn how to get out of them. These just took a mite longer." Reuben approached Mary.

"Get away from me!"

"*Grandmother*," Reuben said, his voice soft, still respecting Mary as an elder despite what she had done, "your arm. I will hold it immobile until the ambulance gets here," he looked at Lumpy. "At least you can call for the paramedics to come and treat Mary."

"I'll do more than that," Lumpy said. He holstered his gun and dug his cell phone out of his shirt pocket. "I'll call for a nice young officer to sit with Mary for her ride to the ER. And for her ride to the lockup afterward."

Chapter 40

Manny never liked meetings. From the time that he was a tribal cop to his time at the Bureau, he detested them—they were usually conducted by arrogant, beside-themselves bureaucrats trying to justify their positions. Such a bureaucrat walked through the door and—with a pregnant pause for drama—looked around and decreed the meeting started. "We can finally begin on time for once," Lumpy said, and shut the door before plopping his big butt into his chair. "We haven't been able to do that since—"

"Since Agent Henderson was alive," Manny said adding, "what I wouldn't give for him to be alive and holding up our meeting right now."

"I... I didn't mean anything by it—"

"I know you didn't," Manny said. "Let's just get this debriefing over with so we all know what to expect when Mary's case comes to court."

Lumpy nodded and opened his briefcase. He handed each around the conference table a file: Manny and Willie and Pee Pee Pourier, half-sleeping as he slumped in his chair.

"Your report outlines," Lumpy said to Manny, "that the... trouble with the Black family began when Hanson Becker stole the phony map from Everett's safe and ran out the door with it. That's the official line we'll take?"

Manny nodded. "At least as it pertains to the case of Everett's death. I think the seeds of the scheme with the map began with Mary long ago, when Everett began taking her for granted. Treating her more like one of his ranch hands than a woman who was once his lover. Just someone who kept the household in one piece, including the thankless job of keeping Jimmy and Tantra from tearing each other's throats out."

Lumpy flipped pages and said, "Are we absolutely sure it was Becker who stole the map that night? Is your theory supported by anything other than Mary's statement?"

"We have Tantra Black's version of the argument Everett and Becker got into prior to that night. He would have known about the map in Everett's safe, especially since he stopped by Tantra's studio some weeks before and wanted to know if she could convince Everett to sell it," Manny said. "When I interviewed Tantra again, she said that a couple of hours after Becker talked to her, Everett caught him and put the run on him. But she hadn't figured it was him that Everett was chasing until later, since Becker had a hard time waddling, let alone running. That, and she didn't think Becker had the *cajones* to come back."

Lumpy flipped a page and scanned it quickly. "I hope Tantra's recollection holds up because it says here Mary has already recanted her statement to you."

"Hard to recant what she said the night she nearly killed me and Reuben," Manny said. "I suspected she'd take her statement back once she hired an attorney." After her broken arm had been set and cast at the hospital, Manny waited until the next morning to interview her so that any attorney she eventualy hired couldn't argue her confession was the result of pain killers given to her at the hospital. "She refused an attorney while she laid out how she saw Becker run out with the map that she thought was *the* Crazy Horse map the night of Everett's accident."

"How did she know it was the genuine map if she never got close enough to Becker to see it?" Lumpy asked.

"She didn't actually see the map. She saw Becker with the cedar box tucker under his arm and knew *one* of the maps was inside." Manny popped a piece of gum and sat back. "That night when I showed her the map Everett had hidden between the magazines, she said it was fake. I thought it was to throw us off, but in actuality, she didn't know if it was Black Heart's map or the one Tantra painted, because Tantra's was that good."

Lumpy rubbed his stomach. He had just had the staples removed and said it itched like the dickens. "If she didn't know which map was real, she couldn't take a chance on the one Becker stole being authentic."

Manny nodded. "It was then that she concocted her scheme and got hold of the Kramers. 'If you get that map, we can sell it and split the profit. *After* we find where Crazy Horse is buried,' she told Buddy Kramer. 'After we have possession of the bones, we can profit from them as well.'"

"For curiosity sake," Lumpy asked, as he selected a glazed donut and dipped it in his coffee, "when did Mary find out about Everett's original will?" He held the donut up and smiled. "This is actually fresh."

"For once," Pee Pee said, sucking air through his ill-fitting dentures.

"Where'd they come from?"

"The Donut Fairy," Willie said. "Who cares where they came from?"

Lumpy washed a bite down with coffee and said, "Did Everett tell Mary about the first will?"

"He did," Manny said, "about twenty years ago. He never told her the specifics, but he said she would have nothing to worry about if he died. But," Manny broke a Long John in half, "she knew she would be cut out of the new one if Mellis ever filed it."

"Because she and Everett had grown apart?" Lumpy asked.

"That, and because she said his brain cancer was making

him goofy, is how she put it. She feared she would never have anything to live on after putting up with him all those years. She grew desperate in a criminal kind of way."

Lumpy wiped frosting off on his uniform trousers and flipped to the next page of the report. "It says here that you also asked the U.S. Attorney to charge Mary with conspiracy to commit murder for that time the Kramers fired on you and Reuben from the hill."

"She let it slip that 'we' ambushed me and Reuben that day. I think we can make a case that she was with the Kramers that day on the hill."

"If there's no doubt the Kramers were the ones who killed Agent Henderson, we can bolster Mary's confession."

"Explain the prints," Manny asked Pee Pee.

Pee Pee gummed on a filled pasty, his teeth sitting on the table in front of him looking like a mini audience. "I finally got the results back on the prints I lifted from the Kramers at autopsy and compared them to those I lifted from the Coke cans in the government apartment. They matched." He put his teeth back in and thumbed through his papers, handing one to Lumpy. "And the Kramers' prints were all over Becker's house in Hot Springs from when they trashed it."

"They figured Becker hid the map in his house. When they didn't find it there, they started looking for him. They found Becker and followed him to Destiny's Door where they chased and killed him."

"So he was killed just where that hunter found him?" Lumpy asked.

Manny nodded. He knew what was coming.

"You were wrong then when you thought he was killed somewhere else?"

"I was," Manny answered.

Lumpy grinned wide and said, "Mark this day—the great

Manny Tanno was wrong in his assessment of a crime scene."

"So he's human," Willie quickly came to Manny's defense. "Give him a break."

"I'll drop it," Lumpy said, "for now." He ran his finger over the statement Manny had obtained from Hobart. "You're positive he killed the Kramers in self-defense and not to protect his mother from them implicating her in the scheme?"

Manny stood and stretched as he walked to the far side of the room and back. He wasn't as young as he once was, and the hike with Reuben to Destiny's Door the other day had left his muscles stiff. "For all Mary's conniving, she has one saving grace—she dearly loves her son. That's why I figure she told him nothing just so that we could never come back and accuse him of being involved with her plan. No, I believe that his rendition that he killed them in self-defense is accurate. He just fled out of fear, his first reaction. After all, he's really never been involved with the law his entire life."

"Still," Lumpy said, "I think we can get the U.S. Attorney to charge Hobart with at least obstruction of justice for pushing their truck into that ravine."

Willie shook his head. "Boss, like Manny said, the guy overreacted. Give him a break, too. Sure, we could convince the prosecutor to charge Hobart with obstruction. But for all intents and purposes, he just lost his mother. She'll be in prison so long, he'll never be able to hold her again. Never be near her after she is convicted, which is a mathematical certainty."

Lumpy folded his hands in resignation. "I see your point. But I also see here that that map you are so certain is the authentic one came up missing."

"It did."

"But the map is such an integral part of the case. The U.S. Attorney will be furious you lost vital evidence."

Manny picked up his cup and tossed the rest of the cold coffee into the garbage. "He was furious. Even when I explained to him that somehow the Kramers found the genuine map and hid it—and that they went to their graves with its whereabouts as well as the one Becker stole—he was still angry with me. 'Somehow we'll have to make the case against Mary Comes Flying without that piece of evidence,' he told me."

Lumpy looked over at Manny, and Willie, and Pee Pee sticking his dentures back into his mouth, and said, "Okay. *Now* I can go to the tribal council and tell them that these murders have been solved, and that prosecution will be successful."

Lumpy put the file folder into his briefcase and started for the door when he stopped and turned around. "I forgot to ask—there's nothing connecting the Twins to any of Mary's schemes, is there?"

"There is not," Willie said.

"But Everett's estate is still up in the air between them?"

Willie chuckled. "I can almost guarantee that until the estate is settled, we will get called to the Black Ranch again and again for family fights between those two spoiled brats. Which will be in about three years, according to the federal court docket."

"How about the problem of Mary owning the house?" Lumpy said. "Even if she's sentenced to prison, she will still own the ranch house according to Everett's original will."

"I delivered a message to the Twins from Mary," Manny said. "For some reason, they both want to stay in the house, and Mary said that if they would make a reasonable offer for the house, she would sell it."

"Why the hell would she do that?" Lumpy asked. "Not like she'll need much money in jail."

Manny smiled. "Because she intends to put the money from the sale of the ranch house into a trust—for Hobart's heritage center. I think he'll actually get it off the ground this time."

Epilogue

"Are you sure you don't want to join us?" Manny asked Hobart.

He looked through the twin spires, through Destiny's Door, then to Manny and Reuben and Willie before saying, "I don't even trust *myself* to know where *Tashunke Witko* is buried." He nodded to the map in Manny's hand. "It has been so long since I saw that... it was in the safe before Everett decided to hide it." Hobart had seen the authentic map when he was but a youngster, back when Everett caught him looking into the safe. Before there even was a second map to muddy the waters. "I am happy just knowing the map and the location of where the sacred man's gravesite is will be hidden forever."

"Understood." Manny did understand Hobart Black Heart better since he first interviewed him last week in Scottsbluff. Mary's version of Hobart's fight with the Kramers had been correct and supported by the evidence at the death scene, a story that matched what Hobart told Manny. That Hobart knew nothing of his mother's scheme to find the map and sell it was evident when Manny began interrogating him. Hobart had one agenda—finding the Crazy Horse map his grandfather's father had drawn and making sure no one ever found it again.

"For the record," Hobart said, "I wasn't even here with you guys."

"I think that goes for all of us," Manny said. When the U.S.

Attorney had told Manny he needed to enter both Crazy Horse maps into evidence for Mary's trial, Manny told him they had been stolen. "Had to have been the Kramers who found them when they tossed the apartment," Manny told the prosecutor. "Believe me, we've turned over every rock on the reservation and still haven't found where the Kramers stashed them," he lied. In this one regard, he trusted Hobart as much as he trusted Willie and Reuben concerning the map. He had to. If the U.S. Attorney learned that Manny had lied and still had the maps, or that he had destroyed or concealed evidence, Manny's job would be on the line, and he would be facing criminal charges. But it was important to ensure that Crazy Horse's resting place would never be found. As he looked at Hobart and Reuben and Willie, he knew they were all on board with the tale Manny had told the U.S. Attorney about losing the maps. "Ready?" Manny asked them.

"I am," Reuben said, "as long as you two ladies don't talk anymore about your marriage plans or about your... how'd you put that, Willie—your little swimmers losing their breaststroke?" On the drive to Destiny's Door for this ceremony, Willie told Manny his doctor had prescribed medication that would help build his sperm count and open the door for him and Doreen to have children. And Clara had finally worn Manny down and he had agreed on a wedding date—next Fourth of July. "I figured I'd never forget our anniversary with that date," he said.

They started down the slope toward Destiny's Door, Manny clutching his folder containing the map, camp shovel tied to his backpack, grateful he had both Willie and Reuben at his side. With such a powerful symbol of the Lakota—the map—he would need the protection of *wicasa wakan*. Holy men. Reuben and Willie.

As they neared Destiny's Door, strange stirrings within Manny emerged again, strange thoughts entering his mind.

But this time, there was no feeling of dread. No feeling that he was being warned away. This time it was as if Destiny's Door beckoned to him. Welcomed him. *Take care, little brother,* the voice of *Tashunke Witko* said inside Manny's mind. *Take care that no one ever knows where my bones are buried.*

Author's Note

I hope you got a sense of the powerful stirrings that the mere mention of Crazy Horse brings to many people, especially people of the Lakota Nation, even now. He was, indeed, the holy man of the Oglala, and was true to living the life of a free Lakota even when he was forced to surrender to spare the lives of his *tiospaye,* his band.

As for "Destiny's Door" leading to the grave of Crazy Horse, I can say with certainty there is no Destiny's Door on Pine Ridge. Such was a literary prop that I used to reveal to my characters—and readers—the power and austerity of being close to the sacred man's final resting place. A place that is still unknown.

As for the conversations Crazy Horse and his followers had, these within the book were based on speculation as to what they might have said at the time. Lakota history was—including the annual winter counts—passed down in the oral tradition from generation to generation and, thus, no conversations were recorded in the Old Time.

As for young Black Heart accompanying Waglula and the others, I could find no reference to such a person, and so, used him as a literary device as well. If he had been with the others and tasked with silencing the woman following the grave detail, I am certain he would have completed his mission to ensure that the sacred man's body was never found and desecrated.

If you visit the Crazy Horse Monument carved out of the granite mountain in the Black Hills of South Dakota, you may experience the same feelings that my characters did. The carving is not finished, yet even with what is depicted, one feels the need to stand reverently when looking up to the mountain top. With the always-present gentle wind in the Black Hills at your back, you can almost feel the power that Crazy Horse had, and his devotion to the four virtues of the Lakota—bravery, fortitude, generosity, and fidelity. That we may all follow his path in our everyday lives.

About the Author

C. M. Wendelboe entered the law enforcement profession when he was discharged from the Marines as the Vietnam war was winding down.

In the 1970s, his career included assisting federal and tribal law enforcement agencies embroiled in conflicts with American Indian Movement activists in South Dakota.

Curt moved to Gillette, Wyoming, and found his niche, where he remained a sheriff's deputy for more than twenty-five years.

During his thirty-eight-year career in law enforcement, he served successful stints as a police chief, a policy adviser, and other supervisory roles for several agencies. Yet, he has always felt most proud of "working the street." He was a patrol supervisor when he retired to pursue his true vocation as a fiction writer.

Curt writes the Spirit Road Mysteries, the Bitter Wind Mystery series, the Nelson Lane Frontier Mysteries, and the Tucker Ashley Western Adventure series.

If you enjoyed reading this book,
please consider writing your honest review
and sharing it with other readers.

Many of our Authors are happy to participate in
Book Club and Reader Group discussions.
For more information, contact us at info@encirclepub.com.

Thank you,
Encircle Publications

For news about more exciting new fiction, join us at:

Facebook: www.facebook.com/encirclepub

Twitter: twitter.com/encirclepub

Instagram: www.instagram.com/encirclepublications

Sign up for Encircle Publications newsletter and specials:
eepurl.com/cs8taP

Printed in the USA
CPSIA information can be obtained
at www.ICGtesting.com
LVHW090229020724
784468LV00028B/254